Rockabye

ROCKABYE
LAIRD KOENIG

November 16, 1981

For Mother
with love,

your son,

Laird

ST. MARTIN'S PRESS
NEW YORK

ROCKABYE

1
=

DECEMBER 21, 8:15 P.M.

"You don't have anything for less?"

"Cheapest room I got," the hotel clerk said, "twenty-eight dollars."

The young woman's thin raincoat was soaked black. Her two-year-old son's blond hair dripped rainwater down his face. They had dashed through the icy downpour from the bus terminal to this hotel in New York's Times Square area. Her red hands shook when she tried to smooth the wet from the boy's head.

The clerk, a pale man with dyed-black hair, peered back into an office where sleigh bells jingled happily on a television set. "Twenty-eight dollars," he said again. "Take it or leave it." On the wall a dime-store wreath of plastic pine needles circled cut-out letters: SEASONS GREETINGS.

"We only need it for one night."

"Cot for the boy will be three dollars extra."

"He's only two. He can sleep with me."

The clerk pulled on gold-rimmed glasses and leaned across the counter. The woman's blond son seldom failed to bring a smile and a kind word from strangers. This pale man frowned. He was not looking down at the little boy, he was searching for luggage.

"I left our things at the Port Authority Bus Terminal." She

ached to get the boy upstairs and warm and pull off his soaking Adidas, pop him into a hot tub and dry his wet hair with a fluffy towel. "I'll take the room."

The clerk turned back to the television's burst of sleigh bells and wild laughter. "I'll have to have a major credit card."

"I'll pay cash."

She drew her wallet from her raincoat pocket and carefully counted out a twenty, a five and three singles.

"Plus tax," the clerk said. "And a New York City surcharge of one dollar."

Without breaking his gaze back at the little rectangle of merriment, he slid a registration card across the counter. She signed her name, "Susannah Bartok," and added "and son." At the space for her home address she hesitated. Despite her red and freckled skin and the boy's warm tan from the California sun, she completed the card with a postal box number in upstate New York.

The man tossed a key on the counter, making it clear that no one would take them up to their room. That was all right with Susannah. She had no luggage to carry and going up alone would save on a tip. As she picked up the key she saw the man glance at her hand. Did he notice she wore no wedding ring? That was something new in her life. No wedding band.

She took the little boy's shoulder but stopped and called twice to the clerk, who had returned to his television. She asked how late the stores stayed open for shopping.

"Ten," he called above the television's Christmas carol.

A tall man in a raincoat dark with wet hunched through the lobby clutching a small bag of groceries. He glanced once at the woman and her son, but she avoided his red eyes.

"Ten o'clock," she repeated to the boy as they crossed the dingy reception area. She tried to ignore the plastic furniture and the burn hole in the lamp shade. "Doesn't give us much time to shop." Midway she stalled to avoid getting into the elevator with the man in the raincoat. They waited. At last, in the car alone with her son, Susannah was relieved that Laddie could not read the graffiti scratched deep into the walls.

Their floor smelled of stale cigarette smoke. The one dim

light bulb forced no cheer into the shadows that filled the long hall. In the gloom, sleigh bells still rang out on someone's television set. A door slammed.

Before Susannah and Laddie reached their door, footsteps creaked somewhere on the worn carpet. She didn't dare look back down the hall. Her heart pounded until the key opened the door, and she slammed it behind her, turned the lock, and slipped the security chain in place.

In their room she pulled off Laddie's wet tennis shoes and balanced them on the radiator. She took the biggest towel from the bathroom and rubbed his hair. Before she settled him on the bed against the pillows, she tugged off the pink chenille spread spattered with stains and hurled it into a corner. His hot bath would have to wait until after one telephone call.

She sank down beside Laddie and, while she dialed upstate New York, she dried his hair with one hand. She let the phone ring nine times. Her father was watching television—the same Christmas program with sleigh bells probably—and the phone was in the kitchen. At his age, with his cane, he moved slowly.

"Dad, it's Susie."

"Susie, where are you?"

She could picture him in the kitchen leaning down over the phone the way he did when a call was important.

"Still in New York. We have to stay the night, so we won't be home till morning. Nothing's wrong. The dumb plane was late getting in so we missed the last bus."

"Wish you didn't have to stay down there in that city. It worries me."

"Don't worry. We're all tucked in for the night."

"How's Laddie?"

"Fine. He loved the flight. I'm just about to put him in a hot bath."

"I've got a big fire in the fireplace and I mulled some of this year's cider. It's a shame you're not here. Let me talk to my grandson. Laddie?"

Susannah cradled the boy closer to share the phone. "It's your granddad."

"Can't hear him. Is he there?"

"We've decided to be shy." She cradled the phone on her shoulder and rubbed the boy's blond hair dry till it shone in the lamp light.

"Laddie," the voice said, "listen—if I can ever get this danged thing out of my pocket—I've got my harmonica handy to surprise you. . . ." Instead of a voice, Laddie heard a reedy song. At the first note he looked very serious. He listened closely. He frowned and looked up at his mother. It was a song, a song over the telephone. He giggled.

"He loves it."

"Tell him I'll teach him to play. Tell him what song it is."

She rested her chin on Laddie's silky hair and kissed his neck, tanned as his surfer father's. "'Bandage on My Knee.'" Laddie giggled and snuggled close. "Laddie, can you say hi to your granddad?"

Laddie giggled.

"Say hi."

"Skip it. He can say hi tomorrow."

"He can't wait."

"It's snowing up here. Laddie, you ever seen snow out in California?"

"He doesn't know what it is."

"You and your mom can build a snowman and drink hot cider. And I'll teach you how to play 'Bandage on My Knee.'"

"We'll get up there about eleven."

"I'll call someone to meet you—"

"No. I'll take a bus from town."

"I've got the schedule on the other wall. I'll check. Hold on."

Her father could no longer drive, and she didn't want him to call the neighbors to pick her up. She didn't want him to call her old friends. She wasn't ready to see anyone but him. She had lost touch with all but two of her old high-school classmates and doubted that any others had stayed in town. The truth was, right now, she couldn't handle the questions about what happened to her marriage and what she was going to do. As her father had said, she'd build a snowman, they'd drink mulled cider, the three of them would have Christmas together—then she'd think.

"Nothing till one-thirty."

4 . . .

"I'll take a taxi. Just this once."

Her father didn't argue, but she knew his silence said he felt a taxi was a wild extravagance. He apologized that he hadn't been able to get out of the house for Christmas shopping and buy anything for the boy.

"I'll pick up something here and get a few things for his stocking. The main thing is for all of us to be together."

"This is costing you a fortune."

She smiled. She knew what he was thinking: Kids these days—don't know the value of money. That was the reason for his silence when she said she'd take a taxi. Taxis and picking up the phone to make long distance calls were no part of his life, which hung by the one slender thread of Social Security.

"Dad, I love you."

"I love you, Susie Girl."

"I hope it keeps on snowing up there."

"It will."

"Night, Dad."

"Night—Merry Christmas, Laddie!"

"Merry Christmas, Dad."

She waited for him to hang up the phone—to hear his click so he wouldn't hear hers. She hung up and the boy nuzzled against her.

"What's bandage on my knee?"

"That's a song your granddad always played and sang for me. My song—'Oh, Susannah.' The real words go 'Oh, I'm going to Alabama with a banjo on my knee' but even when I was a lot older than you I still thought the words were 'bandage on my knee.'" A joke between herself and her father. Now she was passing it on to him. "Family joke." She squeezed him.

She wondered if the back porch where they pressed cider in the fall still smelled of apples.

She felt her own hair, which was almost dry, and she was beginning to feel warm again. Better. She smiled. She had not done much smiling lately. She might be crawling home in defeat but at least she had Laddie to show for those years in California.

"Ready for your hot bath?"

"Okay." He twisted around to smile straight up at her and

for a minute Laddie shut out New York and the icy rain and the hotel sign outside the window with its broken neon letters. Was there ever a more wonderful little boy? He was not perfect, of course. On the airplane he had kicked the seat and managed to slosh thousand-island dressing down his Laguna Beach T-shirt, and wet himself before she could rush him to the toilet.

They slid from the bed and padded into the bathroom where she carefully tested the warmth of the water she ran into the tub. She knelt on the bath mat, staring at him, trying to see him as her father would see him for the first time tomorrow. So blond. No one in their family had been so blond. He got that from Scott. Blond hair, gray-blue eyes, and flawless skin that warmed to a hazelnut brown after one afternoon in the sun. The perfect, radiantly healthy, California boy.

The West Coast had never worked its magic on *her*. She had flunked California.

Nine years ago she had come out to Los Angeles, found a job in an insurance office on Wilshire Boulevard, gone to night school and spent every extra moment struggling to turn herself into one of those ravishing girls in television commercials and on hair-coloring boxes—tall and slim and tan with shining yellow hair flying, white teeth flashing. But she faced facts. She was average height, not model-tall. Susannah feared she was average in too many ways, but with unceasing diets—every new one that came along—she had come close at times to having a slender, sexy body. She had seldom eaten a decent meal; she had skimped, poking through salads and yogurt and nibbling bits of lean fish. Before today's two vodkas on the plane, she had seldom drunk more than one glass of white wine. At the end of a love affair, however, or during no affair at all, or when changing jobs, or when everything seemed to go wrong, she would sit down and devour an entire package of corn chips or eat a bag of junk dime-store candy. These binges, followed by remorse and penance, meant sweating through different gyms, dance classes, and yoga. By living close to starvation and exercising constantly, she had trimmed down her thighs and kept her breasts up, young and pointed as any starlet's.

Her hair, however, was a disaster. The first week in

California she began by lightening it from mousy brown to blond. But no matter how much she paid to have it cut or whatever shade of blond she chose, her hair never took on the proud glow of those California golden girls on the packages. Scott said she worried too much about her hair. But when she cut it short he said it made her look like a dyke.

To hell with her hair. Now that she was leaving California for good she was letting it grow back to its natural color.

Scott Bartok worked out of the same insurance office. For the first couple of years of their marriage they laughed a lot, smoked grass with friends, drank too much wine and never missed a weekend surfing. That is, Scott surfed. Susannah slathered herself with suntan cream and stayed out of the sun.

When they were alone, when Scott, with his perfect body and rugged power, took her into his arms, she knew no man could ever bring her greater joy. His vibrant health, what he could do with his body, gave him his reason for being. Surprisingly, at times, he could be more thoughtful and understanding of her as a woman than any man she had ever known. With Scott she overcame her small-town inhibitions and shyness and came close to finding that same physical joy within her own body that meant so much to him.

In the office and at the beach, she talked about rock stars and movies and women's rights and made few references to her reading, a habit she had never been able to break. She didn't talk about books, but the paperbacks stacked up in the corner of the bedroom.

During their entire marriage she could remember Scott reading only one. *Jaws.* Reading was not mellow. In those years "mellow" was Scott's favorite word to encompass everything good in life. "Mellow" and "laid-back." For nine years Susannah had worked very hard at living the mellow, laid-back life with people who cared little for books or classical music, seldom read a newspaper, and never saw a foreign movie.

For nine years she had pretended to be as laid-back as any of them. And if she ever felt she failed to match his glowing health, she never told him, for Scott hated illness and anything that kept the body from delivering totally. She seldom complained, she read without talking about it, and only listened to classical music when she was alone in the Triumph she had bought with her own money.

Scott didn't stay long in insurance, tried becoming a television actor, and sold used sports cars. Every time they got a few dollars ahead, they flew to Hawaii, to Oahu's North Shore, where he rode the Pipeline: an aging surfer smoking more and more weed. She gave up her job, wore larger and larger hats, and began to read more books.

At first she felt irked at the injustice of a world in which Scott could tan and she could only burn and freckle, or he could chugalug a sixpack of beer, wolf down hamburger by the pound and a mountain of french fries, followed by a pint of ice cream, and still strip down muscular and unblemishedly brown, the captain of the volleyball team. It was all in the goddamn genes she decided. And finally, all that dieting and the different shades of blond hair, whether long or short, and—her one unqualified success—her straightened teeth, had not held Scott. He had simply walked out, left her with a Thanksgiving dinner in the oven in that cheap little tract house near Laguna and flown to Hawaii with a nineteen-year-old named Sharon with a perfect body and an even darker tan than his. After he called from Haleiwa, she had locked herself in the bathroom and cried until it was time to come out and give Laddie his dinner. Then she had gone back to the bathroom, cried for another hour, bathed her face in cold water, thrown herself into a frenzy, cleaned the stove, and finished wallpapering the bedroom. But the next day she had realized she couldn't face Christmas in this house, so she sold the Triumph and spent almost all her money on two airline tickets to New York for Laddie and herself.

California had defeated her, but she still had Laddie. She helped him scramble out of the bathtub, wrapped him tightly in a towel, and ran her cheek over his silky hair. He looked like his father. Those clear blue-gray eyes were bluer than Scott's, his hair blonder and straighter. The snub nose—his only less-than-perfect feature—he had gotten, of course, from her.

Several times on the plane and once during his bath he had asked where his father was. Susannah kept changing the subject.

That was another question Susannah would have to face after Christmas, explaining to him that he wouldn't be seeing his father anymore. She took some cheer in the fact that, at least, for now, he would have a grandfather to show him how to press cider and play the harmonica.

Wrapped in his towel and smelling of soap, he held her hand at the window where she pushed back the curtain to peer beyond the hotel's broken neon sign. The city sky flared red. The rain had stopped. The stores out there were still open and their bus was leaving early in the morning. This would be her last chance for Christmas shopping. She fought the idea of putting on Laddie's tennis shoes, which would still be damp, and taking him with her from this warm room, but she could not consider leaving him alone.

She sounded cheerier than she felt. "You want to see Santa?"

He studied her face. Could he?

"Right now. Come on, we'll get dressed."

Back out on the sidewalk in the glitter of bright lights, the December wind cut through their thin California clothes like razors. Mother and son stopped, paralyzed with cold. Susannah took the boy's shaking hand and pulled him close to her side and they pushed into the wind together. After those years in California she had forgotten about winter. She pulled his blue windbreaker collar up around his ears. She would have to buy him heavy clothes. That meant spending more money, money she did not have.

At the corner the whip of icy wind that shrieked off the Atlantic and howled up the city's cement canyons slashed with such fury that they stumbled back. A torn newspaper whirled and slapped Laddie in the face. He shook off his surprise with a blink, then a laugh. He sounded exactly like Scott.

Auto headlights flashed. Horns blared. A taxi roared close and though Susannah pulled Laddie back in time, muddy water splashed her beige pants and raincoat. They stood on the curb shaking with cold. Laddie felt her sense of defeat and looked up at her with pained eyes. She had to decide. Was Christmas and the few gifts she could get here in the city and not in the village after they got off the bus worth this trip?

"Just a couple more blocks," she said as she hugged Laddie's shoulder. "Santa will be at the store."

"Santa." The boy's hand tightened on hers, and he hunched his shoulders against the wind and led the way, trudging across the street. In spite of being startled and shrinking back from a manhole cover, where steam breathed up in feverish gusts, he pulled on her hand. At a pothole Laddie stumbled, but recovered in time to keep from falling in the wet street. He had gotten that coordination from Scott.

The ground shook. Below, a subway train rumbled.

"It'll be warm once we're in the store. Okay?"

The boy's teeth chattered with cold but his hand tugged hers. "Okay." He sounded exactly like his father dashing in from the surf, blue with cold.

Susannah wished she could pick him up and run through the freezing night into the warm, but Laddie weighed thirty-one pounds. "First thing we do, is we get you some warm, woolen mittens. You want some nice, warm woolen mittens?"

Laddie, shaking with cold, bobbed a nod that meant yes.

"You know what mittens are?"

He shook his head. No.

"Come on. You'll see. Let's race!"

Together they ran through a crowd of black shapes, more people than Susannah had ever seen in one place in Los Angeles. All of them were out shopping late in the icy night.

"First we get you your mittens, then we get your granddad a nice warm sweater."

At one corner the lights spangled brighter and the icy wind carried the sharp tang of frying onions from a luncheonette. A speaker blared Christmas carols. Bells rang out on the cold air. Crowds hurried in all directions. Laddie's small hand locked tighter and tighter on his mother's as he shook with the chill and shrank from the throngs of people. His solemn eyes looked up, stunned. The still-tanned little boy had never seen so many people or heard so much noise or shook with such cold.

Outside one of the biggest department stores in the world his hand clenched his mother to a stop. He stood wide-eyed pointing at a Santa Claus tinking a little bell, and Susannah got him away only by promising they would come back and talk with Santa the minute they had finished their shopping.

The enormous store was, as she had said, warm. Warm and full of light and music and jammed with shoving people in thick coats carrying packages.

First she bought the boy a red wool cap, which he pulled down over his ears, giggling. She couldn't resist a pair of matching red woolen mittens. She showed him how to pull them over his cold hands. Having never seen such things as mittens, Laddie stared at his covered fingers. He uncovered them. Covered them. Gazing at his red mittens and grinning with glee he pranced around, bumping into people.

Susannah didn't let him see her buy a harmonica. She found the soft, warm sweater she wanted for her father, but slid it back across the counter. It cost more than she could afford. Leaving the counter, she changed her mind, and opened her wallet on her few remaining dollars. She had paid for tomorrow's bus ticket and set aside money for the taxi in her home town. She calculated she had enough for Laddie's sandwich and an orange drink after Santa, if all she had was coffee. The only thing she would need money for before they got on the bus was breakfast.

Laddie approached Santa Claus slowly. He finally overcame his shyness to look past the froth of white whiskers, directly into the red face, and solemnly vowed that he had been a good boy. Santa grinned at the boy's mother. What a radiant, tan little boy he was. Susannah again felt her eyes sting and fill with hot tears of pride and love and sudden happiness. She felt guilt at dropping only a quarter into Santa's pot.

A band of street kids in too-large overcoats and swirling floppy hats shading dark glasses pushed by. Dark glasses glinted. Yes, dark glasses on an icy, black night like this in Manhattan. Susannah shook her head and wondered why people would dress like that.

Out in the icy wind Susannah crouched down and tucked Laddie's blond hair under the wool cap. The little boy flexed his mittens, waved his hands, and grinned.

"You ready for a sandwich?"

He nodded. He would eat a sandwich, but he stared at his mittens, which interested him more than food. Susannah straightened up and looked across the street at a lunch counter. At the corner they waited for the light. Crowds surged around them. Several people pushed close. Dark glasses glinted. Were these the same kids she had seen before, with their wild hair and swirling overcoats and floppy hats?

Suddenly a wet spray of something even colder than the icy wind jabbed her eyes sharply as needles. She gasped, dropped her father's sweater, her hands raised to her stinging face. Writhing in agony, she stumbled blindly.

One hand went out for the boy.

"Laddie!"

Squinting and choking from the stinging spray, she rubbed one hand at streaming tears, the other clawed desperately beside her for Laddie. She reeled, fighting to keep her balance. Helpless in her blindness, she stumbled in a circle, frantically groping for her son. She found nothing.

12 . . .

2

DECEMBER 21, 10:03 P.M.

"Laddie!"

As she turned her face streaming with tears into the icy wind, the woman's cry was raw animal fear, her hands grabbed wildly.

"Laddie!"

Christmas shoppers clutching packages recoiled from this frantic woman in the raincoat, lunging among them like a blindfolded player in a game of blindman's buff. This was no game. This woman was screaming with horror and the others hurried past with frightened eyes. Craziness. City craziness. Mind your own business and stay clear of such craziness, the first reaction in a city where addicts and drunks lurch by, crones scavenge garbage into shopping bags, blank-eyed men and women babble to themselves, lost souls suddenly shout out, kids with transistor radios in their ears, hearing nothing but their own music, bop along to a wild beat, switchblades ready to flash. Crazies. Everyone in the city knew enough to stay away from crazies.

The blinded woman stood in one place, rocking back and forth, shrieking her howl of pain.

"Laddie!"

No one seemed less eager to approach such hysteria than a young policeman whose bushy black hair sprouted out from under his blue cap. Hardly more than a kid, with a muddy complexion and scared eyes, he made too much of a show of squaring his shoulders and marching fearlessly toward her. Now that someone had taken on the job of facing the woman, onlookers began to slow. He let her howl as he picked up a dropped package—an offering he could thrust forward—a way to approach her. He clutched the sweater in the bag and waited for the woman to gasp for air, a moment of silence.

"Lady," he began in a voice the wind whipped away. He began again. "Lady, I'm a police officer . . ."

"My son!—" Susannah's body jerked in the direction of the man's voice. Her hand lashed out, swung, scraped past the scared young man. Her hand banged his face.

"Lady, we gotta get you somewhere you can wash out your eyes. Let's hope it's Mace or ammonia. They do that sometimes. Spray people. . . ." He reached for her arm but the blinded woman wrenched away. Her hand warned him off. She was signaling that no one would move her from this cold and gritty sidewalk.

"Lady." His voice was loud now, almost a command. "Before we do anything, we got to wash out your eyes."

"My son! He's gone. Somebody took my son!"

The police officer found himself standing dumbly, his hand wadding her package. He made a sudden grab for her arm, but this time she flailed wildly as an animal that has lost its young. She thrust away. She would not move from this place.

A skinny black youth with a long, sad face under a purple wool hat and inappropriately dressed for the winter night in only a Levi's jacket and pants, shoved his way through the crowd toward the officer. "Use your fuckin' radio, man. Call a fuckin' ambulance while I get some fuckin' water."

"Right!" The young cop, helpless as a scared kid, nodded vigorously, eager and visibly relieved to be told what to do. He unhooked the radio from his belt as the black man loped off, dodging like a basketball player through the cross-street traffic to a lunch counter.

A blue-and-white patrol car flashing lights screeched to the curb. The door opened on a radio chattering police calls. An older policeman in a shiny gray raincoat climbed out and pushed through the crowd to the young cop, who had found himself reduced to keeping the frantic woman from banging into onlookers. The young man cast the officer a look of enormous relief and managed to wait for the older man to reach him before he spoke. "They sprayed something in her eyes. She says somebody snatched her kid."

"If it's her eyes she shouldn't be here. She needs emergency care."

"She won't leave."

Susannah groped toward the men's voices. From her wet and shining face she spoke in their direction.

"He's only two. He's blond—with a brand-new red cap and red mittens. Please . . ."

She waited, leaning her body toward them, listening.

The tall policeman led the younger man a few paces away so the woman would not hear. "How do you know she's not a crazy?"

The skinny black man in the purple hat pushed through the crowd carrying a white plastic bucket sloshing water. His other hand gripped paper napkins. The cops watched him plunge a handful of paper into the water. When the sopping wet reached her eyes, Susannah stiffened. She reached for other wet napkins thrust into her hand.

"Just water," the black man said. "Wash your eyes."

She did not move fast enough for him and he dipped more napkins in the bucket and daubed her face.

Susannah stood absolutely still. The black man leaned close. "Guys do that. Ammonia probably. Sprayed me once. You got to wash it all out. It'll sting for a while, but once we get it out you be all right."

"My boy," she gasped to this man who leaned close. "They took my boy . . ."

The lights in the department store dimmed. The black man handed the bucket to a startled fat woman in a plaid coat and laid a second wad of fresh water on Susannah's eyes. The older officer slowly crossed the sidewalk to the woman and the black man as he signaled the hairy officer to hold back the curious.

"I'm a police officer, Ma'am."

"Please— My son—"

"The department will do everything we can." The older officer turned a tired, gray face to the black man. He flattened his voice, as if any flicker of emotion would betray unprofessionalism. "You see what happened?"

The black man ignored the policeman. "Hold still," he said to Susannah.

"You see anybody take her kid?"

Except for a shake of his head with the purple cap, that said no, the black man continued to ignore the officer.

"Okay. You've helped." The policeman moved a step closer. "Now take off."

The man bathing Susannah's eyes peered into the woman's face. "Can you open your eyes? Come on. That's it. Can you see?"

Onlookers, who had slowed, now surged closer. The older policeman, the black man with the dripping napkins, the crowd, and the young cop shared a long silence waiting for the woman to speak. Susannah nodded. The crowd murmured. She reached out, took the package from the young cop, tore it open and dried her face with the sweater. Her eyes met the black man's.

"Thank you."

The older policeman made it clear he was taking over. "That's all," he said quietly to the black man. "Take off."

The man grabbed the bucket from the fat woman, poured the last of the water on the sidewalk, splashing it onto the officer's shoes. He twisted away through the crowd. Susannah reached out in an attempt to stop the man. Too late. He was gone. Susannah moved away from the police to stand alone. She turned. The two officers waited but the onlookers, convinced the excitement was over, eddied away as she pushed aside the last of the crowd to peer up the sidewalk. The pavement in the dim light from the store windows had nearly cleared and only a few shadows moved through the light. Susannah stopped, turned, rubbed her eyes to look in the other direction. The older officer reached the curb and the waiting patrol car with its blinking lights. He held the door open.

"If you'll come with us, Ma'am. Let's have a doctor look at your eyes."

Susannah stood in the middle of the sidewalk, where only a few people hurried. Another set of lights in the store dimmed. No carols rang out on loudspeakers. No bells rang.

"Ma'am. Let's go."

Susannah hugged her packages with one hand. With the other she signaled the men away. "I can't leave till I find him—"

"At precinct we'll get people right on it."

Against the light the police and the few who lingered could see her shake with cold.

"It's warm in the car, Ma'am." The older officer reached out his hand.

Susannah shook her head. "He could come back and I wouldn't be here."

"The other officer will stay right here."

Susannah turned to the light, wiped her shining face with the sweater. She pushed her wet hair back from her glittering eyes. The young officer moved toward her to post himself on the sidewalk where she had first stood. He was showing her he would stay here. Answering a sign from the officer at the car, the young man clicked on his portable radio. Static crackled.

"We'll be in radio contact," the man at the car said.

Susannah looked at the older officer, then at the younger. "He won't leave?"

"No, Ma'am. He'll stay right here."

Susannah suddenly ran to the man with the portable radio and grasped his arm. He could not fail to sense her raw life-and-death urgency. "He's only two. Blond. Straight white-blond hair. He still has his tan from California."

She took one step toward the patrol car, but stopped. "He's wearing a blue windbreaker, red cap and red mittens."

The men waited.

"Laddie." She spoke carefully as if the men might never have heard such a name. "His name's Laddie Bartok."

Susannah found herself being helped into the back seat of the warm patrol car. The older man slammed the door. She pressed quickly to the window and wiped a clear patch in the mist to stare back at the man on the sidewalk.

3

DECEMBER 21, 10:53 P.M.

Susannah shook. Her scalded eyes streamed. She shrank at the noise and heat of so many people milling through a room that seemed to be brick and concrete. In a blur she trailed the officer through the crowd—mostly teenagers, black, white, and brown—few of whom looked dressed warmly enough for the bitter night. Around her some pretended swaggering arrogance and sullen bravado; most looked stunned and confused, eyes betraying naked fear. A thin girl with bare, white, skeleton arms raked at stringy black hair and sobbed. A boy, no more than fifteen, in a leather jacket studded with Nazi SS skulls and swastikas, a bloody red cross gashed into his forehead, jabbed obscene gestures and shrieked vile curses at the world.

Susannah's wet eyes saw colored lights flare, and she dodged around a glowing Christmas tree.

On the second floor she found herself moving down a hall past offices where silent kids slumped in chairs. A man and a woman screaming in Spanish burst from a door, a tangle of slapping and clawing. A baby wailed.

Susannah tried to resist being led into a washroom where two policewomen bathed her eyes. They insisted she see a doctor, but she tore away from their help shouting she was losing time, that every second was taking her further from her son. One of the women led her to an office where a detective in his early thirties was putting a container of coffee on his desk and pulling off a duffle coat, just coming on duty for the night. This pink-faced man with short red hair had the all-American grown-up-boy look shared by some of the astronauts, and a shy smile that had been no little help in advancing him from the street into this office. At the moment he kept his smile under control. This was a woman in trouble. He looked concerned. Friendly, but concerned. With rather old-fashioned manners and with a soft and calm voice he introduced himself as Detective Lieutenant Ernest Foy and suggested Mrs. Bartok take off her wet raincoat. Susannah refused. She felt that to take off her coat would prolong her stay in this office. She ached to be out on the streets. Every instinct urged her back out into the bitter night to search for her son.

Foy slid a plastic chair to the side of his desk and motioned for her to sit. She hesitated. He drew a silver automatic pencil from the inner pocket of a sports jacket of artificial suede. He straightened the collar of his brown turtleneck sweater. Only when she sat did he sit.

An hour later the silver pencil cross-checked between a Report for a Missing Person and a Worksheet for Missing Persons under Ten Years of Age or Retarded.

Foy sent out for more coffee.

For Susannah these questions were an interminable agony. The man allowed no hurrying. Each exchange had been as precise as his silver pencil, the point carefully adjusted, printing carefully.

Foy said he was sending out an all-points-bulletin by teletype and radio—a full description of Laddie that would go to all police. An immediate and all-out search of the area, he assured her, was now under way. Because she was a resident of Southern California he had teletyped the police there and was awaiting their report.

California? Didn't he believe her?

He showed her the Worksheet for Missing Persons under Ten Years of Age or Retarded and the agencies he would automatically check, including the Children's Shelter, New York Foundling Hostel, Bureau of Child Welfare, Callagy Hall, The Runaway Squad . . .

She stopped him. She fought giving way to shrill desperation. But why, why were they sitting here? Every second that ticked by took her farther away from her son.

Foy worked on.

And the FBI? Didn't they come in on kidnapping?

Foy explained that her son was a Missing Person, Child. She fought to understand. Kidnapping had yet to be established. She could produce no witnesses who had actually seen the boy torn from her. Wasn't he going to call in the FBI?

No. No FBI. Not at this time. Foy spoke of presumptive evidence, use of force, a missing child under unusual circumstances. All words and terms she did not understand.

"You said 'use of force.' What else would you call that spray?"

"We'll check with the Bureau."

Seconds, minutes, precious time ticked by.

Lieutenant Foy ripped open four saccharin packets to stir into his coffee. Susannah refused to touch hers. The goddamn coffee gave them one more excuse to sit here.

Lieutenant Foy adjusted his silver pencil precisely and moved it slowly down the report. Susannah prayed this must be, this had to be, the end of the questions.

He frowned. He considered. Susannah shut her eyes and fought screaming. Please God, don't make them sit here any longer. Why didn't he help her find her son? He was as bad as that hotel clerk who did not trust her even when she paid in cash for the room. A sudden thought chilled her heart. "He doesn't believe me. He isn't even convinced that I have a child. He doesn't even believe anyone sprayed my eyes." She had shown him Laddie's picture, a grinning Laddie she let them photocopy but promise to return to her.

"You almost act as if you didn't believe me," Susannah said in a weak voice.

"The important thing is to get the facts down now." He spoke without looking at her. "Saves time in the long run." He leaned back, swiveled his chair, and faced a pot of red Christmas poinsettias on the corner of his desk. He pinched off a dead leaf. Susannah thought of home. In Laguna, alongside their garage, these red flowers grew in masses as tall as she. Here in New York they grew in little pots.

The detective continued, as deliberate as his shiny automatic pencil. He was asking Susannah about her husband, how long they'd been separated, if there was a chance the father might feel the child had been taken from him unfairly, if he might do something desperate. Susannah ended that. Scott Bartok was surfing on the north shore of Oahu in the state of Hawaii. He didn't give a damn about her or the boy.

"We're wasting time!" Susannah surprised herself at the sharpness in her voice and cautioned herself; if she wanted this man's help, she must appear to cooperate with him. "I'm sorry. Look, I've answered all these questions—" She drew in a long breath. "I told you, I didn't plan on being in the city. Not even one night. The plane was late getting in. No one in the world but my father knew we were coming. Only he and the clerk at the hotel knows we're here. No one could plan it for ransom. Like I told you, right now I only have three dollars to my name." She leaned forward and tried to force the man to look at her.

Foy studied his shiny silver pencil.

"So please. Do we have to go on and on? My son's gone. Until we get out of this office and start looking we're just wasting time!"

"I can understand how it might seem that way to you—"

"Goddammit! Every second is life and death. Laddie's out there and we're sitting here!"

Foy returned to his report.

"Look." Susannah fought to sound reasonable. "Please." She knew enough about men from working in offices and from Scott that she must never, never give a man an excuse to accuse her of being hysterical. God, who wouldn't be hysterical at a time like this? She stifled her every impulse to cry out; she prayed she sounded controlled. "This is a kidnapping. If you're not going to call in the FBI, can't we at least get started?"

The man's clear astronaut eyes met hers.

"Start looking," she begged.

"I told you. We are looking."

"No. I mean you. Me."

"Where?"

Susannah failed to stifle a gasp. She stared at the hand with its tiny orange hairs that returned the silver pencil to the reports.

"I don't have to tell you, Mrs. Bartok. This is a big city."

"Jesus." Stunned, Susannah felt drained of any power to move. She shook violently. Her stomach ached so terribly she bent double. "Jesus Christ—is that all you've got to tell me?"

Foy said nothing.

She shoved back her chair and rose. She pulled her raincoat, still heavy with damp, around her.

"My son is out there!" Her cry was loud enough that a tall officer passing the office stopped.

Outside the door a woman with a wild tangle of shining black hair slowed. She looked in. Gypsy-dark eyes flashed from Susannah to Foy as the woman reached into a leather shoulder bag that hung across the rawhide side of a sheepskin coat. White fur curled at the collar and cuffs. Foy glanced at the door. His look made it clear he knew this woman. His frown made it more than clear he did not want to see her standing there.

His voice was still quiet. "Please sit down, Mrs. Bartok."

"So I can keep wasting time answering your goddamn questions? When you're not doing a goddamn thing? Please—if you can't—or won't help me find my son—then for God's sake tell me now so I can find someone who can!"

"Mrs. Bartok, please." He gestured toward the chair.

She shook her head. Her hands clenched into fists deep in her raincoat pockets. She fought tears.

Foy returned to his silver pencil rather than look at Susannah or the woman at the door. "I don't want to unnecessarily discourage you, Mrs. Bartok, but I don't think you realize what we're up against." His eyes never left the pencil. "You don't know this city. You can't possibly have any idea what it's like out there." His orange head tilted in the direction of the precinct's front door.

The black-haired woman still stood at the door staring straight at him.

"Out there on the street it's—it's a lot rougher than you can possibly imagine."

He waited. Did she understand? She struggled to speak, to ask the one question she had been too frightened to speak aloud and had avoided until this very moment—the terrible question she could scarcely force herself to ask. "What do they want with him?" She choked back tears. "I don't have any money so why did they take him?"

"We have a lot of questions and we're going to help you find your son, but it will help if you let us handle this our way." He reached inside his imitation suede jacket, pulled out a wallet and pulled out two Polaroids. He held out the two pictures, bright colors of a summer day. A red-haired boy grinned broadly, a girl with red hair and blue eyes smiled her father's smile. "Just so you'll know. I have two of my own. Believe me, I know how you feel—"

Hands still in her pockets, Susannah turned from the summertime children. "No. You don't know." Her voice was more bitter than the night outside. "Yours are warm and safe at home. My boy's out there in the black and the ice-cold rain with God knows who and you're still sitting there filling out papers and drinking coffee . . ."

Standing there in her damp raincoat, she blinked back tears. She shook. She raised her head, threw it back, and in a shocking animal cry sobbed her pain.

Before Foy could rise and run after her, Susannah had pushed past the woman at the door, dashed down the crowded hall, and shoved through the crowds to reach the front door. She lowered her bare head against the blast of freezing rain and ran into the night.

4

DECEMBER 22, 12:12 A.M.

The glow from the department store windows glittered through streaks of rain. Across the sidewalk a taxi pulled away from the curb where Susannah drew her raincoat close and hunched her shoulders against the cold. She took her place on the pavement where she had clutched out into the emptiness crying her son's name.

The young policeman with the radio was nowhere in sight. That did not surprise her. She guessed that he'd probably left soon after the patrol car eased away, for now she felt that everything the police had done was only an effort to placate, to smooth over another crime they knew to be unsolvable. That kid cop with his radio? Why should he shiver here in the freezing cold? It wasn't his son who was stolen. And the lieutenant with his coffee with four saccharins and his damn automatic pencil? His kids were safe and warm at home. What did he do? He wasted her time. He told her this was a big city and rougher than she could imagine. What could they do?

What could she do? She peered up and down the nearly empty street. A bag lady lugging bulging shopping bags shuffled through the light. A drunk with his coat flapping open lurched past. Three black boys pressing transistor radios to their ears, bent low, sprinting against the wind, filling the night with music.

She clamped her jaw to keep her teeth from chattering and stamped her wet and freezing feet in their thin California shoes. Slashes of icy rain drove her back against the store window's glow.

This was the last place she had held Laddie's hand. What could she do?

Instinctively she found herself performing a number of rituals. She prayed to God for help. She shut her eyes and willed that when she opened them Laddie would be standing in front of her waving red mittens and giggling. She chanted his name. Over and over and over she chanted his name.

At the sound of footsteps she fell silent. She opened her eyes and listened. A man in a long coat was slowly moving in the light, tracing an arc crossing the sidewalk toward her. Unmistakably, each step brought him nearer and nearer. She closed her eyes and held her breath. His footsteps slowed. Each beat of her heart slammed in her ears. A sidelong glance showed a face under a wide-brimmed hat, bright eyes shining. His steps scraped close enough now that she could hear rattling breaths. She felt her back against cold glass.

Other steps, running toward her, pounded louder and louder.

"Mrs. Bartok!" It was a woman's voice.

The voice spun the man around. A woman in a sheepskin coat clutching a shoulder bag charged straight at him. "*Cabrón*— get the fuck out of here!"

The man's face, catching the light, flashed startled eyes; a big wet mouth dropped open with surprise. Susannah lashed out an arm but the man crouched and pitched back with a thud into the window. Under attack and at bay he twisted from the two, recovered his footing, and plunged past them, his coat swirling wildly.

Standing with Susannah in the light listening to the sound of his footsteps fade on the cold pavement, the woman in the sheepskin coat pulled her bag up on her shoulder. Her face was dark. Spanish, Susannah guessed. A strong, unsmiling face with heavy black brows and huge eyes almost entirely filled with brown pupils sparkled in the window's light.

"It's okay," she said with no accent. "Don't be scared."

Susannah searched for her own voice, a voice she was not sure would be there. She managed to stammer, "Are you a policewoman?"

The woman swept coils of black hair away from eyes that looked straight at Susannah and nowhere else. She said nothing.

"If you're not with the police, how did you know my name?"

"Back there. At the precinct. With Lieutenant Foy. I was at the door. When you ran out I tried to stop you. After I missed you I read his report. I put myself in your place. If I were you, where would I go next?"

Susannah glanced past the woman, at the corner where the store windows spilled light on the empty sidewalk. Now that she was here she realized her return to the scene of the crime looked futile. Futile or not, what else could she do?

"You need help," the woman said flatly.

"But you're not with the police."

"They're helping?" The woman's sarcasm that dismissed the police was the voice of this city.

"Why don't they?"

"Help? They'll try. They'll do what they can. As Foy says, 'it's a big city.'" The brown eyes left Susannah long enough to glance across the shining wet street where a taxi passed the lights of the luncheonette. "Come on. I'll buy you a cup of hot coffee."

Susannah made no move.

The dark eyes returned to Susannah's. The woman held out her hand. "My name's Victoria Cruz."

"Are you a reporter?"

"I do some writing."

"A reporter," Susannah's voice was an accusation.

"There are worse things I could be. Come on."

Susannah shook her head, shrank into her raincoat, and backed against the window.

Victoria Cruz went inside the luncheonette and sat at the counter under the dead-white glare of the fluorescent light. She pulled open her sheepskin coat on a black wool turtleneck sweater. The place with its steamed-over windows where car headlights flashed was stifling. When at last the other woman had come in from the cold, as Victoria knew she'd have to, they sat together. Victoria sipped a cold drink from a paper cup. "On TV and in the movies they always show reporters drinking booze." She did all the talking. A cup of black steaming coffee she ordered for Susannah went untouched on the counter. Susannah, her raincoat still buttoned, slumped on the last stool, facing the wall.

"As you will notice, I don't drink. Except for these piña coladas. Piña coladas and sometimes beer from China."

She put the drink down to forage deep into her leather bag until she found an enameled metal Art Deco cigarette case in black and silver, which she snapped open. "But I smoke. You smoke? Terrific Colombian gold."

She offered the open case to the woman's back. She did not expect conversation: She did not expect the other woman to turn. "No? Then how about showing me his picture?"

Did Susannah shake her head?

"You gave the cops his picture, but you made them copy it and give it back. Apparently you don't trust them." She drew a box of old-fashioned kitchen matches from her bag and struck flame from the sandpaper side. She lit the joint and drew deeply, holding the smoke.

"Is it people you don't trust or just cops?" She spoke without exhaling smoke. When she didn't get an answer she went on, undeterred. "So what did you plan to do over there across the street? Stand in the icy rain till you got mugged or raped or at the very least came down with double pneumonia?" Only now did she allow a trickle of smoke to curl up in front of her shining brown eyes. "Get sick and that won't do that kid of yours much good."

Susannah spun around on the stool. Her wet face shone. "Why don't the police help?"

Victoria held smoke until she was ready to exhale, her turn not to answer.

Susannah fought tears. "That damn cop doesn't care."

"Ernest C. Foy? Boy detective? *El carajo?*"

Susannah slid back wet hair from her glistening eyes. "In that office. You said you saw us. You tell me. Why? Why did he treat me like that?"

Victoria offered another joint which Susannah refused. She snapped shut the case and ran fingers with nails chewed down to bloody stumps lovingly over the angular design, a 1930s motif that made its owner think of the Chrysler Building. "You don't know?"

Susannah searched the other woman's face.

"He treated you like that because he can't help you. Don't get me wrong. I don't like cops, but in this case, believe it or not, he thinks he's being a good guy—kind." She smoked. "To a nice lady like you, Ernest C. Foy doesn't want to be a shit."

Susannah waited. She knew the reporter would explain.

"What do you expect him to tell you with two thousand homicides a year, two hundred thousand muggings, five thousand rapes? This city's under siege. He's losing the battle. He knows it better than you or I. He's surrounded by a city full of killers, junkies, thieves, pimps, perverts, you name it—the total spectrum of weird scum. You come in with your story about your boy— what is that? That is one case out of who knows how many he hears every shift. Even if he really wants to help, he knows the odds against what he can do." She shrugged indicating the detective's hopelessness. "Not much."

"He lost all that time filling out that report."

"You'd rather he told you the real odds against finding your kid?"

"Will he call the FBI?"

"What can they do?"

Susannah found the woman sliding the coffee down the counter, something to hang onto while she talked of things a mother hadn't dared think about. "Would you rather he pulled out his stack of photos and asked you one by one if you'd seen any of the faces from his collection of weird scum with police records who prowl these streets? Jesus Christ, their looks alone would scare you to death. Would you have liked him better if he'd made you guess which one of those would want a little boy and what they'd want him for?" This thought apparently chilled even this reporter who so clearly prided herself on her big-city hardness. She stopped long enough to sip her drink. Susannah did not touch her coffee. "You really think you'd like him to tell you about religious cults in this city that use kids' blood?" The hand with the smoking joint signaled she had more to add. "True, nobody's actually proved the existence of such cults, but that's what you hear on the streets." She smoked. "Might even be preferable to the creep sex fiends who do worse things." Victoria stopped. Her eyes locked with Susannah's. Did the boy's mother want to hear more? "He sat there asking himself if you were a lady who was up to looking at the faces of crazy ladies who've lost kids of their own. Or worse, those others who have it in their whacked-out heads that they've lost kids they've never even had—so they have to go out and steal someone else's. Would you have liked to look at their faces?" Victoria watched Susannah claw her raincoat around her and hug herself with red hands. "Did it occur to you that maybe your boy's in one of those bags you see those old hags dragging around? Or maybe by now he's stuffed in a garbage can. Or floating with chunks of ice in the river along with the dead dogs and cats—"

"No!" Susannah's face, white in the light and splotched with freckles, drew back. She held up trembling hands to put space between herself and this woman.

"Foy held off telling you. So will the Feds—the FBI—if they come in. And right now you hate me more for making you face what you're up against than you hate them for doing nothing. I'm telling you that if you plan to do anything beside hang around that corner you're going to have to think about who you're dealing with, because, believe me, Mrs. Bartok, when it comes to thinking what you're up against, the wildest, most obscene thing I can suggest can't begin to match what is going on right now out there in these streets."

"Shut the hell up!" With a cry of utter loathing she started to push past the woman.

"What's your plan? Where are you going?"

30 . . .

Blocked and drained of the strength to be able to answer, Susannah turned to the wall.

"You talk about wasting time. You're going back over there and stand on that corner in the dark? Keep warm and ask yourself why one of those crazies out there in the night wants your son. Figure that out because that's the only way you can do yourself and your boy any good." She waited. She reached out, but stopped herself before she touched the other woman. "Unless you've got a city full of friends, it looks to me like you're all alone in this—"

"Get out of my way." Susannah twisted around and slammed hard, but Victoria had sensed the thrust coming and blocked her. Trapped, Susannah's eyes faltered and she dropped her forehead against the misted glass.

"The cops and the Feds won't tell you. I'm telling you."

She drew in smoke.

"Cheer up, Mrs. Bartok. I happen to be starting with the worst that can happen. It just might be that I can help. When I go to work on a story I put myself in the position of the victim as well as the criminal. Read my work. You'll find out I know what I'm doing. After all, I did find you on that corner didn't I?" She drew in more smoke. "When I go to work I don't stop till I find a pattern—the reason that brought you and those others together on this dark night." The steamed-over windows flashed with lights. "There's got to be a reason. At least you better hope to God there is a reason, because if this is the wild work of some maniac—"

Susannah covered her face with red hands. "Shut up."

Victoria pulled one red hand from the other woman's face and turned her by the shoulder. "Look at me."

Susannah twisted from the woman.

"I can help."

"So you can write a story?"

"Yes."

"Get out of my way!"

"I'm every bit as serious about this as you are. Okay," she conceded, "I'm not his mother. Almost as serious. What matters is I can help." She couldn't see the woman's face. Had she moved her? "I don't even know where you're staying. Without going back to the police, how the hell do I get in touch with you?"

Susannah found the strength to push past the woman in the sheepskin coat. Victoria scribbled in a notebook. "Here. My address and telephone number." She ripped out the page and caught Susannah at the door where she thrust the paper into her raincoat pocket.

5

DECEMBER 22, 12:47 A.M.

The rain had stopped but the wind shrieked, a fiercer, icier wind that had driven everyone but Susannah from the sidewalk. It was here Laddie had stopped her when he first heard Santa ringing his bell to the hurrying crowds.

That had been less than three hours ago. Three aching hours. Three hours in which each second that passed took her one more beat of eternity farther from her son.

"Laddie?" The wind snatched away her voice.

Any warmth from the luncheonette had chilled. She hunched her shoulders, thrust her bare hands deep in her pockets, clamped her chattering teeth and peered up and down the street. She hated that damned reporter for telling her those things, for telling her she was alone in the city. Alone. But she realized she was not entirely alone. There she was. That damned reporter was standing there now, outlined against the light of the luncheonette. She was watching Susannah, accusing her of wasting time shivering here in the dark.

To hell with the reporter. Susannah knew why she had to be on this corner. She had to keep her link to that last moment in her life three hours ago when she had held Laddie's hand and her world made sense, before this agony of terror and dread closed her off from everything else. This corner was her last link.

Susannah searched the sidewalk. If she could find the smallest thing that proved she had been here with Laddie, she would have something to hold onto, something besides memory.

The sweater? Where was that sweater? That could be proof she had been in the store with Laddie. She remembered holding it against her wet eyes.

The wind-scoured sidewalk showed nothing.

The reporter, standing against the light, smoked.

Susannah hurried to the curb where black rainwater glinted in puddles turning white with ice. Then she saw it. One red mitten lay half-sunk in a frozen puddle.

In her hand Laddie's mitten crackled with ice. She thawed it against her cheek and a rush of hope warmed her against the night. Laddie! Laddie had been here. He was real. He was real and he had been here. He had dropped this mitten and he could not simply have disappeared from the face of the earth. He was somewhere in this city. The hotel. A sudden urge compelled her to the hotel. Laddie was at the hotel!

The mitten made all the difference between despair and hope. She would run to the hotel. She dodged through the lights of a screeching cab and raced through the dark streets, certain, absolutely certain, that her son was not only alive, he was waiting for her, sitting on a torn, plastic couch in that grim lobby. By some miracle the police had found him and brought him there. Yes, he was there now. That was what this overpowering urge was telling her. She would dash into that lobby with its burned lamp shade and there he'd be—sitting there on that torn plastic couch, pink and tan, gold hair glowing, waiting for her, laughing, madly dashing to her with outstretched arms.

She raced. She flew like a wild scrap of newspaper lashing by in the wind. Her footfalls rang out on iron grids in the sidewalk where hot air gushed as subway trains rumbled in a world of concrete and steel far below.

Her heart slammed. Cold air burned her lungs but she ran, gasping and staggering, her wet hair whipping her eyes. When she saw the hotel with its broken neon sign she drove herself even faster.

Laddie.

Laddie would be there waiting for her in that hotel. She clutched the mitten; her other hand clawed back freezing hair. Even if Laddie did not run to her in that lobby, she would find the police had left a message for her that he was waiting for her at the precinct. Not far to go now. The sleazy bars, the shops full of cameras, the pornographic bookstores blurred in the wind and rain as she stumbled to push open the hotel door.

Not a golden little boy, but a gray old man reading a newspaper sat on the plastic couch. Breathless, she ran to the desk barely able to gasp out her call for the pale clerk to leave his blaring television.

Her heart sank. Before the clerk left his show's rattling gunfire she could see the empty pigeonholes behind the counter. 307. Her room. Empty. Nothing there. No folded paper. No message. Still, the clerk would tell her the good news . . .

The man stood in the office door. Her heart slammed. She struggled for breath. She scarcely dared ask: "Three-oh-seven. Bartok. Any messages?"

On television horses whinnied and hooves pounded. He shook his head.

"Please. Will you look?"

With a martyred sigh, the man drew on his gold-rimmed glasses and glanced at the pigeonholes and a counter beneath the SEASONS GREETINGS sign. He picked up a package. He studied an outsize envelope. He shook his head. Nothing.

What made him avoid her? Was he like this with all people or did he have a special reason to want to have as little to do with her as possible?

"You have the room key." His voice was an accusation. Why was she disturbing him? Susannah struggled for breath. No message. No Laddie in this lobby. The worn red carpet, the very ground she stood on, was opening beneath her. Her shaking hand clutched the key in her pocket as she found her way to a chair. Ice-cold hands with the mitten and the room key covered her eyes.

What now? Go back out into the bitter night? And do what? Go to the police, of course. But she could call them from her room. She sprang to her feet. Yes. Her room. Another surge of hope drove her. Yes. Of course. She would call the police and discover Laddie was with them.

In the slow elevator she told herself that Laddie being with the police made the most sense of all. They had the boy. Foy would be happy to tell her that the golden-haired little boy was with him right now, lapping an ice-cream cone. You see? There had been nothing to worry about after all. She could shut her eyes. She could laugh. The nightmare would be over.

Damn this slow elevator.

One thought made her tremble. Someone had sprayed her eyes to grab the boy. Who would steal a child? If they did, why would they ever give him back? Was that horrible pale man at the desk avoiding her because he had something to do with this? Had he seen the boy and called the others? She couldn't think about that now. She'd think about something else. Anything else.

She and Laddie had stood in this car three and a half hours ago. She remembered that she was pleased he couldn't understand these scratched walls. The FUCK. The crude figures. Who were these people, so obsessed that they drew things like this on walls? Who were the people who stole children?

People kidnapped for money. That made sense. Cruel, terrible as it was, it made sense. But they didn't steal Laddie because she had money. This thought made her shake with worry.

She held her breath as she waited on the telephone for the lieutenant. Fear closed in when she learned that Foy was off duty and she found herself talking with a Sergeant Braverman. Fear gripped her in cold sweat when the man volunteered no word of a message. Shaking badly she had to force a deep breath before she dared ask for any news. The man was pretending, exactly as Foy had done, that the police were on top of the case, that he and the entire force were moving heaven and earth, doing everything humanly possible to find the boy.

He talked on.

There was no message.

Victoria Cruz had been right. Like Foy, the man was lying to her because he felt it was kinder to lie. He was stroking her. But Susannah refused to be stroked. "But what are you doing?" She found herself shouting. She had broken the rules. The man met her cry with silence. Now she was expected to join in the lie and tell him she was sorry. She couldn't, she wouldn't do that. Sergeant Braverman spoke in that professional way police handle desperate people. He told her she was not to lose hope; she was to feel free to call him anytime. He added that simply because Lieutenant Foy was not here at the moment did not mean that he himself was not every bit as concerned. And that concern included the entire department. Everyone was working on this case. They would be talking with her.

Talking.

She clattered the phone back at its cradle, but she could not make it fit. For a full minute she stood unable to move. She stared at the receiver in her hand. Should she call her father? What possible help could he give? Call Scott on his goddamn Hawaiian island? He was surfing. He was sliding over the water and running through the sun with Sharon.

With both hands shaking she concentrated her efforts and managed to place the receiver carefully back in its place.

Her shoes were soaked but she did not pull them off. Her feet ached, numb with cold, but to take off her shoes meant she had decided she was not going out again, and not going out meant she was not looking for Laddie. What in God's name could she do here?

The overheated room had not changed.

There lay the bedspread where she had hurled it—in the corner. Outside, the broken neon sign blinked on and off. Freezing rain spattered the window. She picked up the towel she had dried Laddie's hair with and burst into tears. If she could not hold her son in her arms she wanted to wrap herself in this towel, crawl into the bed and pull the blankets overhead and shut out the world until the phone rang or a knock banged on the door to tell her that Laddie was safe; Laddie was back.

Clutching the big towel like a whimpering and scared child, she shuffled into the bathroom. She stared at herself in the mirror. She blinked in the bright light. The cold terror, the gut-churning dread, the terrible fear didn't stare back. This night had shattered her life, so how was it possible this same face she had always known stared back at her? It had to be a different face to show that change. But this freckled face with the dripping wet hair was the woman she always saw.

Her knees shook. She grabbed the sink. Her legs let go and with a howl of pain she sank to the tile floor until she felt her face slump against the cold porcelain of the sink.

She wept for an hour.

She prayed.

In the rest of the dark hours of the night she managed to pull herself to the phone three times and call the police.

One thing and one thing alone roused her from despair. Anger. A fierce drive kept her from crawling into bed and pushing all else aside. Nothing in the world mattered but this furious drive to get back her son. Damn the police who pretended concern. They'd say anything. They only wanted her off their backs. And most of all, damn that reporter. Goddamn her to hell for the gloating pleasure she took in telling Susannah the worst that could happen. The woman didn't care. What the damned woman wanted was a story.

Susannah wanted her son. No one in the world wanted anything as much as Susannah wanted her son.

Still shaking with terror, she ran the coldest water from the tap and splashed her face. She dried her eyes on the towel.

She ran to the window and looked out at the dark buildings. Lights flared the sky red about Times Square.

Lights? Or dawn. In the east the sky was still black. Dawn was hours away. Never mind. She told herself night would finally end. What was more important, she told herself to save her tears. No one out there in this city gave a damn about her tears. She searched the city's towers. Her son was out there somewhere. Tears would not bring him back. If she wanted her son she—and she alone—had to go out there and find him.

6

DECEMBER 22, 7:30 A.M.

Dawn.

Brilliant icy sunshine cast long shadows in the cross streets, making Susannah squint as she hurried to the precinct. For the last hours of the night the reporter's words about looking for a pattern haunted her.

Lieutenant Foy, sipping coffee, offered to share his prune Danish. When she spoke of the importance of finding a pattern, he not only agreed with Mrs. Bartok, he assured her that his police were working along exactly those lines at this very minute. True, they couldn't report anything tangible yet, but—in almost precisely the same words Sergeant Braverman had used— he told Mrs. Bartok she was not to give up hope.

Though Susannah had eaten no breakfast, she refused his offer of pastry. Another kindness on his part. Victoria's words haunted her. Like the sergeant on the phone last night, Lieutenant Foy was not reporting any moves, any results. He was offering her pastry, stroking her, simply being kind. She smothered a flash of rage when he gave her a number to call so she could talk with a social worker. A social worker, he said, might help. Or Traveler's Aid. Susannah wanted to scream in his face that she knew what he was doing. In his smooth, kind way he was still refusing to admit he was powerless to help. Susannah did not scream. Did she want him to admit that? Of course not. This man was all she had; she needed him and his police. Helping or not, they were her only hope and she dared not antagonize them.

She knew better than to speak of her meeting with Victoria Cruz, for the reporter and the detective clearly hated one another. And yet the reporter's driving interest in her story had given Susannah the idea of looking for a pattern. If the reporter was so eager to cover her son's disappearance, other reporters must have been just as avid to cover other cases like hers. If Susannah and the police compared what had happened to her with these others, wasn't there a chance they'd find similarities; even, if they were lucky, a pattern? Newspaper offices kept back issues on file which would report those other cases. Didn't Foy think this was a lead worth following?

Indeed he did. He said it would speed things up if Susannah herself would start this research. He even smiled. She knew it was a tactic for getting rid of her. She nodded. She would start. She watched this man eat his prune Danish and sip his coffee and she hoped its four saccharins would give him cancer.

A few streets away, the front door of the *New York Times* building was closed to visitors. A guard with a strong Spanish accent was telling her she could not go inside to find bound volumes of back issues when a woman her own age, going through the door, stopped. The woman with straight brown hair, who struck Susannah as being very likely a graduate of one of the good colleges, asked her why she needed the papers. Susannah said nothing of her driving need, but when she told her the kind of stories she was looking for the woman sensed her urgency. She told her there were newspaper files at the New York Public Library, but she was blunt. "The *Times* doesn't cover this kind of story in detail. Not the way the *News* or the *Post* or the *Press* does. The others go in for more human interest. We're complete but compared with them we're about as colorful as the *Congressional Record*. Don't quote me on that." She wrote down addresses of the papers. She even gave Susannah the name of a researcher, a friend, at one daily who, if she had time, could give her expert help. Otherwise, looking up the stories at the library would take days.

40 . . .

In a Times Square drugstore Susannah ran to a telephone and pulled a scrap of paper with its number from her raincoat pocket.

Victoria Cruz did not answer. To Susannah's amazement a machine spoke to her directly: "Mrs. Bartok? Susannah? I'm out. You'll find me a few doors down the street from my place at the Cafe Marlene until ten-thirty." Click.

"Damn her." Susannah slammed down the phone. "Was she so absolutely sure I'd call?"

In the Village, Susannah hurried through the freezing sunshine past garbage trucks banging and churning until she saw the silver sign, CAFE MARLENE, as glitteringly Art Deco as the reporter's cigarette case.

Inside the cafe, amid palms and ferns, mirrors reflected the black and white of huge photographs of Marlene Dietrich. In the white wicker chairs at glass tables, women—many as flawlessly and professionally beautiful as models—ate fruit salad, or omelettes, and smoked.

A stunningly beautiful waitress, graceful as a little doe coming through all this foliage, smoothed gleaming black hair pulled tight into a bun. She adjusted a white bow tie within a white jacket as she passed Susannah with a tray of orange juice.

"I'm looking for Victoria Cruz."

The waitress gave Susannah a full smile of perfectly even teeth as white as her bow tie. She nodded toward a corner in back.

Susannah thanked her and indicated she could find her way.

One poster-size photograph of Marlene Dietrich in white tie looked down through hanging ferns. In another, smoke curled up from shining wet lips and in front of half-closed eyes.

Susannah slowed.

There was an unmistakable feeling about lovers ending an affair that can be felt across a room and Susannah felt it unmistakably. The black-haired Victoria ground out a thin, brown cigarette on a pink slice of melon. A blond girl, as glowing as any of those on the boxes of hair color, scraped back her chair and rose. Victoria held her wrist. The girl waited, staring away from the woman seated at the table. Suddenly a look of pure hate twisted the beautiful face as she hissed something Susannah could not hear. She broke free, dragged a beige artificial fur from a chair, picked up a model's portfolio, and hurried through the palms out into the morning sunlight.

It was too late for Susannah to retreat, to pretend she had not seen the two. She found Victoria looking straight at her. Victoria nodded at the empty chair, an invitation for Susannah to sit.

Susannah, reluctant to join the woman at the table, hovered without sitting. Victoria still wore her black turtleneck sweater and a large, carved wooden Greek letter lambda. Her black pants fit closely; they were either tailored or expensive ski pants that tapered into high shiny black boots. She drew a Kleenex from her shoulder bag. "Give me half a minute." She blew her nose, checked her face in a purse mirror. She frowned. Did she feel the face was beyond repair? She ran her fingers through masses of black hair.

Susannah stood without moving.

"Even when you know it's coming, it's never easy." She picked up the black-and-silver cigarette case. "She gave me this." Victoria lit a cigarette, another thin, brown cigarette.

"You and your old man fight like that?"

Susannah, her hands in her raincoat pockets, waited.

"In your nice little tract house there somewhere in the shadow of Disneyland, did you fight?"

Susannah looked at Marlene Dietrich's smoldering eyes staring down over a velvety shoulder wrapped in white fur.

"You didn't answer my question."

"For your newspaper?"

"I'd like to know."

"Did we fight?"

"Yes. Did you and he fight?"

"Yes, we fought."

Susannah looked down at the woman who was waiting for her answer. She should not be surprised, she supposed, that the reporter could talk of how others felt at a time like this. After all, part of being a good reporter was finding out how people feel.

"Did you love the *cabrón*?"

"Yes."

"And now?"

Susannah was no reporter. She had had enough of this kind of talk. She simply stood there in her raincoat. If the other woman cared how people felt, she would know that a mother in her kind of trouble couldn't give a damn about love stories and broken hearts. She had a son to find.

"I still love her." Victoria raised a glass of orange juice. "Merry Christmas." She did not drink. "Right. I'm gay." She dangled the large wooden symbol, the lambda that hung on a leather thong against her black turtleneck sweater. "Gay. The term's generic—nothing to do with my mood." She pointed with her cigarette to the chair opposite. "For Christ's sake, sit down."

"No time."

"Okay. Hover." Victoria pushed away the slice of melon with its drowned cigarette stub. "First thing this morning you went back to the police?"

"Yes."

"More sympathy? More stroking? Those *cabrónes* suggest a friendly social worker? Traveler's Aid?"

Susannah felt her eyes sting with tears. The reporter had been maddeningly right about the cops. She nodded. "Damn them." Then she spoke about going to the newspapers and asking to see their files.

"That's pretty smart." Victoria signaled for the check and tossed down a couple of bills. She pushed back her hair and struggled into her sheepskin coat. "Come on!"

7
=

DECEMBER 22, 10:41 A.M.

On the street Susannah found herself running to keep up with Victoria.

The newspaper office was here in the Village. They hung their coats and Victoria led Susannah through a room where men and women bent over telephones in deep and urgent conversation. Others sat in silence, gazing into green readout on computer consoles. In the newspaper library the dailies lay on a table alongside huge bound volumes of back copies. Victoria called fiercely, "Jeffrey!"

A thin young man thumped through the door on aluminum crutches. He leaned there—tall and blond, with a skinny neck and a pointed Adam's apple he had not succeeded in covering with a scraggly beard. He wore a knitted disc of black-and-white wool that barely covered the crown of his head and was held in place by bobby pins.

"Get her the files on kidnapping," Victoria said. "Children. Also missing. Ours and other papers." She suddenly connected the woman and the young man at the door with a wave of her cigarette. "Susannah Bartok—Jeffrey Mendelsohn."

The two nodded.

Jeffrey shifted his weight on his crutches. "How far back do you want me to go?"

44 . . .

"Two years," Victoria said dismissing him, turning the pages of a rival paper. "And move your ass."

"Up yours." Within his beard Jeffrey smiled at Susannah and his crutches thumped off.

Victoria announced that every day she read every paper in town. The way her eyes sped up and down each page it was clear she missed nothing. "Jeffrey's very good," she said. "He'll be back with everything the metropolitan papers have covered. Give him ten minutes. I know. I started out with that job. Only difference is, I could do it in five."

Victoria tossed a paper aside and with one glance took in the first page of another. She had said ten minutes, but to Susannah it seemed much longer before Jeffrey thudded back with bulging folders grasped against his crutches. He dropped the files on the table.

"All for now?" Jeffrey asked.

"We'll let you know," said Victoria, still leaning over a paper.

The young man propelled himself from the room.

"You get started with these," Victoria said. "I'll be right back."

Susannah sat at the table. She picked up the first clipping in which a three-year-old girl with white hair in a pony tail tied with a ribbon smiled tentatively out of a blurry portrait. She knew the kind of picture—one of those J. C. Penney or Sears specials to bring mothers into the store. Now black headlines shrieked, MISSING GIRL FOUND DEAD. Susannah quickly turned over the clipping. She took a deep breath and forced herself to turn it back and read the story.

In a large windowed office with little other than a white Formica-topped table, a ficus in a white pot, and white wall files, Victoria sat in a molded white plastic chair. A man in his early thirties with a carefully trimmed beard and a three-piece Brooks Brothers gray suit stirred a package of instant soup into a white cup of steaming water. The only blaze of color in the room filled an entire wall. Huge black letters on yellow: NO FUMAR. NO SMOKING.

The man tasted the soup with a white plastic spoon and carefully wiped his lips with a white napkin.

Victoria leaned back, scratched a kitchen match and lit a cigarette.

The man at the desk picked up five pieces of paper-clipped typed paper. As he read he sipped his vegetable-beef soup.

Victoria smoked.

The man finished reading and placed the papers precisely in the middle of his vast and empty desk top. "I love it. What's the problem?"

"It's rough," Victoria said. "Just an idea of how to break the story. I did it late last night. I won't turn it in till I work on what she tells me this morning."

"You have a picture of the boy?"

"I'll have one."

The young editor and publisher whose name, Donald F. Donald, was on the door, shook his head, impressed and amused. "You even managed to get Santa Claus into it." He sipped more soup. "You missed only one thing. Doesn't the boy have a dog?"

"Still time to get one in." Victoria did not smile. She smoked.

Donald F. Donald, one of those people who never expected things to go smoothly, glanced at the first page. "This Susannah Bartok. Are you sure you can get her on an exclusive?"

"She's sitting here in the office right now." Victoria made a display of slowly exhaling smoke. "But it'll cost."

"She's asked for money?"

"No. I'm asking for money."

"You just had a raise."

"Not salary. I'm talking about money to do this story right."

"As I said. What's the problem? Draw expenses."

"I didn't come in here to get your permission to do the story or to get your permission to draw petty cash, asshole. You're the publisher. This story takes money."

Most reporters do not call their editors, let alone their publishers, assholes. Victoria was proving to her boss that she was so good she could call him an asshole and get away with it. He was showing her that though he wore a Brooks Brothers suit with a vest he was still one of the boys who was not shocked by salty talk. "For the holidays I'm taking the family to Aspen: Before I take off I'll tell petty cash to let you draw money for taxis, phone calls—a few meals—okay, including a good one. Reasonable expenses."

Victoria ground out her cigarette in an ash tray she held in her hand. "Don't be a *coño*, Donald. Don't petty-cash me. This can be a hell of a story. Bigger than anything we've broken in months. However, I do not get down on my knees—not for a few lousy dollars." She watched him sip instant soup. "No way. Not for a story as juicy as this."

"You don't have it yet."

"You have me. You have her sitting in the next room." She snapped open her skiny black-and-white cigarette case. "She came to me. She's scared and she's broke. She knows the police and the Bureau—if they come in on it at all, which I doubt, aren't going to be much help. She doesn't know a soul."

"She knows you."

"I'd like to bring in a psychic."

"Readers like psychics."

"I get the money?"

He stirred his instant soup.

"Have I ever let you down?"

Donald F. Donald studied Victoria, who smoked as elaborately as Bette Davis in her old movies. He smiled.

"Okay, asshole. Tell me. This is so goddamn funny?"

"It is funny, Rosalia Victoria Alicia Ampara Consuelo Infante y Cruz because I remember your letter of application seven years ago—"

"Seven years, three months and eight days."

"I never met such an ambitious Cuban since I interviewed Fidel Castro at Harvard. You said you'd have the Pulitzer Prize by the time you were thirty."

"I've still got one year."

Donald F. Donald picked up the five pages to show her he was considering her request but nevertheless, good publishers do not throw money around.

"Front page. For how long?"

"For as long as our readers are interested. Today the search begins. Every step of the way with the mother. I want the full shot, Donald. I want to bring in a top psychic."

The publisher stirred his instant soup and found a fleck he

scrutinized. Was it beef? "How does the mother feel about that?"

"The mother wants to find her kid."

"Is one allowed to ask if one believes in psychics?"

"You just said our readers do."

The publisher wiped his lips. "Tell your psychic that he—or she—will get pages of publicity money can't buy. Pages of exposure. Top visibility."

Victoria spewed a long trail of smoke. As a teacher struggles with a not-overly-bright child, she exaggerated the slowness of her explanation. "I'm not talking about some cut-rate Rexall Drugstore mystic, asshole. I mean a Cayce or a Hurkos or a Zellner. That's right. I'm talking about a superstar like Zellner. As for knowing what he's worth, he knows he sells papers."

"And his own books. He's been on every TV talk show from here to Australia."

"I want him and he's going to cost."

Donald F. Donald turned to look out of his window at the cold December sunlight glinting sharply off a glass wall across the street. "You're absolutely sure you've got an exclusive with the mother?"

"I'll get it."

"And the psychic?"

"It's our story first. Naturally he'll want follow-up rights."

"The mother can't pay him?"

"She's got three dollars."

"Interesting woman?"

"She's California tract house, white bread and canned vegetables. Stunningly, gloriously, sensationally average."

"We're not a big paper."

"Talk this way and we never will be." Victoria scratched a kitchen match and lit another cigarette. She packed up her shoulder bag and rose. "Think of this as a public service." But she had given Donald F. Donald enough time to think. "You know your trouble, asshole? You've got no public spirit. You're rich, but you don't feel guilty about it."

8

DECEMBER 22, 1:20 P.M.

Susannah read a report of a baby stolen from a hospital. Another paper had covered the story in greater detail. She carefully placed the two clippings to one side. In the past she had glanced at newspaper stories like these; she had seen mothers weeping on television. Now these stories made her shake with horror.

She did not hear Victoria enter the room, but she smelled cigarette smoke. Victoria stood in the door watching her. When Susannah looked up from her stack of clippings, her eyes were full of pain.

"God." She shuddered as her hands covered the file. In an effort to break the spell, she sat up straight and drove herself to sound positive. "They find some of them alive."

Victoria moved to the table, slid the file from under Susannah's hands, and picked up a clipping. "Anything similar to Laddie?"

"Not yet."

Victoria put a hand on Susannah's shoulder. She drew a chair close to her and sat. For a few minutes they read together in silence. Abruptly Susannah stood.

"The police. I've got the feeling they know something. They can't reach me here." She did not let her eyes meet Victoria's. She did not want—even by gesture—to have this woman tell her that what she was about to do was a waste of time.

Victoria was already on her feet. "Better to go there than to call." She took down their coats. "We'll take a taxi."

Susannah put a strip of paper as a marker in the file. "I'm just about broke."

"It's on me." She cried out fiercely: "Jeffrey!"

The young man on crutches swung himself to the door and Victoria shoved the stacked files toward him. "Break these down. Acts by parents. For ransom. Crazies . . . et cetera."

In the taxi Victoria smoked another brown cigarette and looked across to Susannah, who stared out the window at the crowds on the sidewalk. "You keep telling yourself he's here somewhere, right? That one of them knows where he is."

Susannah did not turn from the window and the people surging past. "He's such a good little boy. How could anybody not be nice to him?"

The taxi slowed to a crawl in the traffic. A drunk staggered, banged into the car, lurched to the window. A scabby face with red eyes peered in.

"God." Susannah turned away. "Some of them are so horrible—"

"There's a rumor that one old guy goes around here with a human head in a hatbox."

Why did Victoria tell her these awful things? She seemed to relish relating these stories, to prove her hardness, to show that nothing in the city moved her.

"Let's see his picture."

Susannah pulled out her wallet, opened it, and carefully drew a photo from plastic. Victoria took the blue-eyed blond little boy standing, looking very solemn in the sunshine, in the same hand she held her cigarette.

"Looks like a Christmas angel."

She drew her notebook from her leather bag and wrote.

Susannah gazed at the picture the other woman held. "His grandfather's never seen him. Oh, wow—" She clamped a hand over her mouth as people do when they suddenly remember they have forgotten something important. "I have to call him. . . . I'm supposed to be home by now."

Victoria leaned to the steel mesh that protected the driver. "Here. Stop here." The cab slowed and she directed Susannah's gaze. "There's the precinct. There's a drugstore on the corner. From there you can call home." She thrust a five-dollar bill into her hand. "Pay me later." She slipped the photograph of the little boy in the sunshine into her shoulder bag. "I'll get a copy of this. You'll get it back. Right now call your father."

The phone rang its familiar ring five times before her father reached the kitchen. Susannah took a deep breath and blurted out the terrible news.

Her father gasped once. She could see him pulling over a chair and sitting. She found herself forcing cheer she didn't feel, telling him the police were really being wonderful and doing everything in the world to help. She lied and said they promised to have him back in no time.

She shut her eyes and leaned her forehead against the wall.

"Susannah?"

"Yes, Dad?"

"All I can do from here is pray."

"I know . . ."

After she hung up she stood looking out of the drugstore at the crowds in the street. More sharply than the crowds she could see her father sitting in the dark kitchen in the eerie light from the snow.

Detective Lieutenant Foy and another young detective, a slender black man, as carefully dressed as a fashion model in a pattern-knit sweater and slacks, abruptly stopped laughing. The two women had entered unannounced to find the men leaning over the desk throwing the switch on a toy electric train that ground in a loop, picking up speed. Foy switched off the power, which shuddered the trains to a halt, derailing a freight car.

"Christmas present," said the black detective. "Ought to make Ernie's five-year-old very happy, right?"

When Foy said nothing, the other man mumbled something

and hurried out leaving the man with the toy train alone to face the two unsmiling women.

Foy moved empty train boxes from only one of two visitor's chairs and motioned for Susannah to sit. Pointedly he left a bag full of brightly wrapped toys on the other. Neither woman sat. He made no effort to pretend he was not ignoring the reporter. His every move made it clear, he owed sympathy and politeness only to Mrs. Bartok. Again he indicated the chair, and again Mrs. Bartok did not move. "I'm sorry, Mrs. Bartok. Nothing so far."

Victoria scraped flame from one of her kitchen matches and lit a brown cigarette. She picked up the fallen freight car. "Why do you suppose, Detective Lieutenant Foy, that Mrs. Bartok here has the feeling New York's Finest aren't doing everything they possibly can?"

Foy took the toy car from her hand. "You're Mrs. Bartok's attorney?"

"You know damn well I'm a reporter."

"What I know is I see you pushing in here all the time."

Victoria pulled a press card from her bag, which the detective ignored. Susannah and Foy also saw her pull out a Sony TCM-121 cassette recorder. She snapped in a cassette, switched on the power, punched a button.

"In the case of Mrs. Bartok's son, Lieutenant, why don't you tell my readers exactly what it is you're doing. First of all, you've caught the case, right?"

Foy nodded. He was the assigned detective.

"Since last night you've had over twelve hours to bring in the FBI. No Feds. You're handling this?"

"That's right."

"As a 'Missing Person under Ten Years of Age or Retarded'?"

"That's right."

Victoria slid the cassette recorder closer to the man.

"No ransom note to establish kidnapping. Doesn't Mace constitute the use of force?"

"You have witnesses?"

"Jesus."

Susannah shot the man an anguished look. Didn't he believe her?

"This is a 'Missing Child under Unusual Circumstances,'" Foy said quietly, leaning toward Susannah, a way to shut out the demanding reporter. He spoke with warmth, compassion. "Without going into *all* the details about *all* the people working with us on this, believe me, Mrs. Bartok, no one could do more. This is an *all*-out search."

"How about some specifics, Lieutenant?" Victoria was harsher than before.

The red-haired man's jaw set. A muscle throbbed in his cheek. He reached for papers clipped together and tossed them on the train tracks. "See for yourself."

Victoria let the papers lie before her. "Which will tell us exactly what? That you've checked the usual suspects?"

"Like the entire city of New York?" Foy fought himself. He throttled his fury. He jerked his head toward the cassette recorder. "Turn that thing off."

"Wouldn't help, Lieutenant. I've also got a memory."

Foy now made a point of speaking only to Susannah. "What we're doing, Mrs. Bartok, is we're checking other cases. Looking for a lead—"

"That's what I'm trying to do by going through those newspaper stories," Susannah said.

"Precisely." Foy seized her willingness to understand his position. He kept his tone professional, but concerned. "We have your telephone number, Mrs. Bartok. Believe me. The minute we get anything we'll let you know."

"You checked the morgue?" Victoria stared straight at him.

Foy nodded.

"And?"

Foy spoke only to Susannah who had shut her eyes and waited, holding her breath. "Nothing that fits your son's description." He picked up his report. "You're still at the Hotel Argylle?"

"Yes. If I leave there I'll tell you where I am."

"Be sure and do that. And keep checking those newspapers."

Susannah ran one hand through her hair, then thrust both into her raincoat pockets.

Foy smiled. "We'll be in touch."

"That's it? All the stroking the lady gets for today?" Victoria's tone had never been so cutting.

Foy put the papers on top of a cabinet and began to clear the toy cars from the train tracks.

"Lieutenant?" Victoria jabbed her cassette recorder at the man.

"For now, Mrs. Bartok, I'm afraid that's it. Of course, we won't stop working on it for a minute. The whole department."

"And the FBI?"

"We'll handle this one."

Victoria snapped off the power. "Sorry we interrupted you, Lieutenant. Now you can go back to playing with your toy trains."

The reporter dropped the recorder into her bag, pulled out a camera, and shot several pictures before she took Susannah's arm to lead her from the office.

"Mrs. Bartok?"

Susannah slowed.

"May I see you for a minute, alone?"

Susannah looked to Victoria whose acid smile said that she would wait in the hall. The lieutenant shut the door and returned to his desk where he unhooked the loop of train tracks.

"Miss Cruz found you last night?"

"Yes."

"She's promised to help?"

"She already has. She's opened her newspaper's files and has somebody there doing research right now. You said yourself that was a good way to look for a pattern."

"We're working too, Mrs. Bartok. You may have noticed, it's our policy not to make promises to people in trouble that we can't keep."

"She hasn't made any promises."

"She's dropping everything to work with you to find your son?"

Susannah tried to evade with a shrug.

"Why?"

"I guess to write a story."

"You want her to do that?"

"I want help. From you. From her. From anybody who will help me get my son back.

"I can understand that."

"But you don't like her. And because you don't like or approve of her, are you telling me to have nothing to do with her?"

He looked up from unhooking train tracks. That was precisely what he was saying. He dropped the metal sections into a box. "You don't know anything about that woman."

"I know she's a lesbian. Does that bother you?"

"In these days of live and let live and all that, yes, it still bothers me. But what really bothers me is that she lies. You saw her push in here. She pushes in any place in this city where she smells trouble. Once she's in she rides roughshod over human feelings like decency and privacy—anything to grab headlines."

He picked up the last sections of track. "She comes from a rich Cuban family of exiles she hates. In the late sixties she was one of the students who tried to burn down Columbia University. You'd see her in the forefront of every cause—the wild, radical-left reporter. Some of her friends mellowed out. Not her. If there isn't trouble, she starts it. Lots of hate. Especially for cops. Ask her about me. She'll tell you. She tried to get me suspended. A story of hers. After the police commission reviewed the case I was completely cleared, no thanks to Ms. Cruz. You wonder I don't like her pushing in here, writing lies, filth—hurting people?"

"She says you're afraid to tell me the truth."

"What do you want to know?"

Susannah felt her throat close; she couldn't answer.

"Your friend says I won't admit I can't find your son? Your friend says I'm not doing everything I can?"

Susannah stared at her hands. "I don't want to believe her," she cried, "I just want somebody to help get him back—"

"Please believe me, Mrs. Bartok, we're doing everything we can."

The two women walked the few blocks to Susannah's hotel. "There's a four-dollar charge for not turning in your key," the pale clerk said.

Victoria dropped her camera and shoulder bag on the counter, establishing a beachhead for her invasion. "Look, creep. This woman's son has been kidnapped. I'm her attorney. I'm having the law on this flea-bag hotel as an accessory to the kidnapping!"

"Please," Susannah said to the clerk. "This is my only contact here in the city. I've got to count on the police reaching me here—"

"I don't know anything about that. We got our rules."

"My son had things . . . toys—"

"Anything you had's locked up."

"Is Mrs. Bartok paid up till now?"

"Not till she turns in her key."

"First, give Mrs. Bartok her things."

"See the porter."

"Call the porter, asshole."

The pale man grabbed the telephone and half a minute later a withered black man limped from a door behind the elevators with a paper bag. Victoria snatched the bag from the blinking man and thrust it at Susannah. "See if everything's there."

Susannah peered into the bag. A coloring book. A pilot's wings.

"Everything there?" asked Victoria.

"I guess," Susannah said.

Victoria tossed the key, which bounced off the desk and fell. "Now I use your phone."

"Pay phone's over there—"

Victoria strode behind the counter, shoved the clerk aside, and grabbed the receiver of the desk phone from its hook. The surprised man glared at her as he stooped down out of sight to look for the key.

"The police," Victoria told him, "have to be in constant touch with Mrs. Bartok. I'm telling them where they can reach her." She scribbled and ripped a paper from a memo pad. "I'm giving you my name, address, and telephone number. If the police—if anyone at all tries to reach Mrs. Bartok, she'll be at my place. I have an answering machine."

By now it was mid-afternoon and a solid gray sky hid the sun. Light snow fell as the two women approached Times Square. Cars honked, fighting their way, parting the crowds of the Christmas rush surging through the crossroads. As taxis appeared, frantic hands waved, people yelled trying to stop them. Susannah clutched the paper bag full of Laddie's toys and stood on a corner with Victoria, dismayed at the crush of humanity, the helplessness she felt at the prospect of ever getting a cab. The city-wise woman beside her peered around, assessing the problem, planning her attack. Susannah, watching Victoria, failed to see a tall teenage boy in black leather, hair flying around dead eyes in a white face blotched with angry red pimples until he banged into her, then spun on, oblivious of the assault, out of control, stumbling through the crowd.

"An addict?"

"Probably angel dust." Victoria frowned, never looking anywhere but up the swollen river of cars and foot traffic of Seventh Avenue, and its trickle of yellow cabs.

A fat black man, blind and slashing a white stick, slapped Susannah with his cane. Snowflakes hit his black, upturned face as he hollered the blues at the top of his voice. A humpbacked bag lady, bent double with age, her coat trailing the pavement, lugged greasy shopping bags stuffed with garbage. Susannah, who could not bear the thought that she would touch her, shrank out of her way.

At the faces coming toward her, Susannah stifled a gasp of horror. She drew into her raincoat. They terrified her. Had faces in crowds—every color and race, every size and shape, every age, every need and passion and drive—always shown so many people so frighteningly desperate, so clearly on the brink of howling madness, so ready to explode?

"So many of them," Susannah whispered, "look so dangerous."

"Crazies. The city's full of crazies."

One of them could be the one who grabbed him. Susannah did not say this. Instead, she said, "Don't they scare you to death?"

Victoria concentrated on finding a taxi. She ignored the faces. "If they scare you, don't look."

"You were the one who told me I had to face facts."

"Don't let them make eye contact. Don't give them a chance to single you out of the crowd. You don't know who you're up against."

9

DECEMBER 22, 3:00 P.M.

Victoria lived in an apartment that looked like a book store. Except for one window facing a back garden where the snow fell between a tree's bare branches, the walls, floor to ceiling, were shelves packed, jammed, stacked, overflowing with books. The living room was even more cluttered than the tiny entrance hall, where every inch was covered with glossy news photos, awards, curling newspaper clippings. A Cuban ballet poster shared the place of honor along with a photograph of Alicia Alonzo. Susannah had no time to look closely, but all the other photos included Victoria sitting or standing with famous people who ranged from rock stars to politicians.

In the living room Victoria pulled off her sheepskin coat and dropped it on a coach of imitation leather already heaped with books and sweaters. She reached out for Susannah's raincoat which she threw on top of her own. She swept an armchair clear. Newspapers, paperback books and empty Tsingtao beer bottles clattered to a filthy flokati carpet already deeply strewn with litter.

"Sit."

But Susannah stood.

Cut into one wall of shelves was a black metal fireplace.

"That's nice," said Susannah, searching for something pleasant to say about the woman's home. "A real fireplace."

"Which won't even burn love letters."

On the floor by the couch Victoria uncovered the telephone answering machine from scattered pages of the *New York Times*. Susannah looked at a shelf of books, paperback and hardcover—all worn, all obviously opened and read and read again. Many were in Spanish. Borges. Neruda. Marquez. Susannah had once started reading an English translation of *One Hundred Years of Solitude* by Marquez but found it exasperatingly difficult. She still felt a pang of guilt about abandoning it halfway through.

From working the machine, Victoria glanced up. "You read?"

"Sometimes."

"I know. You're not a reader. You're a Californian. And a mother." Victoria switched on the machine.

Susannah thought she had read enough that it might surprise the reporter, but she felt no need to defend herself.

On the machine Victoria heard only herself telling Susannah to meet her at Cafe Marlene. She rose. "I'll make us a cup of tea."

"I'm really grateful for your help," Susannah said. "But I don't have time."

"For Christ's sake ease up."

"Now you sound like Lieutenant Foy."

"I mean it. You didn't sleep a wink last night. You must be dog-tired."

While Victoria put a kettle on, Susannah picked her way across the clutter to stand by the window. The sky was cold. White snow fell through the scraping black branches. She hugged her arms around her thin brown jacket. "All he had was a windbreaker. And red mittens." She choked back tears. "One red mitten."

"Sit down."

It was the second time Victoria had told Susannah to sit, and Victoria was clearly a woman whose orders were obeyed. But

Susannah stayed at the window watching the snow. Victoria crossed the narrow room to stand at her side. She felt Susannah draw away. Worst of all, Susannah knew the woman had sensed what she felt.

"Do I scare you?"

"No."

"Yes, I do. You don't know many lesbians."

"I guess not in Laguna. At least not in tract houses."

"We're even in tract houses. Don't worry. You'll be safer from rape here than you were in that flea-bag hotel—"

"I can't possibly stay here."

"As I said, 'ease up.'"

A brown bird flickered through the branches. Cold bird. Cold day.

"Susannah, face it. You have nowhere else to go. Stay here and we'll work together. We won't waste any time."

"I'm losing time right now."

The winter light was fading. The room was dark behind them. Susannah turned from the window. "I can't just sit here drinking cups of tea. I'll go crazy. I have to look for him. Maybe if I go back to that store—"

"And what?"

"Look for him!"

"There's something we could do right now. Frankly, I haven't brought it up because I don't know how you'd feel about it."

Victoria went to a shelf and pulled down a new book, which she held but did not show Susannah. "How would you feel about bringing in a psychic?"

"ESP?"

Victoria nodded. She brought the book to come and stand at Susannah's side. "I interviewed this man. He really does have a remarkable record for finding things . . . people."

"Would he see us?"

"You're willing?"

"The sooner the better."

"Have you heard of him?" The name on the dust jacket was larger than the title: ALOIS ZELLNER.

Susannah's eyes were wide. "I've seen him on TV lots of times. I've read about him. If he'd only help. But he's famous. Wouldn't he want a lot of money?"

"Don't worry about that. The question is, he might stir up all kinds of feelings you wouldn't want to handle. It could get pretty rough. You willing to go through it?"

"I just told you. The sooner the better."

Victoria handed the book to Susannah, a way of saying that now they could share Zellner. "I've already called him."

Susannah had been with her practically every minute. When could she have called? Victoria explained. "When you called your father."

In the fading light Susannah looked at Victoria, waiting to hear of their next move.

"He can only give us a few minutes."

"Today?"

"Yes."

"That's marvelous." Susannah reached for her raincoat.

"Hang on. He can't see us till five."

"What time is it now?"

"Three."

Susannah paced the cluttered room. "God, that's another two hours." She stopped and looked into the hall at the Cuban ballet poster.

Victoria lit a cigarette. "We're all set with Zellner at five. That doesn't mean we can't follow through on other ways to go at the same time."

In the kitchen Victoria moved a Christmas present wrapped in shining black-and-white paper and a bottle of champagne from the little table. She unrolled a ballet poster's blank back side. With a big black marker pen she prepared to list their plan of attack.

"Shall we call it COUNTDOWN? Okay?" Victoria was already boldly lettering at the top of the large sheet.

Susannah did not touch her tea; a few minutes later, under

the bright kitchen light, the two women assessed their work—the poster filled with a list in big, bold letters:

POLICE
FBI
RESEARCH
PSYCHICS
ADOPTION AGENCIES (Black Market Babies)
SOCIAL WORKERS
STREET PEOPLE
OUR OWN INTUITION
KEEP COMMUNICATIONS OPEN!

Under the last item, Victoria slashed a double line. Most of the ideas were hers, but in every case Susannah agreed. They reviewed this plan of attack. They had already gone to the *police*. Victoria doubted the FBI would take on the case, but she'd make a few telephone calls. Susannah had begun *research* at the newspaper office.

"Jeffrey's good," said Victoria. "I'll call and keep him working while we're following other leads. The only problem is fucking Christmas—or in his case, Chanukah. Holidays. The office will be open but he won't be there."

The newspapers would cover kidnappings and child-stealings. As for things that never got into the papers, *adoption agencies* and *social workers* would be able to tell them all kinds of things that went on when it came to kids in this city. Victoria had started to say she had once been close to a social worker when she ran from the kitchen, inspired to telephone. The friend was not in her office and Victoria left a message. "Tell her it's urgent!"

"The more things we can keep moving, the better. It's like working on a story. Do it by triangulation. Zero in on it from every possible angle."

Street people Victoria listed because she had done a recent article on hustlers, the male prostitutes who worked the Times Square area, those young men Susannah had seen, inadequately dressed against the bitter cold, waiting, shivering on corners and in doorways. "They know everything that's going on in the street."

Our own intuition. The two women meant just that. They would stay open to any feelings they picked up, no matter how seemingly illogical. They would follow every clue. *Keep communications open* meant they would keep constantly alert and assume nothing. They would check and recheck with the hotel, the police, the FBI, even the social worker Victoria had just called. They would leave nothing to chance.

Susannah added *classifieds* at the bottom. Victoria lettered it boldly. She agreed that if someone wanted to reach Susannah, he or she might use the personal columns of the papers to do it. Thousands did.

Victoria tacked the poster on the wall and Susannah studied their work. She felt sick with worry, but against that gnawing empty, cold, and scared feeling that kept her trembling, their work had kindled the tiniest glow of warmth. Hope. At least she was doing something. Best of all, as Victoria had said, most of the areas they could work on at the same time.

Victoria had also said that if Susannah stayed here they would lose no time checking back and forth, staying in touch with each other. She came from the bathroom with a bottle of pills. "They're not strong. Why don't you get two hours' rest before we see Zellner?"

Susannah refused the pills, but allowed Victoria to lead her to the bedroom. "You'll be in there. I'll be on the studio couch in the living room."

"My stuff's still in that locker at the Port Authority Bus Terminal."

"I've got all you need."

Susannah thought of the beautiful blond girl running from Cafe Marlene. Had she slept in this room?

"Get some rest," Victoria said. "Right now I've got work to do."

But Susannah did not go into the bedroom; she closed the door, returned to the living room, and picked up her raincoat from the couch. Victoria watched her and waited for an explanation. "The classifieds. I'm going out and get all the papers."

"Wait."

Victoria ran to the closet and pulled out a sheepskin coat identical to her own. She held it and Susannah struggled into the heavy wool. Victoria smiled as she buttoned the rawhide up the front until the wool reached her friend's chin. Susannah felt snug in its tight warmth. She picked up her raincoat and from a pocket drew out a red mitten.

"Hang on." Victoria rummaged in a desk drawer, found a sewing kit and safety pins. With a big pin she secured the red mitten to the coat.

Susannah went out the door onto the landing where Victoria was brushing her cheek with a kiss when someone grabbed and hurled her aside. Only by clawing at the railing did she stop herself from plunging down the stairs. The blond model she had seen so briefly at Cafe Marlene spewed hard, bitter words at Victoria. Curses broke into sobs. The model begged the woman in the door to take her back; choked wimpers confessed she couldn't face Christmas alone.

Susannah shut her eyes and held her breath. She needed Victoria so desperately. Was this the minute when all she could count on, her only real ally in this cold winter city, would now desert her? Her heart sank. "She'll take her back and they'll want me out of here. The last thing in the world she'll have time for now is my story." She grasped the railing and waited to hear the worst. Without moving, she could not see the two women; they could not see her. Neither woman at the door spoke. Why not? Were they already reconciled and in each other's arms?

"She had my coat," the model cried. "You gave it to me."

Did Victoria answer? Susannah could not hear.

"Who is she?"

"No one. Not that way."

"You've never lied to me before—"

"I'm not lying now."

"Get rid of her."

"I'm on a story."

"It's Christmas."

In the silence, Suannah prayed the two on the landing above would not look down and find her eavesdropping.

"Please. Let me in?"

Susannah strained to hear.

"I'm working. I'm sorry."

"I won't be in your way."

"You know you will—"

"Just over Christmas!"

"I've got a present for you. Wait here. No. Wait out here."

Susannah heard the door shut. The model began to cry. As noiselessly as she could step she began hurrying down the stairs.

10

DECEMBER 22, 4:45 P.M.

It was dark before five o'clock, when they left the apartment. A few snowflakes fell. City lights flared bright in the sharp cold. On their walk to Zellner's place in Gramercy Park, the two women in sheepskin coats stopped at the newspaper office so they could encourage Jeffrey Mendelsohn. They found him hard at work, scratching his pale beard and stacking clippings in folders. Victoria brought her piece on Zellner which she suggested Susannah take a moment to read.

According to Victoria's rather lurid article, the man had performed miracle after miracle. His prophecies astonished world leaders and superstars of show business. His ability to find lost persons through his insight alone left the police gasping with amazement.

Susannah read as they walked. She brushed snowflakes from the newsprint. "You make him sound absolutely incredible."

They reached Gramercy Park and a looming Victorian apartment house of huge blocks of deeply carved gray stone. In some of the windows Christmas lights gleamed.

Susannah folded the article. "Is it all really true?"

"Thoroughly researched. Jesus, it's cold."

"Seeing that little Italian girl in the used-car lot . . . I mean, did that really happen?"

Victoria hunched her shoulders against the cold. "You just read it, didn't you?"

"I guess what I'm asking is, what do you yourself think? Do you think he can really do all these things?"

"My readers do."

Halfway up the stone steps, Susannah stopped. "You told him I can't pay?"

Victoria grabbed her arm and hurried Susannah to the door. "I told you, let me worry about that." She pressed a button in a shiny brass nameplate. The heavy front door opened on half-light where a Christmas wreath with tiny lights reflected on old wood paneling and shining marble floors. An Oriental carpet led them to an elevator with a wrought-iron gate they clanked shut. The car with mesh sides open to a stairwell lifted them up through the gloom.

Susannah plucked nervously at the red mitten.

"Probably," Victoria said, "he'll want to work with that."

Susannah nodded.

"Scared?"

"Terrified."

Down a carpeted hall they found a thickly carved mahogany door with a brass plaque: ALOIS ZELLNER FOUNDATION. The bell sounded deep within.

Susannah's fingers sought the red mitten.

The door opened on Zellner himself, a small man with bright gray eyes and plump scarlet cheeks, a figure from a Dutch painting, round from years of good eating and drinking. A yapping Yorkshire terrier bounded toward the women and jittered excitedly until Zellner scooped it up in a pudgy heavy hand with a huge ring—a glinting gold cross surrounded by rubies. He pressed the wriggling dog against his deep-red velvet suit and red silk shirt, collar open on more rosy skin and a glinting gold chain.

"Sshh, Madame," he pressed his face on the excited dog. The rosy face turned and beamed happily on Victoria, whom he kissed. The hand that held Madame extended one finger for Susannah to carefully shake.

"Mrs. Bartok." His accent was European. The plump red face, which needed only white whiskers to outdo Santa Claus in jollity, set itself in a look of studied severity. He shut his eyes to block out the pain and spoke in a lowered voice directly to Susannah. "We are deeply troubled about your boy. Take heart, dear lady. We are going to help."

A slender young man in a white shirt, black bow tie and tight black trousers appeared noiselessly to take the coats. The man was as blond as Laddie.

Susannah had a moment to glance at the entrance hall filled with framed photographs of the round Zellner smiling with three Presidents of the United States, a Prime Minister of the United Kingdom and a gallery of rulers of countries and instantly recognizable opera stars and conductors. She identified only one movie star, but this was a superstar, the biggest name in the business.

Now she found the often-photographed man bending over a table writing in a copy of the same book she had seen at Victoria's.

"Do we spell Susannah with an *h?"*

"Yes," Susannah said.

He finished writing and laid the book on a hall table. "We will leave this right here so you won't forget it."

"Thank you."

The man's accent was heavy. Susannah supposed it was Dutch.

A pink hand grandly waved them into a velvety cave choked with heavy, upholstered furniture, an antique shop crowded with porcelain and china figurines. Polished wood-and-glass cases held painted plates reflecting the glowing lights of a half-decorated Christmas tree. Boxes of fragile antique ornaments waited to be hung on the fir boughs.

"Kurt. We will have tea."

Without looking at any of them, the blond young man took the quivering Yorkshire terrier from her master's arms and left the room as noiselessly as he had entered. Zellner ensconced himself in a wing chair next to the fireplace's wood fire that wavered out a cheery glow. Susannah placed herself carefully on a velvet-covered chair flanked on either side by tabletops crowded with delicate porcelain.

"Meissen." Zellner smiled at his roomful of figurines.

Victoria drew her recorder and Nikon from her leather bag. Did Zellner object to the reporter? Not at all. His jolly face beamed at his visitors. "The first time our dear Victoria came here she asked if her tape recorder and camera would bother me. I told her nothing bothers me." He coughed. "Except this cough. A lot of something going around. Everyone in Bloomingdale's was barking his head off. Not to worry. Kurt will bring us a nice hot cup of tea in a minute."

The jolly face composed itself into studied seriousness as the man leaned forward to grasp both of Susannah's cold hands into his warm, plump flesh. "I have prayed to *le Bon Dieu* that I can help." This time he smiled a sadder smile that said he might look jolly and well-fed, but he knew only too well that life included much unspeakable suffering and pain.

"Victoria has told me very little about you, Mrs. Bartok. Susannah, may I?"

She nodded.

"You do not live in New York, Susannah?"

"California. That is, I did."

"And you left because of the fire?"

"The fire?" Susannah looked to Victoria. What fire? Then she remembered that last November terrible brush fires had blackened the hills. She did not tell the psychic, but the truth was, the fires blazed far from her house.

"Trees—burning torches. The hills—all on fire. Terrible. Your husband was not with you."

"No—"

"Water." He shrugged as if to chide himself for overlooking the obvious. "Your husband surrounds himself with water."

Victoria and her camera moved among the furniture, catching the man and woman from different angles on her high-speed film. The recorder's power light glowed as bright as one of the Christmas tree lights.

Zellner coughed.

"Please, forgive me." He rose and threaded himself surprisingly quickly through the furniture and porcelain to leave the room. Susannah heard him cough again. A door closed.

Susannah leaned to Victoria who was checking her camera.

"He was right about the fire. I mean he knew Scott—my husband—wasn't there. He was in Hawaii. You heard him say he was—and surrounded by water—" She broke off her whispers as Zellner wound his way expertly back through the velvet and Meissen. He coughed, blew his nose on a pink Kleenex.

Kurt entered noiselessly with a silver tea tray. One plate prickled with holly leaves surrounding a heap of round cookies dusted white with powdered sugar.

"Good boy, Kurt." He smiled at his guests. "You remembered the *pfeffernüsse.*"

Kurt left.

Before Zellner poured the tea he held the plate of cookies he regarded as special to Susannah. "For Christmas. You know *pfeffernüsse?*"

"No."

"Victoria?" He held the plate up to the woman, who made it clear she was working too hard with the camera to help herself to a powder-dusted cookie. "You must have a *pfeffernüsse.*"

"I'm Cuban," Victoria said, squinting into the viewer. "What are they? Dutch?"

"German actually. I make them every year. Give them to my friends. Every President since Roosevelt has loved my *pfeffernüsse.* Callas adored them. Before you two go, remind me to give each of you a bag."

Susannah, who had eaten nothing since she had gotten off the plane, felt she had no choice but to bite into the hard little cookie that tasted of anise and pepper. Zellner watched her closely. He shut his eyes. Apparently he had forgotten about pouring the tea.

He suddenly rose and went to the hall and the two sheepskin coats. He had found the red mitten and was unpinning it when Susannah came to his side and took her wallet from the pocket.

"I have his picture," Susannah said.

Zellner waved away the offer.

In front of the fireplace Susannah put the rest of her uneaten cookie next to a porcelain shepherdess. Zellner rubbed the wool between his hands. "New?"

"Yes," Susannah said quickly. "But he had time to wear it." She sensed the man did not wish her to speak unless he questioned her directly. She brushed the powdered sugar from her hands.

Zellner worked his fingers over the red wool for as long as a minute. Although Victoria photographed him he seemed to commune with the mitten as if he were completely alone in the room. He rose and crossed to the Christmas tree and hung an old and elaborately decorated ornament on a bough. His silence became so long, Susannah felt he might never speak again.

"Gold hair," he said suddenly. He dug almost frantically into a box of tissue until he carefully drew out an ornament wrapped in cotton. "Gold as the hair of this angel."

He did not ask Susannah, but she found herself nodding vigorously. The spun gold hair of the angel flared in the light.

"The boy's father." Zellner stood with his back to Susannah, facing the tree. "Gold hair as well."

Susannah nodded. She realized he could not see her. "Yes," she said quickly.

Victoria crouched beside a chair, shot a picture.

"Gold." The man's voice sounded faraway. "From the sun. And often wet from the sea. The father. Water. Cold water—but the boy does not like the cold sea. The boy loves the warm sea . . . the warm sun." He considered the angel he held in his hands. "Now I see him very far from the warm sea . . . the warm sun. Even farther from his father . . ."

Susannah turned to Victoria, eyes wide, asking the other woman how this man could possibly know these things. They waited for more.

"There is another father I see. An older man who waits for the boy."

Zellner's shoulders shook. He coughed.

"That would be his grandfather," Susannah said. Did he hear her?

Zellner did not turn. "An old man who lives in an open place. With trees—many trees. Not a city."

"Upstate New York!"

Zellner carefully placed the angel back in its cotton and turned to his guests. He rubbed the red wool in his hand.

He frowned. He glanced around angrily. "This boy. Why does this boy have no name?"

72 . . .

Was this a question? Susannah sought Victoria's reaction. Should she answer? Zellner held up the hand with the ruby ring, commanding silence. "You call him 'boy'?"

"Laddie."

"That is not a name."

Zellner returned to his chair, but, too agitated to sit, he paced. He coughed. He shook his head angrily. "No name. But I see this boy so very clearly." He snapped his fingers at Susannah. Gone were his courtly old-world manners; now he moved in response to some stronger compulsion. "His picture. You said you had his picture. Quickly!"

Susannah opened her wallet and carried the photograph of the boy in sunshine to Zellner, who pulled on glasses. She stood next to him. At the first glance he cringed as if the woman had struck him in the face. He clamped shut his eyes but tears welled out and spilled down the scarlet cheeks. He bent with sorrow and covered his face. Rocking back and forth in his chair he moaned.

Susannah stifled a gasp. Her knees shook and she grasped a chair to stay on her feet.

Zellner blew his nose. He gripped the arms of his chair and pulled himself until he sat straight up. "Mrs. Bartok, may I ask you to go into the next room. Please? Leave us alone for a minute?"

She shook her head. She was saying no. Her voice was weak, but she managed to speak: "Because you don't want to tell me?"

Zellner turned from her and stared with wet eyes into the fire. Susannah took a tighter grip on the back of the chair.

"Go ahead. Please," she said.

All the cheer had fled from the ruddy face. In his big chair he seemed small, shrunken, his baby-red face full of fear. He let himself fall back. His fingers plucked at the red mitten. "Cold. So far from the warm sun. Is it a box? I do not know. . . . A drawer. A box? A place where it is always cold. . . ."

No one spoke. The wood fire in the grate crackled.

Susannah did not see Victoria lift her camera and take a picture before she felt the support of an arm circling her. She shut her eyes and tried to see what the man saw. Laddie, lying in a drawer, cold. Dead. After a long silence broken only by the crackling fire, she found her voice, which came out bone dry. "The morgue?"

Victoria stared at the old man.

"I am sorry, Mrs. Bartok."

Susannah pushed Victoria's arm away. She stood alone, separating herself from this man and what he was saying, from this woman and what she believed. Her voice, scarcely to be heard, whispered: "No."

Zellner stared at the little boy's red mitten in his hands.

"No!" This time Susannah's voice was sharp and loud. She lunged and grabbed the mitten from the man.

Zellner struggled to rise from his chair.

"No!" Now Susannah's voice was a shout that rattled the delicate porcelain figurines, the china plates in their glass cases.

Zellner reached his feet. The interview was over. Exhausted, drained by what he had seen, the psychic coughed. He dragged himself from the room.

"No!" Susannah shouted after the shuffling old man. "He's not there!"

11

DECEMBER 22, 6:30 P.M.

On the icy steps leaving Zellner's, both women turned up their collars against the bitter cold wind. Neither spoke.

Victoria found a telephone in a coffee shop on Second Avenue and while Susannah sat alone in a booth, she called the morgue. As she talked, her face showed she was hearing what Susannah feared most to hear.

Victoria sat beside Susannah, who plucked at the red wool of the mitten. Yes. The morgue reported the body of a boy of two years of age. Caucasian. Blond hair.

Lighting a cigarette, Victoria managed to dismiss a waitress who hovered to take their order. She waited until Susannah could steel herself. The boy came in this morning. Sooner or later, it was inevitable, they would have to go uptown to the morgue.

On the sidewalk Susannah brushed back her blowing hair. She flicked a snowflake from an eyelash. "I don't believe those people you talked to on that phone. He isn't dead."

Victoria stopped a cab. In the back seat Victoria watched Susannah turn from her and lean her face against the cold window. The reporter could only guess what this trembling woman was feeling. Before they had left her apartment and at the newspaper office, Susannah had read about Zellner. Her reaction then had been doubt. She had questioned Victoria about the man.

Did Victoria believe in him? That, of course, had been intellect talking. Face to face with the man in front of his own fireplace, Susannah's refusal to believe that this man saw her son in the morgue came from the depths of her soul, a mother fighting against accepting the worst.

And Victoria? Had she ever asked herself what she truly believed about Zellner? She shrugged. She tapped a cigarette on the black-and-silver cigarette case and scratched out flame from a stick match. Zellner? She sent out a long stream of smoke. What she believed didn't matter. Her readers believed in him.

They turned east on 30th Street and, as they approached the river she saw Bellevue, the massive hospital, shining with light. In a few more minutes she and Susannah would know the truth.

They stopped at the corner of a modern, blue-tiled build-ing—CITY OF NEW YORK OFFICE OF THE CHIEF MEDI-CAL EXAMIINER. Victoria rang a bell that summoned a guard who unlocked the glass door.

Susannah had never been in a morgue. She held her breath. The first floor looked reassuringly like ordinary offices. Her hands plunged deep into the sheepskin coat pockets. She hurried alongside Victoria, keeping pace, their footfalls sounding together.

In the basement, blue tile gleamed. They stepped around a metal cart, which Victoria called a meat wagon. In an office where Christmas cards hung over a rope of silver tinsel, voices boomed "Rudolf the Red-Nosed Reindeer" from the next room. Laughter rose. A babble of happy voices erupted from the staff in their after-hours Christmas party.

From that room a medical examiner, a young black man, handsome as a movie star, hurried toward the women as he drew on a white lab coat. He stopped at a desk drawer, took out a small aerosol breath spray, squirted his open mouth, and presented himself to the two. Victoria explained that she was the woman who had telephoned about the two-year-old. The man, profes-sionally solemn against the background laughter, nodded and picked up a file. He nodded again and motioned the two into the hall.

The three strode down the blue-tiled corridor to a room.

Victoria stopped Susannah. "You want me to go in for you?"

Susannah, who had said nothing since they had left the coffee shop, faced the door. She was going in.

The tiled room flared in white light. The two tiers of stainless steel drawers the examiner approached looked as ordinary as office files. He glanced at cards on the fronts of the boxes. He slowed and waited for the women to come to his side. Susannah took a deep breath. Her shoulders pushed back too far as she forced a breath to give her courage. Her legs shook. Suddenly, when her knees all but gave way, Victoria grabbed her arm and held her unsteadily on her feet.

The examiner looked to Victoria. Were they ready? Her slight nod told him to open the drawer.

The sliding tray in this refrigerated box rumbled toward Susannah. She braced herself to see bare feet and a sheet, but at first the drawer appeared empty. What she saw took away her breath. A little boy's clothes. Mittens. Not red mittens, but pathetic, worn little blue mittens. Her heart slammed. She expected to see feet but there lay the head and the naked body of a little boy, small and terribly white and gray. He was not stiff. He was limp. He might be sleeping. The dead boy's hair lay lank, almost brown. She saw that in a glance. His hair did not shine gold. Not even blond. Susannah shut her eyes and thanked God that naked little thing with his clothes wadded up by his head, lying alone in this drawer, was not her boy.

Susannah raced out into the snowy, black night. She ran. Victoria dashed into the cold wind to follow her. At the corner Susannah turned and raked blowing hair back from accusing eyes. "Susannah, please!" Victoria tried to reach for Susannah's arm, but she jerked away. "That part's over. We were wrong. Susannah, thank God. I'm so glad—"

Susannah shook her head and backed away. Victoria grasped her arm before she could run. "Don't hate Zellner. They did have that boy. And those mittens. Give him credit for seeing that—"

"Damn him for saying that thing was Laddie." She snatched deep defiant breaths of stinging, ice-cold air. "Damn that old fraud to hell!"

The wind tore at them and Victoria clawed at her tangled

hair. The reporter had things to say but this was no place to shout at each other against the blast. She searched First Avenue for a cab.

"He's alive!" Now Susannah did not shout. The wind hurled away her words but she did not shout. "He isn't dead. Goddamn all of you! I knew I was right! From now on I listen only to myself. And I swear to God—even if I have to do it all alone—I'll get him back!"

12

DECEMBER 22, 8:25 P.M.

In the taxi Victoria had suggested a Cuban restaurant, but Susannah would not even talk about stopping.

"You haven't eaten a thing since you got off that plane."

Susannah leaned forward and rapped on the clear plastic wall that protects a New York taxi driver from his criminal passengers. "Can't you go any faster?"

The cab leaped with a screech across an intersection.

"Nothing to eat. And you haven't had a wink of sleep since you left L.A.—"

"I've got the rest of my life to sleep. After I get him back."

Until this evening's visit to the morgue, Victoria had made most of the suggestions and done most of their thinking. Now that Susannah had defeated the psychic and successfully attacked Victoria's belief in him, she did not hesitate to give orders. She countered Victoria's directions to the driver to take them to the apartment on Commerce Street. Instead, she would go straight to the newspaper office.

"I'll call the police from there."

"You want me to help with the research?"

"I want you to check the answering machine at your

apartment and call me if there's anything important."

"Yes, Ma'am." Victoria knew her sarcasm was lost on this determined woman. The truth was, Victoria welcomed the time alone. She had more story to write.

The taxi slowed at the newspaper office.

"How late are you going to be?"

"As long as it takes." Susannah bounded out and slammed the door.

In a tiny combination deli and grocery store a block west of the bright lights of Times Square a young woman in a long winter coat and a bright-red knitted cap lifted dark glasses to peer at a rack of dusty little jars of baby food. She clattered up a handful. From a cooler she lifted out two cartons of milk and moved to the counter, where another young woman with a deathly white face waited clutching Hostess Twinkies and a cellophane-wrapped fruitcake against her long coat. Her white hands shook so violently she dropped the cake.

"That crap isn't on her list," the woman with the dark glasses said.

"I thought because it's—I mean, like it's Christmas. . . ."

Behind the cash register a worn old Greek woman in a black sweater frowned at the effort it took her to ring up each price. The young woman's glasses flashed from the woman to glance over her shoulder, back into the store. When she failed to see what she was looking for, she peered up at a mirror in the corner, a monitor that reflected the entire store to guard against shoplifters. She watched a tall, skeleton-thin young man in a shiny black suit, who wore no overcoat but dangled with scarves, cram his pockets with candy bars until he slipped out into the night.

The old woman slowly rang up the second batch of groceries while the woman with the glasses reviewed a typewritten shopping list. "And two cartons of Marlboros."

Out in the icy night the tall man's long black hair whipped in the wind as he gnawed a chocolate bar and pressed his hatchet face to the steamy glass. He watched the two women pay for the groceries and pick up the bags. From his pockets bulging with junk candy he pulled another bar and ripped it open as the wrapper clattered away on the sidewalk. He moved to the women as they reached the door. "You sure you got everything?"

"Joanne's bad," said the woman with the glasses. "She's got to get back."

"You sure you got it all? The Bitch doesn't like it when you forget things."

"We should have gone to a supermarket. The baby food back there was all dusty. Like they haven't sold any in twenty years."

"You know why?" The man sucked chocolate from his teeth.

"Yeah, I know why. Like look around. Not many babies in this creep neighborhood."

The other woman began to shake so violently she would have dropped her groceries but the man grabbed the bag before she lurched to the curb, bent double, and vomited.

The man crunched chocolate. The woman with the glasses waited. "Like I said, she's got to get back."

The woman at the curb turned a white face to them and wiped her wet mouth on the sleeve of her long coat. "Please?"

"Bad?" the man with the candy bar asked.

"Bad."

Down Eighth Avenue, at the corner in the light from a coffee shop, a dark young man in a floppy hat and a long winter coat huddled over a radio. At the sight of the three, he turned eagerly. "Hey, man. I'm freezing my balls off here. You got to tell Shelley it's his fucking turn." The Arabic accent was harsh, in sharp contrast to his soft, boyish face. "Candyman, please?"

"Call the Bitch," the tall man said. "Now!"

The huddled youth's dark eyes peered up and down the sidewalk and into the cross street before he drew a collapsible antenna from the instrument. He uncoiled a microphone and snapped on the sender.

"Tell her it's Joanne," the tall man said. "We're sending her right up."

Susannah telephone the precinct only to discover Lieutenant Foy was off duty. The officer who talked with her exuded professional cheer. He admitted the police had no news. This, he assured her, was not necessarily a bad sign. No news, in a case like this, could generally be interpreted as good news. Susannah hung up on the cop without unleashing her compulsion to tell the man to go to hell. Coolly, she had told him where she could be reached, that she would call back in three hours.

Susannah found Jeffrey had covered the library table with clippings. He sat, furiously scratching his thin beard. Susannah leaned close. He had categorized the stories under file cards carefully printed with a marker pen. *Ransom. Divorced or Separated Mother. Divorced or Separated Father. Psychotics. Sex Offenders. Cults.*

"Getting anywhere?"

"You're not supposed to ask a researcher for that. I'm only supposed to supply the facts. For sheer inspiration, you're expected to ask the hotshot reporter lady to draw the conclusions. She knows everything. She is also something of a pain in the ass." He held up a clipping. "Read this. No. Don't read this. Horrible." He buried it in the clippings marked *Psychotic.* "There's a worse one under 'Cults.' Sacrificing kids in a blood cult in Brazil. What we better hope for is a set-up. A careful plan. The use of Mace. Try to find cases where they've used it before; the hope being that no pervert or complete crazy is going to be bright enough to carefully plan it out."

Susannah read an article about someone who had switched a stillborn baby into a mother's arms and taken the live baby.

Jeffrey shook his head. "I'm going to have to start a new file—kidnapping from institutions—'Hospital Cases.' This one's in L.A. He shook his head, grabbed his crutches to get the last of the files. "People. Wild, huh?"

A half-hour later Jeffrey returned from the library. "I better get home for what's left of Chanukah or my mother will kill me. I've got some good stuff here about illegal adoptions and black-market babies. . . ." He found Susannah, her head on her arms, slumped on the table. He knew the woman was dead tired. Was she sleeping? On the sidewalk below, drunks sang "O Come All Ye Faithful." He saw her shoulders shake. She was weeping.

By midnight Victoria finished typing. She called the paper for a messenger, a kid with glasses who sat and read *The Portable*

Faulkner while she glanced over her story and made a few corrections. She slid the pages into an envelope. The boy shoved his book into his quilted vest and left. Victoria yawned and massaged her shoulders, and switched off the light.

13

DECEMBER 23, 3:05 A.M.

"Turn off the fucking light."

Susannah waved a file-size envelope at the woman burrowing into the blankets on the living room couch. "For illegal adoptions this is all Jeffrey could come up with." Her red face stung from running through the cold. She kicked a pile of magazines out of her way and poked the envelope at the cocoon that held the groaning reporter.

"Victoria?"

The woman on the couch shook black hair from her face and rubbed puffy eyes.

"Illegal adoptions," Susannah demanded, showing the file. "All we could find."

Her eyes still shut, Victoria yawned. "That's because they're illegal. People don't keep records—"

"You know much about them?"

Victoria stifled a yawn. "Not much."

"But they do go on."

"So one hears." Victoria, still in her black sweater, threw back the blankets, shoved her feet to the floor to sit up. "One also hears there's a hell of a lot of money in it. You figure it's a lead?"

"Where do they get the kids?"

"Don't look at me." She reached for a cigarette. Susannah

was still on fire, every bit as determined as she had been on the taxi ride from the morgue. Victoria decided this kind of determination couldn't be faced without a cigarette.

"Seriously." Susannah jabbbed the file at her. "Where do they get the kids?"

Victoria sucked in smoke and tossed the box of kitchen matches on the floor. "From mothers who don't want kids." She shrugged. "They don't get abortions . . . but they don't want to raise the kid alone. Look, I'm hardly the world's leading authority."

"Lesbians have babies."

"Not this one."

"You said you knew a social worker."

"I called. Remember? She never called back."

"Call her now."

"It is now five after three in the goddamn morning."

"Shit." Susannah dropped into a chair. "Call anyway."

"Can we let the lady sleep till eight? Maybe you don't need sleep but social workers and reporters sure as hell do." She found Susannah still pushing the file at her.

"I brought these home to work on. You want to see?"

"Later."

Susannah sprang to her feet, ran into the bedroom, and slammed the door. Victoria snapped off the light. The living room was dark but light spilled from under the door of the bedroom, where she could hear Susannah pacing, stopping and reading, more on fire than ever.

Three cigarettes later Victoria dragged into the kitchen and warmed some milk, a mug of which Susannah took without thanking her. She returned to sit in the dark living room sipping the milk, her cigarette glowing red, when the telephone's ring shattered the silence. Before she reached the phone, Susannah had hurled open the door and grabbed it on the second ring.

"It's got to be the police!" As Susannah listened, Victoria could see her stiffen and grow cold. Susannah said nothing.

"Who is it?"

Susannah held the receiver out to Victoria so she could hear the voice, urgent with the heavy Dutch accent. "Your son, Mrs.

Bartok. Very strong this time." He coughed. "Very close. I must see you!"

"Zellner?"

Susannah held out the receiver and spoke only to Victoria. "I won't see him."

The man on the phone's urgency broke into a cough. "Victoria?" She grabbed the phone.

"Good morning, Mr. Zellner. Yes. That's all right. Yes I see."

"Don't talk with him!" Susannah clawed at the instrument until Victoria twisted away. "Tell him for me he's a rotten old fraud and I hope he rots in hell!"

Victoria clamped her hand over the mouthpiece and spoke around it so carefully that the man would probably never guess Susannah shouted curses at him in the same room. "Absolutely," she said. "Nine o'clock. The corner. We'll be there."

"No way!"

Victoria pushed past Susannah to carry the phone on its cable to her desk.

"Look at me, Victoria. Victoria, goddamn you, look at me!"

Victoria spun around and looked straight at Susannah.

"From the minute we walked into his place he started to autograph his goddamn book—like I was some kind of admiring fan. Then all that name-dropping—all those stories about him and the White House. Maria Callas. You saw him. He's a rotten old faggot phony. He uses people. He only wants to use Laddie and me to promote himself."

Victoria looked through her smoke straight into Susannah's eyes. She shrugged. "That," she said bluntly, "may be perfectly true."

"Are you saying we let him?"

Victoria smoked.

Susannah had the terrible sinking feeling that, yes, that was exactly what Victoria was saying. She felt her shoulders slump. She shook her head, at a loss. "Don't any of you people in this city do anything unless it does you some good?"

"What if he's on to something?"

"How can he be? He's a goddamn fake!"

"He did see that two-year-old boy with the mittens in the morgue."

"That doesn't even deserve the dignity of being called a coincidence. You said yourself they get thirty thousand bodies a year. No, dammit, I don't trust him. I hate him and his fake goddamn vibes."

Victoria rose and turned toward the kitchen. "You want any breakfast?"

"He said Laddie was dead."

"You can skimp on any other meal of the day, but you have to start out with a good breakfast."

"Don't any of you care how I feel?"

Victoria stood in the kitchen door. "Right now you feel sorry for yourself—a very wasteful emotion. As for what Zellner said, he did not say Laddie was dead. He said he saw him and he saw boxes and maybe a drawer. You and I jumped to the conclusion about that body in the morgue."

"You did, dammit. I never—not for one instant—did!"

"I stand corrected." Victoria bowed with mock humility. "Meanwhile, you haven't told me what you want for breakfast."

"How the hell can you be on his side? You saw him hold Laddie's mitten and say he saw Laddie. Boxes. Drawers. Cold. The morgue. Only he didn't see them at all. He was faking the whole thing."

Victoria went into the kitchen and filled the coffeepot. Out in the street a car horn honked.

"Please. Call the social worker now?"

14

DECEMBER 23, 8:00 A.M.

Susannah had been in New York City thirty-seven hours.

On their way to the social worker's office the early morning halls were already full of babies whimpering and bewildered mothers waiting. Susannah had seen people in trouble at the precinct and poor people here in this building. It seemed to her the troubled and the poor spent a lot of their lives waiting.

Victoria rapped on a door and, without waiting for an answer, opened it. At a desk under a bulletin board pinned with Christmas cards and photos of children, a slender black woman munched a jelly donut and gulped steaming coffee.

"Rica Tallmer," Victoria said briskly, "Susannah Bartok."

Rica nodded. Unable to speak, she pointed at her full mouth. She rose and reached a slim hand across her desk to shake Susannah's. Her eyes—long as an ancient Egyptian's—met Victoria's. An awkward silence filled the room. She was so sleek and elegant, her features so slim and aristocratic that Susannah found it impossible to think of her climbing stairs in housing projects, visiting prisons, or counseling pregnant women. This creature who could only peer out of the glossy pages of a high-fashion magazine had long hands made to dangle emeralds and strings of pearls, not hold coffee in paper cups. Yet as Rica stared at Victoria she licked the sticky sweet from her fingers. Her snow-white jogging suit with a brilliant yellow scarf tied at the neck like a man's ascot showed she had come into the office for only a few minutes; she was on her way out of town for the holidays. The silence was too long and it was Victoria moving to the desk who broke it.

"A jelly donut and coffee? Still no time to eat a decent breakfast?"

Rica gulped, wiped her mouth with a napkin. "Sorry," she said to Susannah with a smile as genuine as her beauty. She spoke with far less warmth to Victoria. "I told you. I'm dashing. Practically this very minute." Susannah saw a white suitcase in the corner. On a rack hung a white artificial fur.

"One thing I always told you, Rica. You have to start the day with a decent breakfast."

The woman gave Susannah another smile while Victoria busied herself at the bulletin board lifting the front folds of several Christmas cards and looking for names. "Any from the old gang?"

Rica spoke to Susannah: "As you see, we're old friends."

"Lovers," Victoria said for the benefit of the third woman.

Now Susannah partly understood Victoria's reluctance to telephone the lovely woman, and that long silence when they first saw one another.

Victoria continued to explain. "I got Rica to come out of the closet."

"And now I'd be grateful if you'd get out from behind my desk. I don't know how well you know Victoria, Mrs. Bartok. But Victoria loves to shock. If she can write and make money by shocking she's never happier."

Victoria moved to a visitor's chair.

"Please don't sit, Vic. I really am. In a tearing hurry."

"Millie?" Victoria tried to sound offhand.

"Yes."

"She's waiting?"

"Probably double parked." She glanced at a tiny wristwatch.

"Millie can wait." Victoria smiled her acid smile and opened her leather bag. "Christmas where?"

Instead of answering, Rica swept the desk of the uneaten pastry and paper.

"Where you and I went last year?"

"Do we have to go into this?" Her Egyptian black eyes flicked from Victoria to indicate the third woman.

"Mrs. Bartok is not gay."

"One thing, Mrs. Bartok, that is not so gay about being gay—is holidays. Without families. Not going back home to families you don't get along with. Instead, you go off to some resort out of season and have Christmas Eve in a bar or a hotel room. Christmas Day you get together with other gays stranded in the area and you laugh too much and pretend you wouldn't have it any other way. Not that holidays are such winners for anybody—I hate them. The pits. Professionally, I can tell you that everybody—not just gays—is at his or her worst. People drink more . . . say things they should never say . . . commit more suicides . . . murders . . . beat up on their kids—Victoria, you should do an article about the holidays."

"I have." She placed the cassette recorder on the desk and snapped on the power.

"And now you're doing a story about illegal adoptions?"

"I don't know yet."

Susannah saw Rica glance at her watch, a move she did not try to disguise.

"As you said." Victoria put the acid into her voice. "Millie's waiting."

"Yes. Millie's waiting."

"Let her wait."

Victoria sat. "In beautiful downtown New York someone Maced Mrs. Bartok in the eyes and snatched her two-year-old son."

The beautiful face was suddenly a stricken little girl's. "Oh, God. I'm so sorry—"

Victoria reached with Laddie's picture across the desk so Rica could see. "Is he—or is he not—the blond, blue-eyed little boy everyone who comes into your office wants to take home for their very own and adopt?"

Rica, visibly shaken, studied the picture. She motioned for Susannah to sit. Victoria warmed to her mission, her old aggressive self. "On the open market what would he be worth?"

"God, Vic. Do you have to?"

"Yes. Susannah's ready to hear anything you can tell her." Victoria flared a match on the box's sandpaper. She lit a brown cigarette. "We know your office doesn't charge. No licensed agency does. But if you did. How much for blond hair and blue eyes? Sixty thousand? A hundred thousand?"

"Is that what you think happened, Mrs. Bartok?"

Susannah didn't answer but looked to Victoria. The reporter would do the talking.

"It's one of the leads we're following." She seemed to crave smoke, she drew it in so eagerly. "Am I right about the price? As high as a hundred thousand?"

"That's in line with what I hear."

"How come people are willing to pay so much?"

"You didn't have to come here to ask me that. You live in the world."

"For openers, I'd like Susannah to hear it from you."

"I'm not a newspaper reporter, Vic. I put considerable value on accuracy."

"Okay. Allow me. You tell me where I go wrong." She pulled in a long drag of smoke. "Here we are in a licensed adoption agency. Say Susannah's not a mother, but a gentleman. A banker. An ad man. A buyer in a department store. I'm his neat and clean little wife. In other words, we're an all-American man and wife, true-blue couple, not just living together but married, with all the credit cards and a little house with a white picket fence, a lawn and a back yard with a swing. Only one hitch. No kid to swing in the swing. We come in here and ask for a child. How long before we get one?"

Rica reached to a file cabinet, pulled out a dossier of photos of babies and small children, mostly black. "We have a lot of children who desperately need homes right now. Begging for homes—"

"You didn't understand. Those are minorities. All shapes and colors. We're the perfect mom and dad types. We want a perfect pink-and-white, blue-eyed blond baby boy. How long?"

Rica closed the file. "Four or five years."

"You guarantee he'll have blond hair and blue eyes?"

"No."

"So. In other words, we do it nice and legal and we're out of luck?"

Susannah and Rica conspired to keep their eyes from meeting.

"Now suppose we come in here and we are not the all-American, apple-pie mom-and-dad couple. Suppose I'm single. Divorced. Or unmarried. Not a citizen, but a foreigner. Say I have a record for doing drugs. Or I'm gay."

"You have all the answers, Vic. Why ask me?"

"Hang on. Just tell me where I go wrong, okay?" Victoria tapped Susannah on the knee. "Okay?"

Susannah nodded. Victoria was enjoying herself hugely.

"Say I have the hundred thousand. I want a kid. I want a kid exactly like the kid in this picture. How do I get him?"

"Where do you live?"

"Uh—I live in a suburb of Washington, D.C. Maybe Europe. I could even be an Arab."

Rica no longer employed any charm. Her smile vanished as if she turned a switch. She was serious and Susannah could now imagine her climbing housing-project stairs, doing the dirty work that had to be a big part of her job. "You find a woman—usually a young girl who's going to have a baby—who, for one reason or another, is willing to give it up."

Victoria watched Rica through cigarette smoke. "Like you did."

"A long time ago." Rica glanced at the recorder. "Will you shut that thing off?"

"Wouldn't you rather be quoted accurately?"

Rica sighed her annoyance. She wanted Victoria out of here, but her sympathy for Susannah trapped her. "Of course, you don't need to come to us at all if you have someone inside the family . . . a relative. Or a friend of the family . . ."

"Say I don't have that someone. I'm looking but I can't find that girl."

"You're generally not this slow on the uptake, Vic."

"You have to remember, Rica, that Mrs. Bartok here is new at this. And I am not your average slow-on-the-uptake fucking mother."

"You start by asking around."

"Not me. I want to keep how I went about getting this kid my business and mine alone. Why wouldn't I go straight to a doctor who delivers babies?"

"Why not? Simplest of all. Ask him or her if he or she knows any pregnant girl who might want to give up her child."

Susannah spoke for the first time. "But would this doctor admit he or she deals in babies?"

"Never. Just for his records, he'd ask you to leave your number with his nurse. Next, you'd hear from a lawyer who says word's out you're trying to adopt a child. The lawyer offers to handle the legal side. He asks for money—to show you're serious. You give him the first payment. You wait. When you hear from him again, he calls and says he has the baby and the papers. You have the money. He hands over the baby."

"And practically no risk for the physician."

"No federal law against it. Only statutes in some states that have to do with taking part in the exchange of a human being for money. Slavery."

"Next question," said Victoria. "Now tell me my identity as an eager parent-to-be."

"You already told me you lived in the leafy suburbs of Washington."

"Or Europe. Or South America. If I have this kind of money I can afford to jet here from anywhere. Now just go along with me on this. Say I'd just flown into New York. No prying small-town neighbors here. I wouldn't stay with friends. Even in this city the fewer people who know how I got the baby the better. I'd check in at a top hotel. First thing I'd do is look up obstetricians in the Yellow Pages. I'd start calling. I'd tell them how much a child means to me. Of course, as you just said, the doctors wouldn't take a chance and answer me directly. But I'd leave my number and ask them to get back to me—just in case. Of course, as you say, it wouldn't be the doctor who calls back, but a lawyer. Why wouldn't that work? Hell, call twenty doctors, I'll bet we'd hear back—indirectly—from two, three of them."

"How does that bring Mrs. Bartok her son?"

"Step One. It puts us in touch with people who are dealing in black-market babies. Find them and we're a hell of a lot closer to him than before. It could lead to the big break."

"Then why don't you check into a fancy hotel and start phoning doctors?"

"Since this is just one lead, neither Susannah nor I has the time to tie ourselves up full time on this. We've got other leads to follow."

"And you're absolutely serious?"

"Rica, did you ever know anyone more serious than I?"

"Millie's got a friend on the switchboard at the Plaza. They could relay any return calls here. No one needs to know you're not actually staying at the hotel."

Susannah's excitement had her on her feet. "Please. Let's do it. Right now."

"Of course," Rica said. "When it comes time to meet with the lawyer you should look like you have a hundred thousand dollars."

Susannah and Rica saw Victoria grin.

"From that look on your face, Vic, I'd say we're in for one of your bright ideas."

"Hell, any out-of-work actor and actress would love to play that role for us. And all the actors I know are out of work."

Rica spoke directly to Susannah. "Before I leave town, I'll have my friend set this up with the hotel." She reached for her white fur. Victoria helped her put on the coat. "You've been a big help, Rica." Victoria snapped off the Sony. "Money's always a good angle. If they didn't grab him for some cult thing . . . or sex . . . it might just be money."

Rica picked up her bag but said nothing.

"You don't agree?"

Rica hesitated. "A minute ago, Vic, you said it yourself—you are not a mother. I have to warn you—I see it every day—this city is full of crazy, lost females who will do anything to get a child."

"We'll follow every lead we can. Susannah and I have a few minutes before our next appointment. We'll use your office phones and start with the doctors. And the actors. You think the couple's name—let's see—Raimondo Luis Olmas from Caracas sounds authentic?"

Rica took Susannah's hand. "You'll be in my prayers."

15

DECEMBER 23, 8:59 A.M.

A blast of sleety wind shrieked around the department store corner and lifted the old man's white hair. Kurt, in a driver's uniform and helping Zellner from the back seat of his black Rolls-Royce, let him fall against him. He urged his feverish employer to return to the car, but the old man struggled on a cane to reach the sidewalk and push through the crowd.

Christmas shoppers hurried past. Recorded music blared holiday cheer. Santa Claus stamped his feet against the cold and rang his bell.

Hurrying toward this same corner, Susannah was the first to see Zellner. She slowed. There he stood on the sidewalk, that very place her agony had begun that terrible night. He let Kurt wrap his shoulder with a black fur robe. He turned his red face to the wind. The reporter squinted through her camera and clicked off picture after picture.

By the time the two women approached him, Zellner had bent away from them, his body wracked by a fit of coughing.

"He's burning up with fever." Kurt wound the fur robe closer on the old man. "He should be home in bed."

Susannah hated this man. Seeing him here only increased the suspicion she felt for the psychic. She ignored Kurt to turn to Victoria. "How did he know this was the last place I saw Laddie? Did you tell him?"

Victoria clawed strands of blowing hair from her face. "I don't remember."

"Yes you do, damn you. He didn't get here on his own. Did you tell him?"

"Apparently he found out."

"How?"

"Look!"

Zellner hunched his shoulders. The fur robe slid to the ground. His face twisted in a grimace.

"Jesus," whispered Victoria. "He's really on to something."

"It's a goddamn act. He's using us."

"Then we use him. But it's no act. Can't you at least keep an open mind?—"

"I'm going to the precinct and check with Foy."

As Susannah pulled away Kurt was trying to wrap the man's shoulders. A hand stopped her. "Mrs. Bartok." Zellner's voice rasped. "Quickly. The boy's red mitten!"

Susannah, who hated this man, who had vowed to have nothing more to do with him, found herself unpinning the mitten from her coat and placing it in the plump, hot hand. In the middle of the sidewalk Zellner turned around, circling, waiting, staring with closed eyes. For what? None of the shoppers glanced at the man. They eddied around him, a quiet island on the crowded sidewalk.

His mouth opened and closed. Nothing came out. Suddenly he was stammering. "Why . . . why can I not see you?" Strangled words came apart as he said them and as suddenly as he had spoken he turned, opened eyes watering from the wind, and blinked at Susannah. His face shone with sweat. He shook his head, shrinking at the sight of her. "Yesterday," he raised his hand clenching the red mitten, "you were resisting me. Yes. It is true!"

"You said my son was dead."

"No. Not dead." He turned his face into the wind. His hair was stiff with freezing sweat. "Near. Near this place."

Susannah's heart stopped. Even if this was an act, few things in her life had moved her more. She searched the red face. She prayed for his next words.

Victoria saw the television cameras first. Newsmen with their hand-held minicams and cables were jumping out of a van parked in back of the Rolls. By the time Susannah saw them they were charging toward them like a pack of wild dogs.

Victoria attacked. She blocked the camera crew. "Get the hell out of here!" Her cry of rage, so sharp, so violent, stunned the newsmen. People on the sidewalk shrank back and stared.

Santa's bell still tinkled.

"Kurt, get your boss out of here! Susannah get in the car!" Victoria shoved Kurt, and in the confusion Zellner started to fall. Susannah and Kurt grabbed the man and hurried him to the door.

A reporter dashed toward Susannah. "Mrs. Bartok, has Zellner told you your son is still alive?"

"Get him into the car!" Victoria screamed. She pushed Susannah until she slid across the thick leather back seat against Zellner, huddled shivering and sweating as Kurt wrapped the black fur around him.

Susannah cried out in panic. "The mitten!"

Outside the door, Victoria scraped the red wool up from the sidewalk and flung it at her. She slammed the heavy door and faced the men with cameras.

"This is my fucking story. I've got an exclusive on Mrs. Bartok!"

"Not according to Zellner!"

"He called us!" a woman who tried to look like television's leading female reporter shouted.

Cameras poked closer, but Victoria, hearing the car start, raced into the street and jumped into the front seat as Kurt pulled out, heading down Seventh Avenue. She closed the glass panel between them and the back seat. "So." She turned her full bitterness on Kurt. "We can thank you for that little display. You little *coño*."

Kurt kept his eyes on the traffic.

"What did you think you were trying to do? Drum up a little coverage for your boss on my time? Is that it? You know goddamn well this is my story."

Behind her, a hand banged on the glass. Zellner was agitatingly signaling Kurt uptown and not three minutes later was again banging on the glass until Kurt slowed and stopped the car. Zellner coughed and fell back against the deep cushions, his alarmingly scarlet face pulsing with fever and streaming with sweat.

Susannah's hand clawed for the door handle. She hated this man. From their first meeting her instincts had told her not to trust him. Back there on the sidewalk she had wavered in her feelings. Then came the television people he had called to make sure he had news coverage, publicity. Now she was overwhelmed by her feeling that to find Laddie she must run as far from this wicked old fraud as she could run.

Zellner's hot, wet hand clamped on hers. "Stay!" His voice was scarcely a wheeze. "He is very near." Susannah jerked away and he whined, "Do not fight me. Help me." He heaved himself forward, his hot face on top of hers. "He is here!"

Susannah held her breath. She found Victoria and Kurt sliding back the glass panel to watch her closely. Did they believe what the man was saying?

She twisted away to peer out the window. Across the street, a hundred feet ahead of the car, glowed a hotel's neon sign—a sign with a broken letter. They were passing the hotel where she and Laddie had the room. Again, she saw Victoria and Kurt watching her through the open glass from the front seat. "You told him," she snapped at Victoria. She turned to accuse the old man but he slumped against the seat, panting, his eyes shut. Was this a trance? Was he faking this?

"Lad-die." He called out in such a plaintive, lost voice her flesh leaped on her bones. "Lad-die!"

His eyelids fluttered and sprang open. "Yesterday . . . yesterday I said . . . in a box. Perhaps it was a small room. Yes. Hundreds of small rooms. . . . A labyrinth."

"Could it be a hotel?" Victoria pushed herself eagerly from the front seat so as not to miss his slightest word. She grabbed at Susannah. "Listen to him!" Her desperate croak was unlike anything the other woman had heard from her. Did Victoria believe? This hard, big-city woman? Susannah felt certain that, of course, Victoria did not for an instant believe. She was faking this excitement just as certainly as the old man.

Zellner shut his eyes and huddled deep into his black fur, a sick child. Victoria and Kurt seemed content to wait. Susannah's voice was harsh, bitter. "How long are we supposed to sit here?"

No one answered.

"How long, Kurt?" Susannah demanded.

Kurt lifted a hand from the wheel and let it drop.

"So we just sit here?" Susannah moved to the door. "We're wasting time." Her hand was on the door when she saw the boy on the sidewalk.

Susannah screamed: "Laddie!" She had not finished gasping the name before she lunged from the car. Victoria sprang from the front seat and dashed up the sidewalk after Susannah, who cried out, running madly to catch up with a woman in a blue coat and a boy in a blue jacket walking hand in hand, a little boy with blond hair.

"Laddie!"

The boy turned slowly. He clung to his mother's hand—an ugly little boy with a mashed-in face, a little boy of perhaps six years but small for his age. He glared. Susannah trailed to a stop, but not before the mother turned, the same ugly face with a warning glare of pure hate.

16

DECEMBER 23, 10:15 A.M.

Susannah ran.

Victoria dashed in front of a screeching truck and its honking horn to catch up with her as both slowed to fight the icy wind for breath. They huddled together beside the temporary wooden wall that boarded up the ground floor of an empty building, a skyscraper hotel. Against this wall plastered with posters of Broadway shows and rock groups and revivalists, Susannah fell shaking and gasping. She did not twist away from Victoria.

"You t-told . . . him about the store and the h-hotel."

"No. By now he could have read it in the papers."

"He told the TV he'd be there."

"You can thank sweet little Kurt for that. The *coño* obviously thought it would be publicity for his boss."

Susannah twisted away from Victoria to hurry along the wooden wall, where the sidewalk was heaped with gritty rubbish and broken bottles.

"Filthy city," Susannah said. "Filthy people."

Victoria grabbed her. "Hang on. Before we go back to Foy I've got to call and see if Millie's people at the hotel are picking up any messages from doctors or lawyers. Over there—in that coffee shop—I'll call while you get some breakfast."

"To hell with breakfast!"

They struggled. Susannah bumped into a young man in a long coat bent nearly double over a radio.

Lieutenant Foy rushed to his door to wave Susannah in from the hall. His boyish face upset every professional rule by breaking into his astronaut's grin. Good news? At the sight of Victoria, his smile faded. He grabbed Susannah's arm and led her into his office. He jerked his clean-shaven chin toward Victoria. His smile dropped to a hard line. "Does she have to be in on this?"

Susannah had no time to nod, for by now Victoria had thrust herself into the office. Foy moved quickly behind his side of the desk to pick up a file.

Victoria switched on her cassette recorder.

"Here's a case," he began, "almost exactly like ours. The child was a girl and a year younger than your son. But the thing is—she was grabbed."

"Mace?"

"Or CN."

"Tear gas," Victoria explained.

Susannah threw back her head and breathed deeply with joy. In spite of Victoria, Foy couldn't hold back his excited grin. Victoria, however, folding her arms across her sheepskin coat, shared none of their elation. Her voice cut cold: "You get the child back?"

"Not yet."

The two women waited for the officer to tell them about the case. Victoria lit a cigarette and decided to wait no longer. "Dead?"

"Nobody said that."

"How long ago?" Victoria asked.

Foy ignored the reporter by looking only at Susannah. The question, however, hung in the room and had to be answered. "Almost two months."

Susannah, who had the most to gain, was the first to recover her excitement: "That isn't the point." She was making it clear she didn't want Victoria robbing them of their good news. "The point is, we've got a lead." She nodded at the file that Foy held. "Where do they live?"

"We've got a break there too. The parents live right here in Manhattan. They hired a private detective."

"I wonder why."

Foy talked through the reporter's sarcasm. "If he found anything, we never heard. No report here. It's a little irregular, but I can call these people for you—"

"Right now," said Susannah.

"No." Victoria surprised the others by sounding so sure of herself, they waited for her to explain. "We'll go over ourselves. Susannah and I. Pretty clearly, Lieutenant, they've had enough of you and the department. If they haven't gone out of town for the holidays it'll be better to catch them by surprise. Give them a chance to think up an excuse and they might not want to see Susannah."

"Go in cold?" the lieutenant asked. "Off the street?" He closed his file. "No way. Not these people."

"Want to bet?"

Foy waited for Susannah's decision. Reluctantly he wrote an address and handed her the paper. Susannah was the first on her feet.

Victoria had excluded the detective from his good news. "Give us a report," he said to Susannah. "Okay?"

Before the two women went to the east sixties address, they kept a taxi waiting outside Victoria's newspaper long enough for Susannah to run up and find the newspaper clippings on the case. They read these during the cab ride uptown.

"Not much coverage," Victoria said. "Typical. The rich never let you know any more than they have to."

"What makes you think they're rich?"

"One, they live in the east sixties. Two, when Foy and his pack of backward boys didn't get off their asses, they had enough money to hire a private detective. Three, their names are Arthur and Catherine Reardon. Impeccably WASP. Super correct for the area."

"You don't think we should telephone first?"

"As I said, take the Reardons by surprise."

The driver slowed under bare trees in a street of elegant town houses off Park Avenue. He eased up to an apartment building on the corner.

The old doorman, whose purple face showed a lifetime spent in Third Avenue bars, guarded a recently delivered spruce Christmas tree. As the two got out from the cab he pulled his big face together in a frown. They did not look like anyone his employers would know. Susannah hung back, but Victoria pushed past the tree into the vestibule and to a wall panel of shiny brass buttons with a speaker in the middle.

The doorman, nearly buried behind the tree, watched the two closely through the boughs.

Someone's voice in the speaker clicked. "Yes?"

Victoria bent close to the panel. "Mr. Reardon?"

"Yes?"

"Mr. Arthur Reardon?"

"I'm sorry, but—"

Victoria thrust Susannah close to the speaker. "Please listen, Mr. Reardon. My name's Susannah Bartok and two days ago my son was kidnapped. Mr. Reardon, I have to talk with you!"

She waited.

A delivery boy came and left a case of champagne with the doorman. Victoria pressed next to Susannah to listen at the panel. Had the man gone away?

"Mr. Reardon?" Susannah's voice scraped with desperation.

"I'm still here."

"Detective Lieutenant Foy told me you might have found something that could help me in my search—"

"I'm sorry," the voice said. "My wife and I can't help you. We really can't. We're just leaving town."

"It's life and death and that's God's truth, Mr. Reardon!"

"I don't see what we can do—"

"Five minutes. Please."

The door clicked open. Through his tree, the purple-faced doorman watched the two women enter.

Arthur Reardon, a man in his forties, stood in the door of his apartment with dull, sad eyes and thin, graying hair. In a conservative suit he would look like a stockbroker. In the dark blue cashmere sweater, gray slacks, and suede shoes he looked like an old and very sad schoolboy. His arms barred the door. He was sizing up the two women in their matching sheepskin coats.

"As I told you." His voice was soft as any boy's at a top private school. "We're leaving town. It's our first time out since . . ." He hesitated between the two. He spoke to Susannah. "You're Mrs. Bartok?"

"Yes; Lieutenant Foy told me—"

"Who is she?" Reardon did not conceal the distrust he felt for Victoria.

"A friend."

"A detective?"

"No," Victoria said without her usual push. "I'm Mrs. Bartok's friend. I'm trying to help."

Susannah prayed that Victoria would not show the man the cassette recorder she held.

"I'm sorry. I only agreed to talk with Mrs. Bartok." The gray schoolboy began to close the door.

Victoria whispered, "I'll meet you downstairs. Try to get the detective's report."

In the dark kitchen, which looked like it was seldom used, Reardon offered Susannah a chrome-and-woven-cane chair. He turned from her and gazed out across the rooftops at smoke rising from a chimney. He peered down into a tiny patch of garden. Susannah saw a baby's highchair pushed back in a corner, a white chair with a Snoopy decal. "At first we were frantic. Catherine took it very hard. I stopped going to the office. When the police got nowhere I called some people I know at the Bureau. The FBI didn't come in. That's when I hired a detective."

"Two months ago?"

"Fifty-three days."

"But surely you haven't given up?"

Footsteps left an Oriental rug and sounded on the hardwood parquetry outside the kitchen.

A woman hovered in the door. Her flawless tweed suit, her carefully coiffed brown hair, the way she pulled on tan leather gloves were all part of an act. This woman was only going through the motions of living. She was silent, hollow.

Susannah rose from the kitchen chair.

Mrs. Reardon crept back from the stranger. Footsteps crossed the hardwood floor and hurried away. Reardon called, "I'll be right with you, dear." He waited until Susannah felt her way back into the chair. He returned to his window where he watched a man down in the garden string colored Christmas tree lights in the branches of an evergreen.

"The papers didn't say. Was it in the Times Square area?"

"What? No." He stared at the lights shining in the dark morning. "It happened right here in the neighborhood. Catherine was taking Martha to the pediatrician. In an apartment house not three streets away. They got into an elevator alone and before they knew it two kids—what we used to call hippies—shoved in."

"Street kids? Dark glasses?"

"Yes. And long hair. Strange clothes. Probably on drugs. She didn't get much of a look. They sprayed her eyes."

They heard footsteps pacing in the next room.

"Martha was gone." He kept his voice flat. "The last we ever saw of her." He opened a cabinet and took out a cut-glass decanter of Scotch. Susannah refused his offer to share a drink.

Reardon went back to the window where he wouldn't have to look at Susannah. "I did everything I could. As I said, I stayed home with Catherine. It's become our whole life. I didn't sleep for a month. The police tried, I suppose. . . . You see, what I'm trying to do is get my wife out of here over Christmas . . ."

"Martha." Susannah said the name to herself, a name she would never hear in her part of California.

"Martha Kate."

"You can't give up."

Reardon drank. "No?"

"All the rest of your life you'll wonder if she's alive . . . where she is . . . who she's with . . ."

Reardon turned his amber drink until it caught the dull light from the window. "I'm sorry. As I said, we're on our way out of town. The Hamptons. You know the Hamptons? Quiet this time of year. Lovely. Cold. We'll walk on the beach . . ."

"Do you have the detective's report?"

"Why would you want to see it, for heaven's sake. It didn't help us."

"May I see it?"

He turned. Tears shone on his face.

"Please?" Susannah asked softly. "It might help. I have to try everything."

He put his glass on the counter and moved quickly. "I've got a Xerox copy in my study."

Susannah went to the window and looked into the garden and the glowing Christmas lights. A black-and-white dog barked and leaped on a little girl in a snowsuit. Susannah moved to the highchair and was touching it when Reardon, without a sound, appeared in the door. He held a Xerox copy of a typewritten report. Susannah pulled her hand away from the empty chair, but the man had seen her. They heard the woman pacing in the hall and he called, "We'll leave in a minute, Catherine dear."

He reached for the glass and drained the last of the Scotch. "At first we hoped it was ransom they wanted. Apparently that wasn't it. Seems we could have been poor as church mice for all the difference that made."

Susannah wondered if he would ask her if she had money. But she realized the man's thoughts simply did not include her at all. She had felt his terrible loss would have made him more sympathetic to others. So far, he had done nothing except see her; he hadn't asked her one question about her little boy.

"I guess the day will finally come when we'll get around to adopting another child." He considered the decanter and taking another drink. "The trouble is, going through agencies takes years. There are other ways, of course, but among the sort of people one knows, one doesn't often hear of women wanting to give a baby away. When you have a hole in your heart and want a child more than anything in the world you simply are in no mood to wait the years that the agencies put one through."

"Four years," Susannah said. "That's what a social worker just told me."

"It's enough to lend credence to one of the angles our private detective was working on. Illegal adoption." He went back to the window before he forced himself to continue. "Black-market babies. I rejected the idea. I still can't make myself go along with the idea that someone would kidnap our daughter for that. . . .

The detective said that the people who manage these things get as much as a hundred thousand dollars for a child."

"That's what I hear."

"How old was—is yours?"

"My son was two in September."

"Blond hair and blue eyes?" It was the first time Reardon's feelings had reached out of his dull, gray world to touch anyone but his wife and himself. "God, I'm sorry. You're sure about that drink?"

Susannah wanted nothing. He poured himself a stiff one. "The detective's theory ran along the line that the seller gets the highest price for delivering precisely what the customer specifies. No different, I suppose, from any other business transaction. The fact that the kidnappers had planned their moves, that they lay in wait and sprayed my wife's eyes, the detective considered strong evidence to back up his theory."

"Fifty-three days."

"Not a year old until the twenty-ninth. This would have been Martha's first Christmas."

"How do you go on?"

He drank. "We don't." He looked up at the sky. "I've even tried to tell Catherine that anyone who is going to pay that much money for Martha is going to take good care of her." He crossed to the kitchen and called: "Catherine!"

No answer.

"God," he sighed. "I hope she hasn't lost her nerve. As I said, we never go anywhere. This was to be her first time out of the house." He handed Susannah the detective's report, but the papers fell from his hand and dropped to the floor. His arms went around Susannah and held her close. They clung together, both shaking with sobs. "God help you," he whispered.

17

DECEMBER 23, 11:50 A.M.

The two women ducked into the Bloomingdale's vestibule to get out of the wind and rain and devour the detective's report. Backed against the wall where crowds surged in and out of the revolving door, they turned the pages.

Victoria, who read faster, reached the bottom of each page before Susannah. She became more and more excited. By mutual agreement they skipped much of the report. For now they had what they needed.

"The kids. The dark glasses. The Mace. We asked for a pattern." Susannah was breathless at their discovery. "We got one. Boy, did we ever get one!"

"Which still doesn't get us very far," said Victoria.

"It starts us on a pattern!"

Susannah turned back to the first page. "Here's the detective's phone number. Shouldn't we try to call him again?"

They dashed across the street and waited their turn at a glass phone booth on a busy corner. Susannah watched Victoria trying to reach the man. The reporter listened but showed no sign of encouragement. She hung up and they moved into the chilling rain, which did not keep the New Yorkers from crowding the sidewalks. "Same answering machine as before," Victoria said. "He's probably out of town for the holidays. Or drunk."

"Fuck the holidays," said Susannah.

"Indeed."

Susannah shoved her hands into the coat pockets. "Without him we're wasting time."

"Right."

"Maybe we should call and check your answering machine for messages."

"It's still too early to hear from any of the doctors." Victoria slowed at the curb and peered down the streets. Was she trying to stop a cab?

"Where are we going?"

"You're going back to the paper and work on the clippings."

"Not after this. This is our best lead of all. It all adds up to this black-market angle. I don't want a cab."

"Then go back to my place and get some rest."

"You're going someplace and you don't want me to come with you."

"True."

Against a light they raced traffic in a cross street.

"I'm going back to Times Square."

Susannah stopped. "I'm not allowed to see Times Square?"

"I'm going to be talking to some pretty weird scum." Victoria reached out and turned up the wool collar against Susannah's red face. She slipped her arm through hers and they walked in their twin sheepskin coats to 57th Street. "I did a story a couple of months back on a hustler."

"Right. That's why we put street people on our countdown list."

"The guy I wrote about was living with a girl somebody got pregnant. She said then that she planned to sell the baby. Doubtless, by now she has."

"Could be black market."

"She looked like she needed the money."

"Why can't I talk with her?"

"First of all, I don't know if I can find her. Second, it is a pretty tenuous link between her and that gang in dark glasses you ran into. Third, you're not going to be any too thrilled to meet some of her friends."

"Come on. I bet it'll be faster to walk to Times Square than take a cab."

By crossing Broadway on 46th Street they avoided Times Square, snarled with traffic and blaring horns. At 42nd and Eighth Avenue they looked across at the Port Authority Bus Terminal. Susannah wondered if her things were still in the locker. Together with Victoria she decided it was easier to have her California things put into storage than drag them back down to the Village.

Forty-second Street blazed nearly solidly with sparkling lights of movie houses. Sizzling hot grease of frying onions and hamburgers spiced the icy air. Few people moved along the sidewalk; a pair of cops, a tall black man wound in burlap who wore a paper bag on his head, a pale boy in a cowboy hat who loped by with a blaring transistor radio. In a few doorways boys in leather jackets, worn jeans, and boots smoked, shivered painfully in the cold, and gazed out at the sidewalk.

"Do they ever get customers?" whispered Susannah.

"Some of them do a couple of hundred dollars a day."

Victoria was searching doorways for the hustler she had written about, and Susannah quickly looked away from one boy with a white, angelic face full of blue shadows, but not before their eyes locked. In the doorway of a discount camera store, Victoria slowed. A painfully thin boy Susannah guessed to be no more than eighteen, in a blue Levi's jacket, matching jeans and black boots, clutched himself, wincing, writhing in agony. His upturned face sucked in great drafts of icy air.

"Roy?"

The youth slid wounded eyes in Victoria's direction and they flickered imperceptibly.

"Are you all right?"

"Goddamn toothache."

"I've got some good grass. Might help."

He nodded vigorously. Victoria and Susannah reached the doorway. She asked, "Do you remember me? I did that article about Dennis in *The Press.*"

The boy named Roy bobbed his head. Suddenly he pushed past the two women to show himself to a sallow man with thinning hair bundled in a fake-fur overcoat who smoothed his blowing hair over a nearly bald head. Their eyes cruised each other, but a glance at the two women sent the man hurrying away.

"Lousy cunts. You scared him off." A white hand criss-crossed with blue veins and the deeper blue of a tatooed star massaged his jaw. "Bad enough to be stuck in the city over Christmas with a fucking toothache, you scare off the only john in the last fucking hour." His thin body tightened in a jab of pain. He writhed and his teeth snatched at the ice-cold air.

"Have you seen Dennis?"

"Hell with Dennis." He peered out onto the sidewalk and apparently saw no sign of a customer. "You said you had some good grass."

Victoria took out the shiny black-and-white cigarette case and clicked it open. Roy's white hand clawed up three joints before Victoria snapped it shut.

"If you read that story I did about Dennis, you'd know I'm not here to jerk you around."

Roy's face flickered in the flame from his plastic lighter. He drew the smoke in deeply. "You wanna do a story about me?" he rasped in a closed-off voice.

"After I see Dennis, we'll talk about you."

Roy, seized with a violent shaking, closed his eyes and gave himself over to the smoke.

"It's very important that I see Dennis right away."

Susannah wondered if the boy would ever exhale.

Smoke crept out from his trembling blue lips. "San Francisco." He shuffled out of the door and the two women followed him past a porno book store's window draped with tinsel and a glittering SEASONS GREETINGS.

"He's gone to San Francisco?"

"Hasn't everyone? While I freeze my ass off here." He slowed, drew in smoke, and looked at Victoria through narrowed eyes. "About this story you're gonna do on me. Pictures?"

Victoria pulled out her camera, which Roy wanted to touch, but she dropped it back in her bag. "Dennis had a girl. Michelle. Right? They lived together. She was going to have a baby and said she was going to sell it. Did she go to San Francisco too?"

Roy snickered. Some image filled him with such glee, he had to stop on the sidewalk and jiggle with silent giggling. Two cops passed. Roy smirked at his image of the girl. "Old Michelle's too spaced to go anywhere. Talk about spaced . . ." He stopped giggling to suck in smoke. "She is really spaced . . ."

"You know where she is?"

Roy blinked. The image of Michelle had vanished. No more snickering grin hung on his white face. Now he was onto something else, sorting out confused thoughts. "That fucking story made Dennis a fucking star. A fucking superstar."

"You tell me where Michelle is, you'll see your name in the paper."

A man strode past. Roy turned to look at the man, who slid one glance back at him.

"No shit. My name in the paper?"

"No shit."

"Soho," Roy said.

In the taxi with Roy, Victoria told Susannah about Soho. Painters and sculptors had moved into the lofts in the streets of warehouses. Ground-floor doors opened into galleries. It was, she said, what Paris had been in the past, the art world of today. Roy led them to a battered door that opened on a dark and narrow staircase. Crushing Victoria's twenty-dollar bill in his fist, three times he made her promise she would put his name in the paper. Satisfied, only after she had clicked his picture, he wandered away.

Although the dark loft loomed vast and high as a basketball court, it throbbed with heavy-metal rock music clashing with opposing sound from a television set. All the furnishings of those who lived here huddled in an isolated island next to a sink on one wall. A broken couch had collapsed on a torn carpet and become a heap of cushions strewn with open cans of pet food where cats prowled. A refrigerator stood half open, sharing its light with a projected television picture that played on a nine-foot-square screen. Beyond this nest where people lived, a hundred feet away in the dusky half-light, a sculptor's blue acetylene torch spat a shower of sparks on twisted bronze.

Susannah stumbled over a squalling cat. Victoria approached

the couch, opened her cigarette case to a thin girl in a filthy caftan, which may have once been white. The hand in the robe waved away the joint and pushed back a wild frazzle of orange hair.

"I don't want to talk about Dennis," she shouted above the twin roars of the television and the rock. "I am trying to watch the Pope say Merry Christmas to the world all the way from the Vatican. Will you listen?"

From the other end of the loft slamming rock music crashed above the cheers of the crowd, the words in Italian.

Michelle was talking, but Susannah and Victoria failed to hear a word. Victoria signaled. Did Michelle mind if she turned down the television?

Now Michelle only had the Pope's image and the rock to talk against.

"So why does everybody make such a big thing about selling a kid? People sell blood, don't they?" She gulped wine from a water tumbler. "Blood—babies—what's the difference? Other people sell babies." She looked up past the glass of wine at Susannah. "Who's she? Welfare?"

"Susannah's also a reporter. We're working on this story together."

Eyes peering over the wine narrowed. "You a dyke, too?"

"She's got a little boy."

"Lotta dykes have kids."

"Roy tells us you had the baby."

"'Course I had the baby. I'm Catholic. I love that Polish Pope." She asked Susannah, "Do you love the Polish Pope?"

Susannah nodded. She loved the Polish Pope.

"I don't believe in abortion. Right to life. You can print that in your paper any time you want."

"You handled the arrangements?"

Michelle coiled back on the couch to show the reporter the shock she felt at the use of the word. "Ar-range-ments?" she twisted out the syllables.

"How you handled selling the baby."

"No big deal."

"A lawyer?"

114 . . .

"Catholic lawyer. Gave me five hundred dollars for the baby. What'll you give me if I tell you who handled—the 'ar-range-ments?'"

"Where did you get the idea? Your doctor?"

The sculptor's voice boomed through the emptiness. "Turn up the fucking TV!"

"One more minute," Victoria called into the dusk. She returned to Michelle. "The doctor's got his own clinic, right? He asked you if you wanted to keep the baby, because if you didn't he knew of some very nice people who couldn't have a baby of their own?"

"Very nice people. He said they were very nice people. New Jersey. A very good home. One day I handed over the baby and he handed over five hundred dollars."

"He." Now Victoria pressed. "Meaning the lawyer?"

Michelle sucked red wine.

"What was his name?"

"Wait a minute." Michelle hauled herself up on the couch and began to massage her feet. She looked first at Victoria, then at Susannah. "Like what is this? You two dykes come in here and start this heavy number about how come I sold my baby and how much I got. You want all this for your newspaper. What do I get out of it?"

"You don't know the lawyer's name?"

Suddenly she was a little child who wanted to play, all mischievous smiles. "That—is for you to ask and me to know."

Susannah spoke to Victoria under her breath. "Why would the lawyer give her his name unless he had to?"

"Probably had to witness the papers."

"Don't whisper!" the woman on the couch whined. "It's not polite!"

"Okay, Michelle. What was the doctor's name?"

The woman on the couch burrowed into the cushions, making another childish game of silence. She sipped wine.

"Fifty dollars," Victoria said.

"Let's see it first."

Victoria opened her bag.

Michelle grabbed for the money, but Victoria held it tight.

. . . *115*

"Dr. Vincent Robusti."

"Where?"

"What do you mean where?"

"His address."

"Thirty-six Bleecker Street." She snatched at the bill but Victoria held it high, out of reach.

"Give me my money!"

"First we see if your story checks out. Got a phone book?"

"Gimme my money!"

"You're lying. Show me a phone book or a doctor's bill. Something to prove it checks out." Victoria jerked her head toward the door. Susannah picked up the signal and began to leave. Michelle clambered off her cushions.

Victoria put the bill back in her leather bag. "Merry Christmas, Michelle."

"Don't you try to give me this Merry Christmas shit."

"You're lying, Michelle." Susannah and Victoria reached the door.

"Fucking dykes!"

On the narrow stairs, they breathed deeply to free themselves from the sour smell of cat urine and rotting food. Susannah buttoned her coat. "God what a rat's nest. You could almost convince me it's a good idea for her not to raise her baby."

"Pathetic the way she kept saying 'very nice people, very nice home,' when it's an established fact there's not one nice home in the whole state of New Jersey." Her hand went to Susannah's shoulder. "That's a joke but since you're from California, you wouldn't get it. The truth is, if the people wanted the kid enough to pay, it is possible it is a nice home."

"But it's illegal."

"The mother's choice."

"Still illegal."

"You haven't discovered by this time in your life that almost everything people really want in this world is?"

They walked downstairs. Susannah was asking Victoria if she truly thought the doctor's identity was a fake when they heard heavy footfalls hurrying behind them. They looked up and found the bearded sculptor looming, filling the passage. Both reacted out of pure instinct, ran, and reached the first landing. The man shoved past them to the platform, blocked them, and hurled Victoria stumbling into a corner.

"Give her the money!" He filled the staircase with the reek of sweat and garlic.

Susannah grabbed at him to pull him away, only to see his hand lash out across her face. He clamped her wrist. Victoria twisted out of the man's way to dig into her bag until she held a blade that flicked out with a metallic snap. The lunging man saw the knife glint, slowed in his attack, and jerked Susannah back in his retreat.

Victoria screamed to Susannah, "Run!"

Susannah wrenched but the man held. With her free hand she pulled a knife from her own pocket, fumbled, but only for a second until she found the switch, and a wicked long blade, much to her surprise, snapped out. The man, edging back from the two knives and the two women, stumbled and fell against the stairs. Scrambling to his feet, he pounded up the steps.

Susannah and Victoria dashed down the last flight of stairs and hurled back the street door with a bang.

Plunging out into the bright, cold sunlight of the sidewalk, they staggered, silent, speechless, unable to catch their breath. Victoria pulled in enough air to ask, "Where did you get the knife?"

Susannah signaled to wait until she could speak. "Just before I met you—at the Cafe Marlene." She breathed deeply. "I went into a hardware store. Didn't have enough money so—so I stole it."

"No shit?"

She nodded. "Never stole anything before. . . . I was as scared as I was on that staircase using it."

They faced each other, laughed noiselessly at first, until bursts of victorious laughter bubbled out, sending them falling helplessly into each other's arms. They clung together, rocking back and forth, laughing in the icy sunshine.

Susannah drew back from her friend to shake her head at herself in consternation. What in God's name was she doing laughing? Yes. She was wiping tears of laughter from her eyes.

She looked so perplexed, so confused for feeling even this one instant's release from the cold grip of fear and gnawing dread over Laddie that Victoria, in spite of herself, had to grin, reach out and touch Susannah's bewildered face.

Thirty-six Bleecker Street, far from being a doctor's address, was the Globe Storage and Moving Co. Susannah had to give Victoria credit. She knew Michelle had lied. Victoria, however, was not pleased. "I didn't handle that right."

"With that guy on the stairs? You were brilliant."

"No. I mean the girl. Knowing who the doctor is could make all the difference."

"You want to go back?"

"And face him again?"

"I mean if you think it's that important . . ."

"Not now anyway."

At the newspaper library they sat munching their two nut-filled cream-cheese sandwiches and drinking coffee they had ordered to go from a Chock Full o'Nuts counter restaurant. This was the first food Susannah had eaten, except for Zellner's half a *pfeffernüsse,* since the plane—forty-one hours ago.

Susannah read a telephone message from Jeff saying that he remembered having seen a UNESCO article about black-market babies in *Commentary* or *The New Republic.* About six months ago.

Victoria called the Plaza and their contact, Elaine, only to learn that Señor and Señora Raimond Luis Olmas from Caracas, Venezuela, had received no calls from any of the doctors. Victoria told Elaine they would be here at the newspaper for the next hour. She made another call to the young actors, who took their responsibility for their roles as the South American couple as seriously as if they were stand-by parts in a Broadway play.

Victoria showed Susannah where to find the back issues of *Commentary* and *The New Republic* and while Susannah followed up on Jeff's lead, Victoria walked into her editor and publisher's office unannounced.

"Caught you," she cried triumphantly.

Donald F. Donald, studying his paper's front page, did not even bother to pretend he was not pleased. Black headlines screamed HIS LAST CHRISTMAS? The large picture of the blond boy looking out with his wide eyes bore the caption, *The lost angel from the New York Christmas tree.* In a smaller inset photo, Susannah stared in shock. The writing leaped with such immediacy, such quivering details of the frantic mother's search, that the words seemed to be torn from the heart of the woman herself.

"Good picture of Zellner. TV and all the wire services want the story."

"Didn't I tell you you'd love it?" She grabbed a copy from a stack of papers on her boss's desk and shoved it into a shoulder bag.

Donald F. Donald, who felt a feeble attempt to play his role of the unexcitable executive was in order, made a small effort. He went to the wall and bent his ankles to do leg-strengthening exercises for his skiing trip to Aspen. "It isn't Watergate."

"Yet," said Victoria striking a kitchen match and lighting a cigarette, "to make that happen, asshole, I need money. No games. And don't stall me. Before you take your asshole family to Aspen I've got to get that check, this afternoon before the banks close for the holiday."

While Donald F. Donald lowered himself, back against the wall, strengthening his thighs, Victoria told him about calling the doctors and the fake couple from Caracas waiting at the Plaza. They were set up and now they were waiting for the big break.

"That won't necessarily get back Mrs. Bartok's boy."

"No. Not this time around. The kidnappers snatched Laddie to fill some previous order. This new order will start them looking for some other kid. We go to the contact point when the lawyer meets the would-be parents; we follow them, we find the ring."

"Will it be too late to get back the Bartok boy?"

"Whatever happens, we'll have the ring. We'll be a helluva lot closer to him than before."

"Would be nice if you got back her boy."

"Stop skiing and give me the money. At least five thousand."

Donald F. Donald winced. That was a lot of money.

Victoria picked up a paper and held the front page at him.

"Twenty-five hundred," he said.

"Fifty-five hundred, asshole. Five thousand for the first payment. Five hundred expenses. And hurry up before the banks close."

Donald F. Donald straightened up, went to his desk for a briefcase, which he snapped open, and pulled out a checkbook.

18

DECEMBER 23, 2:30 P.M.

Gasps for breath and footsteps on metal echoed in the dark.
Two men climbed through the black, following the spill of light
from a battery-powered lantern.

"Jesus, I hate these stairs . . ."

The tall man banged open a door and the lantern flashed the
way ahead into a corridor as black as the stairwell.

"Fucking stairs . . ."

A door opened and a blaze of light silhouetted a woman in a
physician's white lab coat who held up a silencing hand. "Quiet. I
just got him to sleep." Her voice was low, emotionlessly
professional, but commanding enough that the men entered the
room without a sound but their heavy breathing. They covered
their eyes from the blaze and turned from the light.

"You're making us run late." The doctor moved from
silhouette into the dazzling light; a woman with dark goggles, a
calm, strong woman with iron-gray hair that fell below her
shoulders—hair of a folk singer, a mountain woman, not a
physician in Manhattan. A nurse, also in dark goggles and a crisp
uniform shining white in the glare, stood behind her. The doctor
slid a silver pen into the breast pocket of her immaculate lab coat
and handed a chart to the nurse. Her tiny, regular features in a
tanned face revealed no more emotion than her voice.

. . . *121*

"I've been calling down to the street for the last half-hour."

"So I'm late." Candyman's hands shook when he stripped the wrapper from a chocolate bar.

"Doesn't give us much time. You deliver at three."

"They wanted the passport, didn't they?"

"Let's see it."

"Beautiful." The man licked chocolate from his fingers and reached past a scarf into his suit coat to draw out a small, dark-blue booklet, which he handed to the woman.

The doctor turned her back to the glaring light and lifted her black goggles to study the document. She held the pages close and nodded. The work was good.

"My brother." Ahmed, the shorter man, grinned. "He does the very best work."

"Can we trust the photographer?"

"I myself took the picture, Doctor," Ahmed said as his grin continued to widen. "A Polaroid. A truly first-rate picture, yes?"

The doctor handed the passport back to Candyman and fitted the black goggles carefully over her eyes. "They leave tonight?"

"Brazil," Candyman said.

"I'll give him something stronger so he'll sleep till they take off." The doctor turned into the light.

"Doctor. Me first," Candyman said.

"And me." Ahmed grinned eagerly.

"After." The doctor had drawn a folded note paper from her pocket. "It's from the answering service. I want you to call right now."

"I'll call when I go back down—"

"You'll call now."

"I just climbed those fucking stairs. You could have at least radioed down so I could have phoned from the street."

The doctor did not bother to remind Candyman that she had tried to reach him for half an hour. "The service said they had a Spanish accent. The number's for the Plaza Hotel."

"Boy or girl?"

"Girl. By Christmas."

"Tomorrow's Christmas Eve. No way," said Candyman.

The doctor lit a Marlboro cigarette. "Call them and tell them you can meet them this afternoon right after you make the other delivery."

"I won't be able to be out that long."

"You'll do it."

"Then you better take care of me, Doctor. Like right now."

The goggles fixed on the man. "Candyman, you know how you look?"

"I know how I look."

"Sickening. You're filthy. How long since you've washed your hair? Look at your fingernails. Black. Go wash up. We'll get the boy ready."

Candyman made no move.

The doctor turned into the blazing light and left the room. "Wash up and then come into my office."

19

DECEMBER 23, 2:30 P.M.

"Victoria!" Susannah's excited voice, calling through the newspaper offices, brought the reporter running. Susannah held out the phone. "It's the hotel. Here's the contact number. They want you to call right away!"

The reporter studied the number. She dialed carefully and grabbed Susannah's hand. "Wish me luck!"

Susannah squeezed her hand.

Victoria spoke with a Spanish accent. She looked up at Susannah and her lips formed the word "attorney." Susannah shut her eyes and listened to Victoria, to hear her as the attorney on the other end of the line would hear. This was clearly a desperate woman who had come to New York with her husband because friends in the diplomatic corps—friends she dared not name—had told her sometimes miracles were possible in this city. The biggest miracle of all would be to have a daughter by Christmas. She and her husband were waiting by the phone. They had money. Yes, money in their hands. They could bring that money and meet anyone, anyplace, any time.

Victoria listened closely. With a moan, she sank to a chair in defeat.

Susannah, her heart in her mouth, watched her every move.

"Please. For Christmas. Please. It has to be by Christmas!"

She was fighting desperately; above all she could not allow this contact to slip away. "We can pay you part of the money now. My husband and I will come to you. How much should we bring . . . just tell us where . . ."

Suddenly the call was over. The other end hung up and she handed the phone to Susannah. "First payment today. They'll call back when they can deliver."

Susannah had never seen Victoria so low, but she herself shared none of Victoria's despair. On the contrary, her spirits soared. "Okay, so our first contact couldn't deliver overnight. Still, we did make contact. It proves we're on the right track—all you have to do is call and there are people out there who deliver. Now we know there's at least one gang who deals in black-market babies. Maybe there's another we'll hear from any minute."

"We want the one," Victoria said, "that took Laddie."

On the way back to the apartment, Victoria stopped at the bank and Susannah did some shopping.

Victoria snapped on her answering machine, opened the refrigerator, and pulled out two clinking bottles of Tsingtao beer from the People's Republic of China. Susannah cleared a place on the floor to lie flat out on the flokati carpet. Lieutenant Foy's voice purred from the machine. "I'll be home over the holidays, Mrs. Bartok, but Sergeant Braverman's briefed and on top of the case. If something comes up, Mrs. Bartok, don't hesitate to call me."

"Merry Christmas from Lieutenant Foy. *Cabrón.*" Victoria said bitterly, lifting a bottle cap and handing the beer to Susannah.

"This is Kurt," a carefully controlled voice announced on the machine. Victoria raised her eyebrows. "Sounds like he's auditioning for the role of Blanche in *Streetcar.*"

"Zellner's under a doctor's care, but he wants you to know, Mrs. Bartok, that he is with you and your son, in spirit."

The tape ran, but they heard no more messages. "That's it?" asked Susannah.

Victoria switched off the machine. "That's it."

"We still have a possible nineteen other doctors to get back to us." Susannah was speaking mostly to keep up her own spirits.

A knock on the door brought Victoria into the hall. The upstairs neighbor and her live-in boyfriend gripped suitcases. Because they were on their way out of town for the holidays, they asked Victoria to keep an eye on the place.

"Right."

"Merry Christmas!"

"Yeah, Merry Christmas."

The sound of laughter and footfalls faded on the staircase. The street door banged. Victoria returned to Susannah and lifted her bottle of beer. "Merry Christmas. Everyone's getting out of town. Rats leaving a sinking city."

"We only need the one telephone call."

Victoria gazed for a long moment as Susannah sprawled on the carpet. "You're dead tired. Why don't you get some sleep? I'll be here if anyone calls."

Susannah rose. "What did Zellner mean when he said Laddie wasn't far?"

"That he wasn't far. Only you don't believe in Zellner."

"Not in Zellner. In us. I've got this really overpowering feeling we're right on the edge of something. You feel it?"

"Absolutely." Victoria answered too fast. Did Susannah sense a hint of Foy's kind of false encouragement? She doubted it. Susannah was too tired to pick up such nuances. "Look. Get some rest. As I said, I'll be here if anyone calls. You've done all you can for now."

Susannah left the living room to go into the kitchen and study the chart. She heard Victoria come and stand by her side. "It's amazing how much ground we've covered. Thanks to you."

"I can't think of anything we're overlooking, can you?"

"Stay right here," Susannah said, and she ran to her coat in the living room to take out a tiny package wrapped in black and white with a red bow. She returned to the kitchen and the chart. She slid an arm around the other woman and gave her the little gift.

"When did you have time to get this?"

"When you were in the bank. It isn't anything, really . . ."

"With all you have to think about, you took time . . ." For one instant there was nothing hard or big-city street-smart about

Victoria. She smiled, touched, happy as a kid. "Can I open it now?"

"The sooner the better. You'll see why."

Victoria read the card. "To the dearest friend anyone ever found. With more thanks than I can ever say. Love, Susannah."

They embraced.

Victoria worked at untying the bow. "It's true," Susannah said, "I don't know how I'll ever be able to thank you . . ."

Defeated by the bow, Victoria broke the ribbon. "Wait till we find him."

"I just want you to know I mean it."

Victoria unwrapped a cheap, black plastic cigarette holder.

"It's a filter," Susannah said. "The black goes with your case."

"You know I smoke too much and I won't cut down?"

"Right," Susannah said.

"And you took more time out to worry about me?"

"Like I said, I love you."

Victoria brushed Susannah's cheek with a kiss. "Thank you."

"What if I hadn't found you?"

"I found you, remember?" She hesitated. "Stay right there." She picked up her shoulder bag and brought it to the kitchen table. Susannah expected Victoria to open her case, fit a cigarette in the new holder, and strike a kitchen match. Instead of the case, she held a folded newspaper. "You're going to have to see this sooner or later." Victoria glanced down at the paper, which she did not unfold. Instead, she decided not to hand it to Susannah. "You look like you're living on nerves. Maybe this isn't the time—"

"Your story?"

Victoria nodded. "As I say, maybe this better wait until after you get some rest—"

Susannah reached for the paper.

"Get a grip on yourself, okay? I told you I was doing all this for the story, right?"

Victoria's dark eyes held Susannah, a demand finally answered with a nod. Yes. Susannah had known from that ice-cold night on the street corner about the story.

"Believe me, my dear, I am not going to apologize for this, although I wish to hell it wasn't about you. What I can deny is that I wrote this shitty headline. Horrible."

The little photograph of Laddie Susannah still carried in her wallet, that cherished little picture, filled the entire front page. The huge black headline hit her like a blow: HIS LAST CHRISTMAS?

In a small news photo inset below Laddie's face she saw a photo of herself gaping in shock—the picture Victoria had taken at Zellner's. Her despair, her tear-filled eyes, stared out of this front page for all New York, all the world to see.

HIS LAST CHRISTMAS?

Victoria held her breath. She'd been honest with Susannah. From their first meeting she'd told her there'd be this story. She also knew that up till now it had been talk, something vague the two could talk about, not this, not a full-page headline of this woman's son . . . not this ghastly headline.

"Please don't hate me." Victoria waited and began to wonder if Susannah would ever make a move. Susannah dropped the newspaper, stifled a cry, and slowly raised her face to stare in disbelief. Her eyes, glittering red from lack of sleep, said it all. They showed heartbreak. Worse for Victoria, they accused her of betrayal. Susannah scraped a kitchen chair between herself and the other woman to keep her from trying to come close. She stumbled to the living room, grabbed the sheepskin, and tore the red mitten from that coat, that coat which had become a hated thing now for it belonged to the one who had betrayed her. In the hall she yanked down her own raincoat.

Victoria sprang to the hall, blocked the hall door, and clamped the handle. Susannah twisted away her face. Susannah would no longer look at her.

"Where do you think you're going?"

Susannah bolted, raced back through the living room and into the kitchen where she ripped the countdown poster from the wall and crumpled it into her pocket.

Victoria blocked her in the kitchen door. "I told you I didn't write the headline. I always told you there'd be a story. You knew I was going to use the picture. I just told you I was sorry. I'm

128 . . .

sorry for you, but not sorry I wrote the story!"

Susannah slammed her entire weight into the woman, who fell back. "Get out of my way!" Her warning was a frightening snarl.

"And go out there?"

"Get out of my way!"

"Go where?" Victoria grasped at the thin raincoat. "In this? Lot of good you'll do your son frozen to death."

Susannah snatched her coat from the woman's hold.

Victoria deliberately kept her voice low, quiet. "You can't leave. You don't have anywhere else to go. All your contacts are here. Find him. Then leave."

"You don't care if I find him. You don't give a damn about him or me. All you care about is what will sell your goddamn papers!"

"Sit down!"

"Your goddamn, lying story that doesn't care how people feel—"

"Shut up and sit down! You can't keep on like this. Any minute you're going to break!"

Victoria shoved Susannah from the door—a grave miscalculation, for that push sent her into a screaming rage. "Goddamn you to hell!" She leaped at Victoria, clawing, screaming, tearing, sobbing. "You goddamn heartless bitch! You don't care because you can't feel what I feel—what a woman—any real woman—feels. You never will because you're a twisted—nothing. You have no life except this shit—lying about people in trouble!"

Susannah clawed and fought but now her rage was spent and she was shaking so violently all she had left were tears and gasped mutterings until she needed no shove from Victoria. She had held up for three days and three nights without sleep or rest, but now she broke. She broke and she sank into the chair and shook with silent weeping.

20

DECEMBER 23, 3:10 P.M.

The gnawing dread of the last two nights and days without sleep, the nonstop agony, had left Susannah too weak to resist Victoria's hot cup of tea and two sleeping pills.

In the bedroom Victoria pulled off her guest's raincoat and eased her onto the bed. She rushed back to the living room, drew on her sheepskin coat, and hurried out the door.

She slammed the door of the taxi and rushed to the stairs of the Soho loft before her courage faltered. She deeply breathed in the frosty air, fighting to gather her courage. A trembling hand dug into her bag and pulled out an envelope.

On the stairs two blasts of music—a stereo slamming out rock and an old movie musical on television blaring a tap-dance number—clashed. The door of the nearly dark loft stood open and she peered at light flashing and blazing, blue and white, down at the far end—the sculptor's acetylene torch. She moved toward the flickering light of the television, avoided a cat, and picked her way to the couch where Michelle drank red wine in front of the enormous projected picture. Victoria held out the envelope. "This time there's a hundred dollars in it. Please, I know your old man can beat me up and take it, but I've got to know the name of that doctor."

The other end of the loft went dark. The acetylene torch was off. The sculptor was walking slowly toward her.

"I'm not a liar," Michelle said.

Victoria held out the envelope. The woman on the couch reached up and took it and looked inside. "Okay," she said. "The honest-to-God truth. And I mean that, 'cause earlier I was just watching the Pope all the way from Italy. When you asked the name of that doctor I really wanted that fifty dollars. But the truth is, there was no doctor. I had the kid myself."

The sculptor stood in the dark beyond the light from the island of furniture and the flickering television screen.

"That shit Dennis didn't even help me."

Victoria knew that one word from the woman on the couch and the hulking man would walk the rest of the way and finish what he had begun on the stairs.

"I mean, since I didn't have a doctor I told you the name of the first doctor I could think of."

"If there wasn't a doctor, there had to be a lawyer. What was his name?"

"No lawyer. Guys from the street. They handled it."

"There had to be papers to sign and make it legal."

"Whatever they had, I signed. I gave them the baby, they gave me the five hundred."

"Have you seen them since?"

"Never once."

Victoria walked away from the television screen and forced herself to think. "When the baby came, there had to be telephone contact. An answering service at the very least. You have the number in your address book?"

"I don't keep stuff like that."

Victoria drew her list of obstetricians and their telephone numbers from her bag. It was a long shot, but she would take it. She held the list out to Michelle. "Any of these look familiar?"

"Are you kidding? Like you expect me to remember—"

The sculptor crossed in front of the television's flickering light and snapped it off. What was he holding in his hand? "The lady answered your question." He came to the couch, grabbed the envelope, and looked inside. His other hand gripped a ballpein hammer.

Victoria wanted to run, but she stood her ground. She asked Michelle to hand back the list of doctors.

The sculptor came so close she could smell sweat mixed with garlic.

"Get the hell outta here!" he shouted.

Victoria stood her ground long enough to show the shouting man she dared face him and his hammer. Then she strode from the loft.

The man grabbed a telephone and, whipping out its long extension cord, carried it to Michelle. "Call them."

"How?"

"She's looking for them and she's willing to pay. There's money in this. Big money."

"I don't keep an address book. Honest. Besides, I never had a number for them anyway so how's she ever gonna find them?" She looked up at the man, a pleading, pouty little girl. "Turn on the TV. Please?"

"Not 'til you find them."

"How am I gonna find them? If they're still around, they're probably up in Times Square someplace. I mean how are you going to find anybody in all that scum?"

"Was there a lawyer?"

"I guess. I mean how would I know? There was some creep who said he was a lawyer. The last time I ever saw him is when he gave me the five hundred dollars and even threw in a carton of M & M's."

Victoria reached the street and thrust her shaking hands into the sheepskin coat. Going up to that loft, she had risked her life and spent a hundred dollars. Now she had left Michelle's with no doctor or lawyer's name, nothing to show for her visit. She looked up and down the street for a pay phone. As Susannah had said, they still had nineteen doctors they might hear from any minute.

Might. The operative word was *might*.

Unlike climbing up to the loft, her next move would cost no hundred dollars, but only a dime to call the Plaza.

Elaine, on the hotel switchboard, gasped her excitement. She had something so important to say that she went to another phone where she could speak in private. "We've been trying and trying to reach you. Your answering machine's off. Do you know that?"

Victoria realized that in her rush to leave she had not turned on the machine, and the ringing telephone would not break through the two sleeping pills and awaken Susannah.

"We got a call. Sounded important. A guy who wanted to make contact with the South American couple right away."

"Jesus!" Victoria cursed herself and hoped to God she hadn't let this chance slip away.

Elaine was still excited. "I got the number and took the liberty of going ahead and calling the actors."

"Good girl." She waited, holding her breath.

"I wrote down exactly what your actor friend, Eugenio, said. He called the number and told them what you told him to say. I wrote down his message. He says he gave a great reading."

"Did he manage to set up a meeting?"

"Four o'clock."

"Today?"

"In twenty minutes."

"Holy Christ—"

"He said they didn't give him any choice."

Victoria glanced at her watch. "Jesus. She's right. It's twenty to four right now. Never mind. Where are they meeting?"

"Better write this down. Ready?"

"Ready."

"Southeast corner of Central Park. By the hansom cabs. At four o'clock."

"I'll repeat that," Victoria said. "Southeast corner of Central Park. By the hansom cabs."

"Correct. I sure hope we did the right thing."

"Absolutely. Only Eugenio doesn't have the money."

"He figured he'd better go ahead and meet them—even if we didn't reach you and he had to go without it. He said he'd try to stall them and keep the contact open."

"Get Eugenio and tell him I'll meet him there. I'll have the money! Before four o'clock. I'm leaving now!"

A couple from Connecticut in matching tweeds left a gallery on Prince Street and crossed the sidewalk to a waiting taxi.

Victoria dashed in front of them, sprang through the door, and slammed it in the couple's startled faces.

The black driver with a gleaming bald head turned with a wicked glare through his plastic partition at the woman who thought she was settling herself in the back seat of his cab. On the front seat beside him a fat dachshund yapped angrily.

"Out!" the driver roared at the woman.

The outraged couple banged on the glass.

Victoria leaned to the steel mesh at the side of the scratched plastic divider, pulled her newspaper from her bag, and held her press card next to her by-line. The driver resisted her bangs on the plastic but found himself squinting.

"I'm not shitting you," Victoria said with great authority. "If you get me to Central Park South in fifteen minutes you save a life."

The driver turned all the way to face his passenger.

"I haven't got the time to explain now, but you'll read about it in the paper." She peered at his name on the meter. "And about yourself. I won't leave you out of the story, Henry Harris."

Tires squealed. The cab dug out. The dachshund barked.

Henry Harris's driving was inspired, unafraid of threats and angry horns from other drivers. In one cross-town street the cab got around a stalled truck by jumping onto the sidewalk for a hundred and fifty feet. The dog yapped happily.

Victoria forced herself to lean back, shut her eyes, and smoke.

By the time they saw the bare branches of the trees in the park the driver was fully committed to accomplishing the impossible. He brought his taxi to the southeast corner at three minutes to four. On the lookout for the couple, he was the first to spot the distinguished Latin gentleman in a camel's hair coat walking slowly with his elegant young wife in a dark mink coat. Victoria had to congratulate the actors. They looked like the richest couple in South America.

The taxi slowed enough that Victoria could lean out of the window and hand the man an envelope. She signed to him that she and the taxi would be waiting within view.

The taxi parked illegally and Victoria and Henry Harris

glanced through the windshield and a line of hansom cabs and horses. She had pulled out her tape recorder and was describing how the horses steamed in the cold and snorted, how in the falling dusk the lights of the city never flared more brightly.

"I can't wait here," the driver said.

"Only for a minute."

"Not even for a minute. See that cop over there?"

"After your driving, I'm convinced you can do anything."

"Yeah, well, we got here." He kept his eyes on the cop. "But you didn't tell me down in Soho that now I gotta follow whoever meets up with that Latin dude."

"I'll make you famous, Henry Harris."

"Just pay what's on the meter." He picked up his dog and scratched her behind the ears. "Following's hard to do. Like the contact could be on foot, you know? Or take the subway."

"I'm counting on you. Whatever happens we can't lose him."

"Yeah, well." After a glance at the cop, he turned to his dog. "Just like the old movies we see on TV. Dude jumps in and hollers, 'Follow that cab!'"

Victoria spoke into her recorder.

Both the driver and his passenger suddenly had reason to peer at the corner.

The driver whispered, "Look!"

Victoria peered through the scratched plastic panel.

"You see that?" The driver did not turn toward Victoria. His tone was conspiratorial. A tall skeleton of a young man in a black suit jumped out of a cab in front of the Plaza. He wore no overcoat and his long scarf tangled with shoulder-length hair flying in the wind. He broke into a run to cross the street in midblock. At the sight of the rich Latin Americans in camel's hair and fur, he slowed.

"That's got to be the contact," the driver said to his dog. "Looks like Abraham Lincoln. Only mean."

Victoria murmured a description of the man into her recorder, perched forward in the dark cab to watch him as close to the windshield as the driver. The tall man wound his scarf around his neck and circled the sleek couple. In a moment the three were talking. Another moment and the rich-appearing man drew something from his coat and slid it into the tall man's hand. This man with the scarf counted the contents, nodded, turned, and suddenly ran back into the busy street.

"Let's go," Victoria urged. The cab was already pulling out to keep the man running across 59th Street in view.

"He's got the same cab!" cried Victoria.

The tall man jumped into a yellow taxi, which turned right and headed downtown on Fifth Avenue.

Victoria almost screamed: "They're turning!"

"I see."

"Don't let them get out of sight!"

The driver pushed down the dog, who jumped around yapping at the windshield.

"Don't get too close!" Victoria cried.

The dachshund picked up the excitement and pressed her muzzle on the windshield, whimpering.

"You're too close! They'll see we're following!"

"They can't see!"

"I'm telling you we're too close!"

"You wanna drive?"

The driver lurched his cab with a spine-crunching thud over a pothole and Victoria found herself flung back against the seat. She scratched out flame on the box of matches, lit a cigarette, gulped smoke avidly, but immediately leaned to the plastic in back of the driver.

"Traffic's terrible."

"Not gonna be no chase in this movie, that's for sure. The trick now, is not to get cut off."

The two cabs turned west from Fifth Avenue, found themselves blocked in traffic, and a quarter of an hour later crawled into the bright lights of Broadway.

"Oh, God," the driver moaned. "Don't tell me that turkey's going down Broadway."

"He's not turning."

"Good." The driver reached over and scratched his dog's ears.

At the next corner they turned north onto Eighth Avenue, where the traffic suddenly thinned.

"Careful."

"I am being careful."

"He's getting away from us!"

"No, he isn't!"

"He's way too far ahead. See? He is getting away from us!" Victoria was shouting, banging on the plastic divider. The dachshund was going crazy.

"I got him—he's right ahead!"

"Get in the next lane. The next lane, asshole!"

"You shut up!"

Victoria hurled herself against the back seat.

"Anyway," the driver said quietly, "he's goin' 'round the block to get back down Eighth. Eighth is one-way."

As the first cab slowed in front of a porno house, Victoria thrust a bill on the driver of a denomination that brought a huge smile. "I won't forget you, Henry Harris."

"Follow that cab!" The man laughed hugely.

The tall man jumped out of his taxi. Victoria, reaching the curb, crossed the sidewalk, dodged an old crone in a bathrobe gabbling to herself. She peered ahead. The tall man. Where the hell was he? She felt icy sweat trickle down her spine. Just as he turned into a coffee shop on the corner, she caught sight of him.

She raced for the shop, but slowed when she saw two young men with paper-white faces passing a smoke at the door. One man held a radio with an extended antenna. She slowed almost to a stop. She didn't have to be told these two were connected with the tall man.

She hesitated to enter the shop, but found it impossible to see through its misted windows. She turned the corner and walked a few paces toward a street of Broadway stage theaters. With every step she was trying to work up her nerve to turn around and walk past those two at the coffee shop door. With each step she was more and more convinced that they were not only connected with the tall man inside, they were guards in radio contact with others like themselves somewhere in the city.

Now, she had the proof. She felt absolutely convinced these two and whoever the tall man inside was were joined in the business of buying and selling children—a black-market-baby ring. She also felt it likely they were into something even more deeply evil, and that was kidnapping. Most important of all, she felt—no, she knew it without any doubt—that if these desperate people realized the trap she had set, the bait she had seen them take, they would not hesitate to kill her.

21

DECEMBER 23, 4:45 P.M.

In her work Victoria had come up against all kinds of desperate people. Why the hell was she standing here trembling, sweat dripping from her hands? The tall man had not seen her following him; none of those with him could possibly know what brought her here.

She summoned a burst of courage and forced herself to walk straight to the door and push past the two guards. Inside, the heat was intense. Stale cigarette smoke mingled with hot grease. Without a glance around, she went directly to the counter, sat, and ordered a black coffee. The waitress had filled her cup before Victoria dared slide her first sideways glance at the table in the corner.

The tall man's black strings of hair dangled over his hatchet face as he heaped sugar from a glass container into his cup. As he stirred the heavy coffee he spread out a newspaper Victoria could see was the *Press*. Beside him a round-faced young woman of perhaps twenty, with a full mouth, smoked and patted a baby that lay against her shoulder. She smoothed its thin brown hair. A second woman, with dark glasses, was buttering toast. Pulled down over her curly black hair, a wool cap hugged her skull, a wool cap of exactly the same red as Laddie's mitten.

Victoria dared only furtive glances. The reporter in her

cursed these circumstances that kept the camera and the cassette recorder in her leather bag. She rehearsed the thoughts she would put on tape the instant she was out of their sight. "Why did they choose this tall man sipping the syrup-sweet coffee to be the contact? Is he a lawyer?" She saw him push up the sleeve of his brown turtleneck sweater to peer at his watch, a large silver-and-black dial, an expensive chronometer. She wished she could see his shoes. Shoes always told her a lot about people. Fingernails supplied clues as well. But these were details too distant to see. The man was devouring every word of her story. Was he reading about himself?

"Who are the others? They're sure as hell careful not to show any reaction to what he's reading. What's the link between them?"

The woman shifted the baby to her other shoulder. Was she the child's mother? At something she said, the woman in the red wool cap nodded and took the child, which she held with the familiarity of someone who knew about babies. A nurse? The round-faced woman rose and without a look back, hurried from the shop.

What tied these two and the baby at the table to those two guarding the door?

Five, now four, people—undoubtedly more at the end of the radio signal—working together.

Were they the same people who stole the other child? Victoria's mind raced. Their work was high-paying but dangerous. Secrecy was important. That meant the first thing they had to share in common was absolute trust in each other. What could inspire this kind of mutual confidence? The money they made? Victoria doubted that. From what she had seen, instead of holding people together, money more often divided them. No, money was not the hold on this group. Sex? When did sex of whatever variety keep two people—not to mention four or more—together? The baby on the woman's shoulder cried. She jiggled him into silence. Children? Do they all have children of their own, children that someone else controls? Are they all some kind of hostages? Victoria had to admit to herself that in this area of parental love she was no expert, but during almost every hour of two days she had been seeing what one mother would do to get back her child. And yet others like the spaced-out Michelle gave away or sold their own flesh and blood. Children as hostages? It was a possibility. Could they be part of a cult? If they were all brainwashed, fanatic, a Manson-gang kind of zombies, anything was possible. Yes, she must consider they might be part of a cult. Drugs? She felt almost certain that drugs played their part. More and more these days drugs played a bigger role in everything and often explained this city's sudden, violent crimes.

She glanced at the tall man spooning his syrupy coffee. Could his craving for sugar be explained by drugs?

She stiffened. The woman with the baby suddenly rose and stood at her side, and even leaned across her to the waitress, to order two coffees to go. The man at the table scraped back his chair and waited at the cash register, where the woman with the red cap took the coffees. The tall man took one cup, filled it with sugar, and carried it, sipping as he walked. He followed the woman with the red cap out the door.

Through the open door Victoria caught one glimpse of the white face of a man on guard out in the rain. If the two exchanged any signal with him, she saw nothing. She tossed a crumpled dollar bill on the counter, slung her leather bag over her shoulder, ached to run, but forced herself to move slowly.

At the door she found the guard bending over his hidden but crackling radio. Damn. She'd give anything to move close and hear what he was muttering. She kept moving. She watched the two cross the street. With her coat the woman covered the baby from the rain.

Rather than follow directly behind them, Victoria angled a few steps back toward the bright lights of the Broadway theaters. She shrank into a doorway's shadows. Here, unseen by the guard, she never let the two out of her sight.

In the rainy street the couple with the baby and the coffees moved slowly. Victoria hoped following them would be easier than chasing the tall man in the cab. She must stay out of their sight, but if they escaped hers, she might never see them again.

Across the street they reached the corner.

She dashed out into the rain. A taxi roared past, showering her with gutter water.

On the sidewalk opposite the coffee shop she found herself facing the wooden wall of the boarded-up hotel where she had quarreled with Susannah that morning. Zellner had brought them here. A band of loud teenage boys thronged by, waving cans of beer, and she shrank back against the wood. The boys slowed, arguing about turning into the cross street. Victoria shoved past them to peer through the rain at the corner. The couple! Where had they gone?

She raced to the corner of the boarded-up hotel. Her heart sank. Had they turned the corner to walk downtown? Huddled men and women hurried by. But where in God's name had the two gone? In the few seconds since losing sight of them they could not have started across Eighth Avenue, for the street was a solid stream of traffic with headlights stabbing the night. The only way they could walk was downtown, and carrying the baby and the coffee they could not run. Victoria sprinted down the sidewalk the length of the hotel's wall, where wet posters peeled from the wood.

Gone.

She turned and squinted through the rain back up the street. Gone!

She forced herself to stop in the middle of the sidewalk. She raked tangled hair back from her face. "Don't panic! For God's sake, think!" In her newspaper work Victoria prided herself on an ability to define problems that led to correct answers. She had learned this technique from a quote from Einstein—if you have five minutes to solve a problem, first spend four of those minutes making sure you understand the question. "Right. Slow down." She forced calm on herself. She stood in the rain. "Okay. What is the question? The question is, can two people simply disappear from a Manhattan street corner? Clearly not. Consider. Where the hell can they go?"

She had already satisfied herself the two had not ventured out against the light into the honking traffic that roared up Eighth Avenue. They had not walked the cross street into the lights that led to Broadway or she would have seen them pass her and the guards. The coffee shop? The boy over there was handing the radio to another young man who had sprinted, head down against the rain, from the hotel. The first pushed into the steamy shop. She had been watching this corner. She was convinced there was no way the couple could have turned, recrossed the street, and gone back inside the cafe without her seeing them.

Downtown. That was the only way left. They had to be walking downtown. As she ran down the street she glanced at each couple she passed. The frosty air stung each breath, her head throbbed from the cold, but she reached the next cross street. She cleared her eyes of tears. They were nowhere in sight. By racing she had proved to herself that the two with the child and the coffee could not have come this far. Stunned, defeated, she looked around. What could she do now but turn and dash back to the corner and start over?

How could they have left this corner so instantly? Had they stopped a taxi and sped away in the rain? Unlikely. Highly unlikely. Even if they could get a cab, the coffees proved they wouldn't do that. Manhattan was full of places to buy coffee. You didn't buy hot coffee to sit and grow cold on a taxi ride. You bought hot coffee after the ride. That was her reasoning. Her hope.

She buttoned the top of her sheepskin coat against the lashing wind. "Where the hell could they go?"

Surely she had defined the question properly. Had she taken the time to exhaust all the possible answers? All but one. They did not go anywhere. Or, at any rate, not more than a few steps.

She turned and looked up at the deserted hotel that rose, dark with coldly glinting windows, thirty-one floors into the night sky.

She stepped back to touch the wooden wall. Plywood. Was there a door in this plywood among the posters? She moved along the sidewalk cluttered with litter and broken bottles. An arc of sidewalk was swept clean. Strange. She looked closer. One plywood panel stood slightly ajar. Her first impulse was to pull it open, for it was clear that it had been this door that had shoved aside the litter. She walked past the panel, careful not to let the guard across the street see her slow. A few feet along the sidewalk she reached a shadow, where she stopped and pretended to dig for something in her shoulder bag.

She peered up and down the sidewalk and shot a quick glance at the coffee shop. The guard huddled over his radio, pulling his collar up against the rain. He did not see her open the panel, slip in, and draw it shut behind her.

One step away, the glass of the hotel doors glinted. Locked. Not surprising. She pressed her face close to the cold shine but she could see only a little way into the dark lobby. Not more than a foot inside the door lay an empty paper cup in its spill, a puddle of steaming coffee.

22

DECEMBER 23, 5:10 P.M.

She reasoned that any time a number of people come and go through a door that is kept locked, a key has to be hidden in some convenient and nearby place. She found it the second place she looked—on a hook at the bottom of a bronze plaque that needed polishing: HOTEL MIDTOWN TOWER.

The key fit the lock.

But now Victoria resisted pushing the door. She clenched the key in her dripping-wet hand and slipped back out through the wood panel with another cautious glance across the street, making certain the guard did not see her. She closed the panel and raced through the rain.

In a musty little hardware store less than a block down Eighth Avenue, she waited impatiently while the only clerk and a ruddy priest plugged in two lines of Christmas tree lights and debated their merits. God, how she loathed their jolly holiday banter, which seemed endless. They even tried to include her in their cheer. At last it was her turn and it took only a minute for the clerk to strike two copies of the key. She left with the keys and a long-barreled flashlight.

From a deli she tried three times to telephone Susannah at her apartment. Each time she got a busy signal. Strange. Why was Susannah on the phone instead of sleeping? Victoria had been worried that she wouldn't be able to waken her. Apparently the pills had not done their work.

In the Hotel Argylle's plastic chair Victoria sat under the burned lampshade speaking into her recorder, bringing her story up to the minute in an account of these last two hours since she had left Susannah. This included the second visit to the spaced-out Michelle, the mad taxi ride to Central Park and watching the actors and the tall man make contact, following that tall man to the coffee shop, and the discovery of the door in the wooden fence. All this in two hours—instead of exhausting Victoria—had fired her spirits till her mind raced. She felt strong and capable of anything she had to do. She snapped off the recorder's power and tried again to call her apartment and Susannah.

The last time she had called the phone had whined a busy signal. Now it rang. And rang.

An enormously fat man in a bowler's shirt, who walked as if his tiny feet hurt with each step, dumped his bulk with a thud against the wall close to the phone. Around a wet cigar he wheezed deeply, making it clear that he had posted himself here to wait impatiently for the woman to get off the phone.

Victoria muttered, "Susannah, for God's sake, wake up!"

The fat man wheezed deep, long-suffering breaths. He wanted the phone and he wanted it now.

"Susannah, please . . ." In her mind's eye Victoria could see her tiny apartment where the phone shrilled. Damn! Had she gone out? How could she be sleeping that soundly when only a few minutes before Victoria had gotten busy signals when she was talking on the phone.

The fat man drummed stubby fingers on the wall. Victoria spun on him and lashed out, "Get the fat fuck out of here!" The bitterness of her sudden attack choked off his wheezing. He rolled his wet cigar in his fat lips and hobbled off on tiny feet.

Now Victoria spat the words into the phone. "Susannah, damn you. Be there. Be there, you hear me! Wake the hell up! Now!" She waited, closed her eyes, and seethed. She slammed down the receiver, fished another coin from her bag, and made another call. The Plaza, she decided, must be a busy place. The switchboard did not pick up until the fifth ring.

146 . . .

"Elaine, please—"

"Victoria? Victoria Cruz?" It was a voice she did not recognize.

"Yeah. Who's this?"

"I'm Laura. Elaine had to go out to finish her Christmas shopping. Thank goodness you're home at last—"

"I'm at a pay phone."

"For the last two hours we've been trying to get you at your place. Ringing and ringing."

At least that explained the busy signal. Laura explained to Victoria that she had been briefed on Millie and Elaine's operation. "The contact has been made. Money exchanged hands."

"I know. I saw it myself. Thank you. Thank everybody there. Now it's life and death to reach my place and I haven't got time to go down there in a cab. Laura, listen. Listen closely. There's no time to explain now, but keep calling my place. Susannah's there."

"Susannah Bartok. Elaine told us about her—"

"Right. At my place. Asleep. As I say, I haven't got time to go down there and get her. So you have to reach her by phone. She's taken sleeping pills. No, no problem. Only two, but apparently she's really out. You have to keep calling till you get her to answer. It really is—life and death . . ." Victoria took a long breath. She was shouting, words were tumbling out. If she wanted to be understood she'd have to slow down. "Once you get her, tell her I've left my cassette recorder for her at her hotel in Times Square. The Argylle. The minute she wakes up, she's to get a cab and get to the hotel as fast as possible and ask for a package. Money will be waiting. The tape will give her a complete explanation of everything that's happened right up till now. You got that?"

"Hotel Argylle. Pick up the cassette recorder. Money and explanation waiting. Got it."

"I can't begin to tell you how important it is for you to reach her. There's no one else to call. My goddamn neighbors, everyone I know—they're all out of town. Keep ringing. Whatever you do, don't stop till you get her."

Silence.

Across the lobby sounds of a television cartoon snapped and jingled merrily from the office.

"Still there?" asked Laura.

"I've got to hurry."

"You sure you don't want the police?"

"No time."

Victoria hung up the phone and slumped against the wall. She shook so violently it took several pokes before she snapped on her recorder. "Susannah, this is my last message until I see you. I'm standing here in the deserted lobby of your flea-bag hotel shaking with fear like some chicken-shit coward putting off what she knows she has to do. I've got to go into that empty, dark hotel now—alone—while the trail's still hot and—just between you and me—I am scared to death. Jesus. It has to be alone. Everyone's out of town for the holidays. I could call that actor who played the South American but at the start of trouble he'd begin screaming like a Girl Scout. The police? You got to be kidding. Foy would throw me out of his office and on my ass. The rest of New York's Finest would keep me waiting forever with endless stalls about getting a search warrant and assigning officers. Even if I could talk the cops into going with me, they'd storm in like the CIA hitting the Bay of Pigs and fuck up the search by scaring them out of that hotel or deeper into hiding. As I say I tried to reach you but it's just as well I can't get through. You wouldn't be any real help, except I wouldn't feel so goddamned on my own. So here I am shaking, trying to talk myself into it. See how I'm stalling? Still. When every second counts. The thing that worries me about the time element is that the new parents will want to get home for Christmas. The minute they get the kid they'll be on a jet for God knows where. And here I am. Still stalling. I'm tempted to wait for you. . . . I'd love to have you with me for moral support. After all, it's your kid, but it's my story. You live for him . . . but I live for my work. Is it possible you get the feeling I'm standing here giving you nothing but a lot of high-sounding talk? Either I go in or I don't. Right? You should see me—really shaking."

She stopped, then started again.

"As you can hear—still talking, still stalling."

23

DECEMBER 23, 5:50 P.M.

Without one light, thirty-one floors of hotel loomed black against the night sky flaring red from the lights of Times Square.

Victoria forced herself to the corner. Her steps dragged. Her teeth chattered. She felt even more cold and scared and immensely alone than she'd admitted to Susannah. And all these people on the street huddled in their winter coats, hurrying past her. Not one of them gave a thought to the board fence, the dark and apparently empty building and what might wait within. She glanced across the street. A taxi blocked her view of the coffee shop. Not bad. The same car would block the guard's view of her.

In a burst of courage, she crossed the last few feet of gritty sidewalk to the panel, cast one more glance to make sure the taxi stood between her and the guard, and drew open the door. Slipping inside, she carefully shut out the street. She held two keys, the original and a bright new copy. Should she return the key she had stolen to its hiding place under the bronze plaque? She hesitated. Was she still seizing any excuse to keep from going in? Why worry about the key? Once she was in, if someone came to this door and found no key they would have to bang on the glass till someone came and opened it. Yes. They'd bang on the door. Or radio. They'd get in eventually. She couldn't stop them. She pushed herself to peer through the glass into the dark shadows.

She turned the key in the lock. She pressed on the glass. The door did not move. Damn! Was something wrong with the key? She jiggled it and the key turned. With her shoulder against the glass she pushed. The door swung in.

Across the street, one of the guards shoved out the door to stand with steaming coffee. He sipped from the cup and peered up and down the street. His gaze rested for a long moment on the wooden fence that boarded up the first floor of the dark hotel.

Freezing cold cut to the bone, even more bitter inside the black building than out in the rainy night. Victoria tiptoed noiselessly across a chilled marble floor to stand in the dark and listen for what seemed hours but was probably less than five minutes. She found her eyes adjusting, complete black becoming shades of dark. Finally she could make out the wall on the Eighth Avenue side, and the boarded-up main entrance. An immense wall of windows rose three stories high. Some were broken. Others flashed with passing traffic and the colored glow from the street signs.

Above her something tinkled in a draft from a broken window.

Satisfied no one waited here in the dark with her, she switched on the flashlight and swept its beam across the marble floor. Her light faded out before it reached a mezzanine balcony that appeared to hang in the gloom surrounding the lobby. At the tinkling overhead, she threw the beam up to sparkle in an enormous chandelier. Broken strands of cut glass dangled and swayed in the freezing wind that rushed in the open window on the street side.

Her beam swept across a hotel desk and a long wall of key boxes. A closer look showed there must be seven hundred rooms.

She turned off the flashlight and listened. In the dark the dangling glass tinkled. From out in the street traffic rumbled. Horns honked.

She considered the hotel desk and the over seven hundred

rooms. Where should she begin her search?

As noiselessly as possible, she moved across the marble, around a broken couch and an overturned lamp. Even on tiptoe, her footfalls echoed in the emptiness like gunshots. The hollow lobby amplified the eerie, tinkling glass, the street noises, the scraping newspapers blowing in the draft, every sound.

"Good," she thought, trying to cheer herself. "I'll be able to hear anybody before they hear me."

Victoria considered the daunting immensity of the search ahead. For an instant she stopped and turned back toward the door. She fought her strongest feelings and again faced the dark. She told herself that if she concentrated on each move, she could keep going. She managed another step. What she must be, she told herself, is systematic. Yes. Systematic. That meant she would go to the top of the hotel and into the hall where, even if she found every door locked, she would listen. In this vast, empty box of more than seven hundred smaller boxes she felt confident that any sound would carry. She would hear them before they heard her.

"Okay." She prodded herself on. "Here we go to the top of the hotel."

To climb, she had to find the stairs.

She tiptoed hurriedly through the lobby toward three doors her flashlight showed stood open. Arches, most likely to more lobby. She hurried to move through one. Was it the change in the echoes of her own footfalls that alerted her? A subtle change in vibes? Some lifesaving instinct made her freeze, stop, and suddenly grab the door frame. In front of her a floorless void yawned. Emptiness lay one step away. She was looking down into the black of an elevator shaft. She slumped against the door frame and gulped down her terror. Her flashlight swept down and showed the top of a car three floors below. One more step and she would have plunged into space.

A strong blast of wind skittered papers across the freezing marble floor.

Trembling with fear, Victoria moved with even more caution. Along a wall strewn with rattling papers she found a steel door and turned the handle slowly, careful to make no sound. She held the door open and shined her light ahead. Yes, a metal staircase. She checked the bolt to make double sure the door would not lock behind her when it closed.

This lock reminded her that she must overlook no detail. One mistake like the next step into the elevator shaft or locking herself behind a door would be her last. One telltale sound or an unguarded flash of her light could mean her death.

In the total black of the metal stairwell her flashlight showed stairs rising to a landing that turned into a second flight and a door. These wound up, up into space around a narrow opening. Thirty-one floors.

She decided against shining her light up the well. She had no reason to believe someone was up there on any one of those thirty-one landings, but it could be seen. This was equally true of the four landings below. The faintest light shining up or down would flash her presence to anyone within this dark well. Just as the light could be seen, one footstep on the metal would ring out, echoing up and down the iron well, and be heard. She listened. She heard nothing.

She kept the light low against the steps and the wall. She climbed. Suddenly, she grabbed the rail and hung on for her life. Her heart leaped. Above her a door slammed, echoing as loudly as the end of all things. She snapped off her light, shrank against the wall, and waited. She sat. She hugged her arms against the cold. Inside her black wool turtleneck, dripping sweat crawled down shivering skin. She listened but no footstep rang out on the stairs. She sat and waited and listened. Never in her life had her teeth chattered in such biting cold, never had she been sealed in such total black. Shaking with fear and cold she began to doubt she had heard the door slam at all. It could have been her own heart. No. Again she was harsh with herself. She must fight against reducing what had happened to imaginings or a dream. This was no dream. Every fiber of her being told her this was too goddamn freezing cold to be a dream.

Still sitting, she pulled off her boots and jammed them into her leather bag. Stocking feet would help her climb in undetectable silence but at the first touch on the chilled metal, she stifled a gasp of pain. She winced. She forced herself to climb with the thought that from time to time she could sit, rest, massage the warmth back into her freezing feet.

In her carefully controlled spill of light she climbed step after silent step. With no elevator there was no other way up. That would be as true for those she saw at the coffee shop. She tried to imagine those three climbing these same stairs. Would the men help the woman carry the baby? They probably had a light somewhere. And of course they would not be shoeless. They would feel no compelling need to creep in total silence.

She reached the first door: MEZZANINE.

"Open it slowly . . . slowly. Very slowly. Easy. Mustn't make a sound. Good. Now hold it open and lean out into the hall. Listen . . ."

The dark on the mezzanine outside the well was less black. She felt carpet under her feet. Standing in the door, holding her breath to listen closely, she heard only rattling papers, the tinkling of the broken chandelier that hung in the vast dark of the middle of the lobby. What was that squeak?

She took her first step and went rigid with horror, clamping back a scream. She felt it before she heard it; sharp claws scratching and fur brushing her stocking feet. Startled by the light, a huge, fat rat had scrambled across her, and then slithered away over broken furniture.

She stopped. Her heart slammed the back of her throat.

"Okay. Okay," she told herself with real harshness. "You've seen rats before. Forget it." The truth was, she hated rats. They scared her to death. She could go to the morgue and stare a corpse in the face, but a rat made her blood run cold.

She eased the door shut.

She climbed.

She reached the next door: 1ST FLOOR.

"Thank God they mark the floors. If I lost count, how would I ever know what floor I was on?" The thought of getting lost here in the freezing black forced a tighter grip on her flashlight.

She stepped out onto the carpet of the first floor. Any rats?

Down at the end of the hall a window glowed with moving light reflected from the theater-filled street. She held her breath and listened. From outside she heard street sounds, but from within the empty hotel around her she heard nothing. Not a sound. Except for the window, she saw no glimmer of light.

On the stairs she quietly shut the door on the fourth floor. She had repeated her fourth search identical to the one she had begun on the first floor. She found herself slowing. Each step that took her up to the fifth floor became more hesitant. Was it the dark? The cold? Something even stronger seized her, and she suddenly knew, beyond any doubt, that someone was up there on the other side of that door.

She approached the top of the stairs.

Increasingly she was relying on instinct and now she had never felt more certain of anything. When she pushed open that door and stood in the hall she would hear them. Was this how Zellner felt when he had one of his visions?

Zellner. Susannah said he was a fraud. That was likely. She slowed. Zellner had spoken of boxes. Many boxes. She had jumped to the conclusion he meant drawers at the morgue. Could he not just as well have been talking about rooms, boxes within this one large box? Or was she twisting what she had learned to fulfill his prophecy. Zellner. Right now Victoria was worried about Susannah. She ached to look at her watch and held the light under her coat to look at her wrist. Almost six. Six o'clock on a cold winter's night. In here time meant nothing. Had the woman at the switchboard awakened Susannah yet? This very minute did she have the message, was she on her way to the hotel to pick up the cassette recorder? Perhaps Susannah was already with the police and they were listening to it now. She hoped so. Foy wouldn't believe her story but if he heard it now it would save time when she joined Susannah and the law to tell them about the fifth floor of this thirty-one-story hotel that looked like it stood deserted in the very heart of Manhattan.

What would she tell them she had found? Her next steps would tell her.

She reached the top of the stairs and felt for the ice-cold

metal of the knob. Its touch chilled and raised her fear close to panic. Before she set foot in the hall, she stood in the open door listening. She cautioned herself. Now was the time to be very, very careful. She peered into the hall. Dark. In the direction above the street where each floor had shown lights reflecting on glass, she saw nothing. Black. The window on this floor was covered.

Hurrying along the carpet, her stocking feet felt something like a rope. She knelt. No. This was no rope. This was rubbery to the touch. She dared one instant's light from the flashlight. The line was an electric cable that ran from one of the outside rooms the length of the hall.

A blaze of light sliced the darkness. At the other end of the corridor a door was opening.

Victoria pressed herself against the nearest door. Her hand found the knob. Locked. She couldn't imagine what kind of a light would glare with such a blaze. Stifling her breath, she prayed this door frame would cast a shadow deep enough to hide her.

She waited.

She listened.

Footsteps. From down the hall? No. They sounded too far away to be on carpet or within any of the rooms. These footfalls, though behind a door, clanged like boots on metal. With a sickening realization that closed her throat and rattled her bones she knew each step that grew louder, each ringing on steel, was climbing the stairs.

The stairwell door opened on a wavering glow. The door slammed shut. This wavering light grew brighter with each footfall, almost silent now on the carpeting of the hall. A black shadow carried a lantern. One of the guards from the coffee shop?

In the other direction, on the inside of the building, the other light blazed bright as the sun on a summer day. A figure crossed the shimmer till he stood in silhouette. The tall man.

"Shelley?"

"Candyman, that you?" The voice came from the other

direction. Between the man in the light and the man with the lantern, she was trapped.

"Hurry up!"

"What does the Bitch have to drag me all the way up here for? I said I'd radio her the minute Ahmed shows—" The lantern's pale light wavered along the wall into which Victoria shrank. The glow neared, then stopped, pinning her against the door. The light rose to her face. Behind the lantern, Shelley, one of the guards, ten feet away, stared straight at her. She prayed she would have the strength to run, even to be able to move.

The tall man striding down the hall was hurrying to see why the guard stared. He stopped. No one, the guard, the tall man or Victoria, moved.

She glanced around wildly. Her only escape was an open door in the opposite wall—one of three doors.

Strangling a cry, Victoria didn't wait for the men to move but bolted from her doorway and dashed for the open door. She stumbled over the electric cable, regained her footing, and lurched toward her only escape. *Jesus, deja ser una puerta!*

One backward glance showed her Shelley waiting for the tall man, who loomed larger against the light with each step. A blast of icy air from the open door stopped her on the threshold. She grabbed the door frame with a gasp of terror. Down in the lobby she had seen these three doors that opened into space—the black drop of the elevator shafts.

"Get rid of her!" Shelley rasped frantically. "I can't let the Bitch know she ever got in here. Candyman, please, you owe this to me!"

The tall man spoke quietly. "Go and shut the door so the Bitch won't hear."

Victoria clutched the frame and twisted away from the shaft and its rush of air. Blackness swallowed them as the door down the hall closed. Only the lantern on the floor glowed.

Heart racing, she gathered breath for a cry for help. Who would hear? Who would help?

"She's the reporter," Shelley breathed.

"The goddamn reporter." The tall man loomed over Victoria. "On the famous Bartok story. You the one who named him 'The Christmas Angel'?"

She couldn't see his face.

"Was your story worth it?" He was stepping between her and the lantern's glow.

"Goddamn all of you to hell! Give her back her son—" Victoria was still shouting as the rush of air tore apart her last words.

24

DECEMBER 23, 5:42 P.M.

Victoria's apartment door splintered. The three locks held. The panel crashed as two policemen battered through the frame.

Susannah stared wide-eyed from the bedroom door, but she felt no fear. She had risen from a dream in which she had heard thuds on the door. Some part of her said what was happening made perfect sense.

"Mrs. Bartok?" An officer thrust his pockmarked face into the hall. He squeezed his bulk through the splinters, a big man with round shoulders in a gray-and-white checked sports jacket, civilian clothes that made him look even more like a cop than the two men in uniform who picked their way across the shattered wood.

"Mrs. Bartok?"

Susannah answered with enough of a gesture to show the law they had broken through the right door and found the right woman.

"You all right?"

She nodded but sensed more was needed. "I guess."

The policemen stared at her, then at each other, asking themselves if this woman was all right or was simply responding with an answer as conventional as their question. The plainsclothesman with the pockmarked face was now in the living room searching. He lifted a spread newspaper and found the telephone, which he looked at as if it explained the events that brought them crashing in.

"Your phone."

With her fists, in exactly the same way Laddie did, Susannah scrubbed sleep from her eyes. She wished she had a chance to splash her face with cold water. Shaking her head to clear the cobwebs, she fought to bring the three policemen into focus. She ran her fingers through her stringy hair and watched the plainsclothesman lift the receiver. Along with the officers she heard the dial tone. The man in civilian clothes looked at the answering machine.

"You turned this off?"

"What?"

"Did you turn off the machine?"

"Don't know."

"It's off."

"Oh?" She felt thick; everything she said sounded stupid.

"Your friend at the hotel knew you were here. She kept trying to call you. For hours. When she couldn't reach you, she got scared and called us . . ."

"Sorry about the door," a pale-faced cop in uniform said.

"The main thing," the plainsclothesman said, "is that you're all right."

"Yes. I'm all right."

"We really banged on the door. Hard," the pale cop standing in the wreckage said, continuing to apologize.

"You didn't hear?" asked the man in the sports jacket.

Susannah shook her head. She frowned. Though she felt no fear she was still not clear why the police were here. What did they want? Where was Victoria?

"Everybody's been trying to reach you," the man in civilian clothes at the phone said. He looked as confused as she. "The precinct. Your friend at the hotel."

The precinct. What little strength Susannah had gathered she felt ebbing from her. In the hollow it left, cold fear crept in. *News from the precinct?* It had to be bad news. Yes. Bad news. The look on his face said the big officer didn't know where to begin.

"Like I said. The precinct's been trying to reach you since three o'clock. Prepare yourself for a shock."

"Oh, God. Laddie?"

He shook his head no. His big face split into a grin. "The second best news you could possibly have. Your husband's here."

"All the way from Hawaii," the pale officer said. "Has he ever got a tan!"

"Scott?"

The three men nodded, happy to be the bearers of good news. "He's been going crazy waiting up there at the precinct. Been telephoning here since three. Didn't dare leave in case he'd miss you. We'll take you to him now. Come on—"

"Scott? Here in New York?"

The men grinned like kids.

"Wait." Susannah grabbed the sheepskin jacket and a knitted cap. "You said my friend at the hotel called." The men scarcely had time to nod before she snatched up the phone and was dialing.

"Can't that wait till after you've seen your husband?"

"Elaine?" Why wasn't this Elaine? It was someone named Laura. "Laura? Right, they're here now. Broke down the door. I'm fine. I guess I must have been dead to the world. Victoria gave me something to make me sleep. . . . Yes. Yes. Yes, I've got that. The hotel in Times Square? Right away. Where's Victoria? I see."

The men in this room watched her still fighting off the pills. She said she understood the caller, but did she?

The blue-and-white patrol cars eased to the curb in front of the Hotel Argylle. Susannah ran in first. The officer in civilian clothes crossed the sidewalk and sauntered into the dingy lobby. He even walked like a cop.

The pale clerk behind the counter pulled off his gold-rimmed spectacles and fumbled along a shelf full of letters and packages behind a Christmas-wrapped bottle of whisky. He peered at a string-tied parcel and tossed it aside. At last he found the manila envelope.

"Mrs. Bartok," he read carefully. Without looking at her he slid the package across the counter.

Susannah grabbed it and under a lamp the plainsclothesman watched her shaking hands tear off the paper and carefully place a recorder on a table. She ripped open an envelope that contained five one-hundred-dollar bills. A key fell to the carpet, which the cop picked up for her.

Ten minutes later the two uniformed officers hurried her down the hall past Foy's empty office to a room where a powerfully built blond man with a deep tan and dressed for the tropics turned from a grimy window and the rainy night.

There was no one like him in New York.

In one bound he was across the room pulling Susannah into his arms. He felt immense, hard, and warm. His skin and hair even smelled the way they always smelled. Scott. He lifted her face but her eyes blurred with tears and she couldn't see a thing.

"You all right?"

"Laddie—" She choked with tears.

"God, I'm sorry, Baby. We'll get him back."

Even in his arms she was shaking so violently he drew her close.

"It's going to be all right. I love you. I'm back for good, Suze. We'll always be together." He kissed her wet face and she let him lead her to a chair. Still clutching the cassette recorder, she slumped. She coughed. For several minutes she was unable to utter a word and was grateful to Scott that he said nothing. He sat on the edge of the desk, his huge, warm presence filling the room. She sniffed back tears and squeezed her wet eyes to be able to see him, to make sure he was actually here.

It was true. He was here. Scott. In New York. Sitting five feet in front of her surrounded by a desk top of empty coffee cups and sandwich wrappers. He'd been waiting for her. She shut her eyes and offered a silent prayer. Thank God she wasn't alone anymore. This was Laddie's father who had just said he loved her and wanted her back. Together they'd find their son. He'd find him. Scott could do the most remarkable things—fix cars that wouldn't run, mend a stereo that had gone on the blink, run a mile on the beach with a baby in his arms to a first-aid station. When he put his mind to it, he could do anything.

Now he was here and he was nibbling ginseng root and

almost smiling at her. Strange. If Susannah had never seen him again she might have gone the rest of her life without thinking about Scott and ginseng. He swore by it and gnawed the little root constantly. When he offered her a piece, did he forget she had never liked its taste of earth and felt he and the emperors of China had kidded themselves about its miraculous qualities? Here in New York it was easier to take it than argue about it.

Any other time she would have thought him comical, this huge man nibbling so delicately. Had he always been so huge, so bursting with life? She knew every inch of him, but she'd never seen how truly enormous and gold and tan he was. His tangle of bronze hair and his pale eyebrows bleached by the sun shone against his dark skin. His gray-blue eyes, Laddie's eyes, looked straight at her while he nodded the way he always did, not quite a smile, but that look he always gave her when he was saying everything was going to be all right. At his throat on a leather thong hung a pearly sea gull carved from abalone shell she had given him three birthdays ago. He wore one of those ridiculous Hawaiian shirts, green palm leaves against black, open three buttons and hanging down over white jeans. Sandals. He wore no socks, only leather sandals here in the middle of the New York winter. His toenails were dirty. He'd often had dirty toenails even at home.

His hands. She looked at his huge brown hands. Yes. He wore the wedding band that she did not.

He was staring at her and she realized how she must look to him. Wet, lank hair. A face smudged with lack of sleep, eyes deep in gray-brown hollows. He'd never seen this sheepskin coat but he remembered when she'd first bought these California pants, now black and spattered with filth, the bottoms soaking. Her shoes were from California, too, thin shoes black with gutter water.

He was here because he'd called California from Haleiwa to tell her he was coming home; he wanted his wife and son back for Christmas. With his second call to upstate New York her father gave him the terrible news and this precinct's number. Now they were both far from home. He reached out to her but she made no move toward him. He smiled again. Poor Suze, she must be as dead-tired as she looked.

162 . . .

"The main thing is, I'm back."

He'd just come six thousand miles. He told himself he couldn't expect her to be as excited to hear he was back as he'd hoped—not with Laddie gone. He reached out a second time and took her hand. She nodded, which meant they'd have time to talk about things between them later. She had desperately important news for Foy. It was here, in this recorder that Victoria had left. Should they start playing it now or hold off until she could play it for the police. She hated losing time.

They sat in silence.

"He's supposed to be back any minute," Scott said. "About us," he began. It was a speech he'd been practicing all the way from Hawaii. "While we're waiting—"

"Later," she begged him.

He nodded to show her he understood how she felt. "But I want you to know that I hardly got out our front door and on the jet before I knew it was a colossal mistake . . . that it was you I wanted. You and Laddie."

Laddie. Laddie was what this was all about. Why wasn't Foy looking for him? Where the hell was Foy?

"I love you, Suze. Nothing could have kept me from getting here."

"Has Foy told you what we've done?"

"He's filled me in right up till now."

She ran her cold hands over the tape recorder. Should they start playing Victoria's tape?

He was looking at her but she stared at the recorder. "I can guess what you've been going through. You'll never know how much I've worried about you—like every goddamn mile on those jets till I got here."

Susannah got up and went to the door. "Where the hell is he?"

"He was here." Scott's voice urged calm, patience. "We were waiting for you, trying to call you. Three hours gave us a chance to talk. He's a great guy, Suze. He knows you don't think so, but he's doing everything humanly possible to get our boy back—"

"Then where's Laddie?"

"Give him a break."

"So we can sit here?"

"He'll be back—"

"Every second we sit here makes it worse. Like right now. He could at least call—"

"Ease up." Scott led her to a chair, knelt beside her, and took one of her hands. "Cold." He kissed her fingers. "Look, Suze, you don't have to deal with this all by yourself. Foy and his police, and me; we're all in this together. You can't go on cutting yourself up like this. I know what you've been going through because I've been going through it too. I know what you feel but believe me, no one's wasting time. This is a big city." He felt her cold hand draw away. "Like I said, we had a chance to talk. He didn't play games with me, Suze. He leveled with me—man-to-man—in a way he maybe never felt he could with you—"

"Because I'm a hysterical woman?"

"Suze, he's got three kids of his own—"

"Who are all safe at home right now munching Toll House cookies and drinking cocoa and getting ready for goddamn Santa Claus—"

"He says you're being very, very rough on yourself. In his estimation, too rough."

"I'm all right." Could he see how dead-tired she really was?

"You don't look too good."

"Damn sleeping pills. After we get Laddie back I'll have the rest of my life to sleep."

Scott drew over a chair, where he sat and put his arm around her.

"Oh, God, Scott, I've been so scared."

"Sshh. I'm here."

"Can't we do something?"

"He says we're doing everything we can."

Shouts echoed out in the hall. A radio went by blaring "Joy to the World," then switched to a burst of *salsa*.

"I got to hand it to you. He's told me about the different angles you and that woman reporter have tried. The newspaper files. The adoption agencies. The telephone set-up—"

"That's another thing. Why don't we hear from Victoria?" She stared down at the recorder and her chapped hands and broken fingernails. Before they played the tape, how long was Foy going to keep them waiting?

"You know I love our son every bit as much as you do. You figure you should be right here where it happened in case anything breaks. Right?"

She let the recorder rest on her lap and plunged her cold hands into the sheepskin coat. "Has he had any word of Victoria?"

"He doesn't like her."

"At least she's out there looking—"

"Only because there's a story in it—"

"I better call. I haven't seen her since three."

"In a minute. She's the one who gave you the sleeping pills?"

"I never should have taken the damn things—"

Out in the hall a boy's voice screamed abuse at a woman who answered with an even louder shriek.

"Look, Suze. We're worried about Laddie, but we're also worried about you. You've been at this every minute for practically forty-eight hours. You've got to get this into some kind of perspective."

"What does that mean?"

"It means we can't have you cracking up on us."

"He's out there and we're sitting here—"

"Baby, don't. . . ." His face touched hers.

She chewed her chapped lips.

"I mean it, and I'm telling you because I love you. You've got to ease up on yourself. You owe it to all of us. Now I'm not saying Foy's right, but when he gets here he's going to tell you what he thinks would do you the most good. He wants you to go up to your father's for a couple of days and get some rest—"

The first to hear Foy's voice in the hall, Susannah jumped to her feet and raced from the room. Husband and wife reached the office before the detective.

25

DECEMBER 23, 6:17 P.M.

Foy, in his Ultrasuede jacket, had always been unfailingly polite. Now he was bitter, mad as hell. As if he accused Susannah of an offense, he thrust a newspaper with its black headline and photo in front of her.

"You seen this?"

Susannah jerked her head. Yes, she'd seen the paper.

"Your friend's story."

Susannah set up the recorder on his desk and made it clear she had not rushed into his office to talk about the newspaper. "We waited for you to get here before we played this."

Foy hurled the paper aside. "Lies. Your dyke friend loves making all of us look like assholes!"

Susannah snapped in the tape. Foy raked his glare from her to Scott, whom he could see had no more control over the woman than he. He slammed the door. Victoria's voice filled his office.

As Foy listened to the hated voice his jaw set and he smoothed out the newspaper to glare at the headline. Susannah showed him the five hundred-dollar bills. When Victoria spoke of the key, she held it in the light to glint. Not once as Victoria's voice reported her every move after leaving Susannah a few minutes after three o'clock did Foy allow his eyes to meet hers.

Victoria's voice finished her story. In a more intimate tone,

166 . . .

she added, *"Susannah, this will be my last message till I see you. I haven't got time to go to the police and go through the whole procedural hassle with those shits. It is now thirty-five minutes past five."*

Susannah saw Foy glance at his watch. Hers read six thirty-seven.

"Look, my darling Susannah, if—and that's still a big if—I've got the guts—I'm going in there." The voice cut off.

Victoria was gone. Foy tidied a neat stack of the hundred-dollar bills. His usually smiling astronaut's face clenched with anger. "That all?" He tossed the bills in front of Susannah. "For the story. I hope she paid you enough." Susannah gathered the bills. "You know damn well that's probably her expense money from the paper."

Suddenly Foy's gaze was piercing. She was looking at a man who had nothing to do with Ultrasuede jackets and PTA manners. A Foy she had not seen before was capable of pitting himself against the roughest, most violent of criminals. His anger showed her that. He ignored her and turned to Scott.

"They pay for their lies. Sometimes I hate them more than the scumbags on the street."

He reached across his desk and punched the wind button and played bits from the cassette. The recorded voice hushed with excitement. *"Remember what Zellner said about boxes? We thought—at least I thought—he meant the morgue. That hotel could be a thousand boxes. And this morning in his car we were actually right outside the place . . ."*

Foy shook his head. This was not the part he was looking for. His impatience said that that was the trouble with cassettes; you could never find what you wanted on them. He punched twice.

"Question: What holds them together? What links these people on the street to what goes on in that building where no lights shine?"

Defeated, he snapped off the power. "I was trying to find the part about the newspaper publisher." He thrust the instrument aside. With Scott he felt he had earned the right to sarcasm. "All very dramatic."

Susannah shoved the money into her pocket next to the red

mitten and the key. She rose. She reached for the recorder but Foy claimed it under his hand. "Can we go into that hotel now?" By making no move Foy showed his command. He leaned back in his chair, studying the recorder.

"Tell me. Do either of you believe what you just heard?"

Susannah stood at the door, waiting to leave.

Foy folded the paper lengthwise and took his time explaining to Scott: "The second time your wife came in here she was with the reporter but I asked her to stay on alone. I warned her then about Victoria Cruz. I told your wife that that reporter tells lies—story after story."

"At least she's out there doing something!" Susannah cried.

"The question," Foy said quietly to Scott, underlining his bitterness, "is whether you're interested in selling papers or the truth."

"All I want is to find my son!"

"Talk about wasting time." Foy's hands twisted the paper, strangling it. "Reading this! Listening to this cassette—this is wasting time. Ask her, Scott. Is your wife really telling me to take all her reporter friend's crap so seriously that I'm supposed to use this as a lead?"

"What have you got to offer? Where's my son?" demanded Susannah.

"Take God knows how many man-hours to follow up on this?" He slapped the offending paper against the desk. "This isn't a lead because none of this is the truth. What this is, is more of her crap to sell papers!" He turned away in disgust. "Of all people, how can you—the boy's parents—possibly stomach such garbage?"

"I haven't read it," said Susannah.

Foy's pale red brows rose and held their surprise. "No? You haven't read what everybody else is reading about you? About your son's last Christmas? Scott, you've read it. You recognize your wife in this story? Or your son?" He ran a finger down a column till he found a line. "I quote: 'The golden-haired Christmas angel lost out in the black winter night.' Cute? Heart-tugging? That is your son, your precious friend is writing about, Mrs. Bartok. And how about, 'The hysterically sobbing mother—already fighting the heartbreak of a husband who walked out on her little family at Christmas—barely choked back tears to beg take precious time from their own holidays to join her in her frantic search for. . . .' et cetera, et cetera. The Bartoks enjoy this, do they?"

"Give me the key to the hotel," Susannah said flatly.

"I don't think what you have in mind is a good idea."

"Are you going to help or not?"

"I don't want to tie up my men on a newspaper story dreamed up by some lying reporter."

"So you sit here?"

Foy pretended to study the key.

"Laddie's at that hotel."

"According to your Ms. Cruz." He pronounced it mizz, with a nasty twist. "Or is this your famous psychic speaking?"

"It's me."

"And you want me to tie up my time and the time of my men searching how many hundreds of empty rooms?"

She sounded harsh, demanding, every bit as pushy as Victoria. "Right now!"

"That would take past Christmas."

"If you won't do it, pick up the phone and call the FBI."

"The Bureau doesn't like to waste time either."

"I asked you for the key."

Foy rubbed his face with his hands. "Scott, for God's sake tell her. If I tried to follow up on even a fraction of what these crazy reporters peddle in their papers—"

"She's done more than you and your whole damn department have."

"She sure as hell has. Did it ever occur to you that if that hysterical dyke is right and there is a gang or a ring—that they can read newspapers too? If this stuff is true, you'll have her to thank for scaring them deeper into hiding, for making it all the more impossible for all of us!"

"She's with them now."

"You want to bet? Right now she's off somewhere banging out the next installment of her story. You want me to call the paper and back that up?"

"She won't be there. As sure as I know anything, I know she's with them."

. . . *169*

"You've been around Zellner too long." He shook his head. He appealed to Scott. "If she could give me the slightest evidence—"

"That money and the key to the hotel aren't *evidence?* Why would she leave the cassette and the recorder if she didn't think there was a good chance something was going to happen to her?"

Foy tightened his angry grip on the newspaper, all the evidence he needed to deepen forever his long-held hatred for the reporter.

"Scott, what I'm saying," urged Susannah, "is, if they do have Victoria they know about the trap we set with the telephone calls and the contact with the first payment. They know that right now we're looking for them. Right? Then, Jesus Christ, why are we still sitting here?"

Foy dreaded hearing what he knew Scott had to say. And, of course, with no choice, Scott said, "Isn't it worth a try?"

Foy snapped out the cassette and turned it over to put it back in the machine. "I want to hear this again—"

"Listen to it in the car!" Susannah buttoned the coat Victoria had lent her. She grabbed the key and recorder and slid them into her coat pocket. "My son is in that goddamn place and we're wasting time."

Foy scraped back his chair. "I'll get a search warrant."

"And waste more time?"

26

DECEMBER 23, 7:01 P.M.

In the patrol car, as rain drummed on the roof, Foy and two cops nibbled ginseng root. The detective decided this was not the time to urge Susannah to leave the city. He did, however, suggest that he take the couple downtown to Victoria's where Susannah could sleep off the pills. He assured them they could leave searching the hotel to him. At no answer, Foy glanced from the front seat. No, she wasn't asleep back there. She was in her husband's arms, staring straight at him.

Scott's arm, in the duffle coat he had borrowed from Foy, had been around his wife these few blocks through midtown Manhattan that dragged the patrol car into an agonizing crawl of honking, bumper-to-bumper traffic. He welcomed the delay. Back in the office, when he first held Susannah, she had postponed hearing what he had just flown six thousand miles to say. To take time for Scott, to talk of their lives together, was stealing precious minutes from the search for their son. Huddled in this patrol car with three cops, mired in traffic, she could ask no one to do more than they were doing. Now she had time for her thoughts to include him.

He began with kisses and whispers about that terrible Thanksgiving Day when he slammed out the door. So many things had really gotten to him that day. Heavy. They'd stacked up on him to the point that leaving really never had anything to do with her. He whispered as he nuzzled her wet hair, the side of her face, which showed him nothing of her reaction. He explained about that girl—Sharon. She had never meant anything to him—not even at the beginning. He knew that on the plane. By the time they reached Oahu's north shore he had discovered she was a whiner, and Susannah knew he'd never been able to put up with whiners. When he went out to surf the Pipeline she had acted as if her ear infection that kept her home was his fault. Even an ear infection was no excuse for not going to the supermarket or cleaning the goddamn house. Her mother and father, who lived in the condo next door and who were really mellow for old people, agreed with him. They, too, had never been able to do anything with that whining girl.

When he had telephoned from Hawaii less than a week ago, he was calling to tell her then about the colossal mistake he'd made and how every minute he missed her and their son. Especially now, with Christmas coming.

He tried to see her face. Did Susannah hear any of this? Even with his arm around her she'd been leaning forward, peering out the windshield where the wipers slapped. Through the rain she could see the coffee shop. "When we get closer to the corner," she told the big black cop at the wheel, "be very careful. See that guard at the door? He's got a radio."

The driver waited for orders from Lieutenant Foy, whose indifferent nod made it clear he was making this call only to placate the hysterical mother. "Do what the lady says," Foy said. "Park here, out of sight." He ordered the little Puerto Rican cop, who'd shared the back seat and spent the trip testing a new moustache with his tongue, to the coffee shop to question the guard. "Hassle him as a drug suspect. Use any excuse but draw him away from seeing us go into the hotel. Keep him off that corner and get back to us."

The Bartoks, Foy, and the black cop left the car and moved through the rain along the wooden fence. The officers pulled on several panels before one swung open. The black cop peered across the street and signaled that no guard stood at the corner.

Foy down-played his surprise when Susannah fit Victoria's

key in the lock of the glass door. The officers brought out their flashlights, ready to enter.

"Awful dark in there, Mrs. Bartok. Scott, you don't think your wife would rather wait for us out here?"

Susannah urged him to push open the door. She kept the key.

The lobby loomed darker than Foy had warned. The cold shook them even more bitterly than the night outside, piercing to the bone. Susannah clenched her teeth and shuddered. Since she was insisting on joining his reluctant search, Foy asked her where she would like to begin.

"Don't talk so loud," she whispered. "They'll hear us."

"Sorry."

Scott drew her to his side, but she hugged herself against the cold and stared helplessly into the black. Above them the chandelier tinkled in the icy draft.

"Did your psychic tell you where to start looking?" His sarcasm demanded no answer. He followed his flashlight's bright beam to the reception counter and the wall of pigeonholes. He wiped a finger in one of the boxes where his light showed dust. "Seven hundred and twenty-three rooms. No keys. The rooms are all probably locked. Which one, Mrs. Bartok, do you want to look in first?"

"Downstairs."

Foy looked at Scott. Did he agree with his wife? He waited for Scott's nod. "Okay. We start downstairs. May I ask if you've got a reason for starting there? Your vibes tell you—"

"We have to start somewhere!"

Foy showed an abrupt change. Until now he had missed no chance to make it clear he resented coming here with his two men and going through what he plainly regarded as wasted motions. Now that the search was on, he dedicated himself to the work. He had his job to do and he would do it as a professional. "Right!" he said and led the way across the marble and drifting newspapers. The big cop made no effort to soften his footfalls. "Try to be quiet," Susannah rasped. "And don't smoke. It'll give us away."

They passed the three open doors of the elevator shafts to reach the wall and a door, which Foy pushed open on a staircase.

The sound of the four walking down the metal stairs made Susannah wince. They were far from quiet.

From what they could make out in the dark, the basement divided itself into storage areas. Their flashlights picked up shelves, cartons, heat ducts leading down dark passages, doors to more rooms.

The big cop brushed against a shelf and a crate crashed to the concrete floor. Bottles shattered. The four froze on the spot, waited, and listened to the sound of one another's breathing.

Foy signaled more silence. He was the first to hear something. He pitched his warning voice so low the others could barely hear. "Someone's here."

Something behind one of those doors shared their dark corridor. Scott's arm tightened around his trembling wife. Foy drew his pistol from his shoulder holster and gestured for Scott to leave Susannah and open the door. Flinging it open, he leaned back. Dozens of rats tumbled out, scurrying with piercing shrieks, racing in every direction across the floor.

Susannah stiffened with horror and clenched her fists. She made no sound. After a long moment she jumped at a touch. Scott was whispering that the rats had gone.

They passed the bottom of the three elevator shafts and the cars behind their open doors. Foy swept his light into the nearest. They glanced into a car, the roof door pushed back to the dark of the shaft. They moved quickly past the other two cars. No one saw a broken body wedged in the open roof of the last car, or the leather bag that had fallen through and spilled its contents on the floor. No one saw their passing light glint on a black-and-silver cigarette case.

27

DECEMBER 23, 7:08 P.M.

Cut glass tinkled. Susannah looked up at the broken chandelier swaying, sparkling in the light of the big cop's flashlight. Foy opened the street door to the little cop who shivered outside. The three policemen, Susannah and Scott, their breath coming out steam, crossed the lobby and climbed the gritty dust of the thickly carpeted stairs to the mezzanine.

A glance around convinced them they could leave. No one had found a thing. No lead here.

In the stairwell footfalls echoed on metal until Susannah begged for quiet.

Foy and Scott led the way, climbing side by side. "Without any heat," Scott whispered through chattering teeth, "they can't hole up here for long.

"They could if they fixed up a few rooms." Susannah paused to catch her breath. "What would keep them from running a cable in here for heat and light?"

"That is what we're going to try and find out," Foy said, struggling for breath. "The trouble is, which rooms? Which floor?"

"I keep thinking about Zellner," said Susannah. "He kept talking about 'boxes.' Boxes are like rooms. Why couldn't he have meant all these rooms?"

"Did he bother to tell you there were seven hundred and twenty-three? A real search could take us through New Year's."

"Damn," the black cop muttered. His light faded and went out. He shook the thing. "Battery's dead."

"You really believe in Zellner?" Scott asked Susannah.

"I didn't at first."

"What changed your mind?"

"I believe in anyone who wants to help."

They climbed. Foy's light picked out the door: 1ST FLOOR. "Just for the record," he said to Scott, "he's as bad as her reporter friend. There's a whole slew of psychics doing it for the publicity. The way the public eats it up it sells millions of books."

In front of the door Foy stopped and signaled the search party that he was snapping off his light. From the total darkness of the stairwell Foy pushed open the door and they stepped onto the carpet of the hall.

At the end of the corridor a window's faint light cut a rectangle of gray in the black. There was a flash of light on the glass, a reflection of a passing glow from the street. Foy led them down the hall to the first door. He tried the handle, found it locked, and stepped aside as the big cop went to work. Susannah stared in amazement at the speed and ease with which the officer slipped a plastic card between the panel and the frame. The lock clicked and he pushed open the door.

"Your old-style lock," the cop said.

"Lucky for us," said Foy. "At least that saves time."

A rush of air howled over them from an open window. Tattered wet curtains sucked into the room and flapped crazily. On the window sill shadows stirred and grumbled. Pigeons flapped.

Scott pushed his shoulders through the open window and looked out into a court. The hotel soared up, black, without a glow in one window. From a few open windows, from black rooms, waved torn curtains.

The big cop tried the light switches. Nothing in the room worked, but in the bathroom, turned faucets coughed and sputtered, then gushed water.

They returned to the hall. Foy announced, "Seven hundred and twenty-two to go."

The two policemen waited in the dark for Foy's orders. Their silence demanded, What did he expect them to do?

Susannah and Scott waited.

"Unless you have any other ideas," Foy said to the Bartoks, "we'll have to settle for a spot check. The best we can do."

"Not if we split up," said Scott.

"You think that's a good idea?" The detective was polite. He let Scott feel that if the idea had been feasible he would have agreed. Scott apologized and told Foy they'd do it his way.

They stayed together, and opened the stairwell doors, and entered the second- and third-floor corridors. Foy chose room doors at random. The big cop opened doors. They entered black rooms. They found nothing.

"We're wasting time," the big cop said.

Susannah hated him for saying that. She knew very well the three policemen felt this search was a waste of time, utterly pointless except as a duty to mollify her. From the fourth floor the cops hurried back to the stairs, confident that Foy would tell them they had done all they could be expected to do; they would leave this ice-cold emptiness and return to the heated car.

Susannah insisted, "One more floor."

In the dark Foy stared at her. She stood her ground, knowing her request was all but impossible to deny. "Like you said—at random. This time we pick the floors at random, not the rooms. The ninth floor." It was simply a desperate guess.

"Jesus," the cop with the dead flashlight muttered.

"You wouldn't say it that way if he were your kid," Scott snarled.

Foy made a display of shining his light on his watch, which showed that he regarded the six-floor climb as a waste of time. "The ninth floor? You get that from Zellner?" But he was already leading the party to the stairwell.

On the ninth floor, in no way different from the others they had spot-checked, Foy said nothing, but his attitude made it clear to Susannah he would go no further. He did not actually say it out loud, but everything in his manner said, "Satisfied now?"

Susannah was far from satisfied. "We can't just quit."

Foy looked at his watch, repeating his silent accusation. He turned to Scott. "There's a building across Eighth Avenue. Come on. I've got an idea."

Susannah felt certain Foy had seized on this plan of visiting the building across the street simply as an excuse, a way to end this search in which he hadn't ever believed. He was getting them out of the hotel. She ached to fight him, to stay here, to search every room in the place if she had to, but the men were already leaving. She found herself surrounded by the four hurrying back to the stairwell door and down the iron steps; behind Foy with his flashlight, next to Scott who took her arm. She longed to wrench away and go back. Behind her the big cop lit a cigarette. Was this his way of saying to her that he took none of her search seriously?

"Damn him!" she cursed silently.

Across Eighth Avenue in the lobby of the office building, the five and a Spanish-speaking superintendent strode through the lobby, their footsteps rattling like machine-gun fire, to an elevator. They followed Susannah into the car, faced the front, and rose thirty floors in silence.

The superintendent unlocked an office door, which Susannah now realized the big cop, who stood and waited, could have opened without a key almost as quickly.

Facing Eighth Avenue, she resisted being maneuvered to stand beside Foy looking at the wall of black windows, the proof he was presenting—that the hotel stood empty.

No chink of light gleamed. Against the night sky the deserted hotel stood unassailably black, mocking her. She did not expect the detective to say, "No lights." By now she knew him well enough that his silence, not his comments, carried the stronger accusation.

"Victoria said there weren't any lights. They wouldn't dare show any." She turned to Scott. "They'd be careful enough to cover the windows. I mean they've got water in those rooms, they could have lanterns . . . even electricity. For power all they'd have to do is run a cable . . ."

"Anything's possible," Foy said. He was also saying that he had done everything any reasonable man could do. The two officers had already moved from the office and into the hall toward the superintendent waiting at the elevator. They had gotten her out of the hotel. They had peered at the building from across the street. This was all the search she was going to get.

Downstairs in the lobby Susannah wrenched away from Scott to grasp at Foy's arm. "Are you saying we just give up?"

Foy did not draw away. He looked to Scott: It was the husband's duty to tell his wife the truth.

"Where's Victoria? Where's my boy?"

Foy, who had been so strong, so decisive in his anger, now avoided looking at the woman or at his wristwatch. The big cop, the black man who could open doors, was the one who peered at the time. He grimaced for all of them. The hour was late.

"Scott, tell them!" In the empty marble hall Susannah's voice rose and echoed increasingly shrill. "Tell them for Christ's sake they've got to do something!"

The superintendent scuttled off to unlock the front door and prepare their retreat. The three policemen looked to Scott to handle his wife.

"Scott, don't let them go!"

Foy spoke only to the man. His tone, unlike Susannah's, maddeningly reasonable, caused no echo. "You know we'll do anything we possibly can."

"They say that!" Susannah screamed to Scott, "but they don't do anything—"

"That's not fair, Susannah. Hold on," Scott said.

Foy continued to speak only to the man. "Where can we drop you?"

"My wife and I have to talk—"

"No! Goddamn all of you, no more talk!" She thrust her angry face close to Foy. "Your job is to find Victoria and get my son back!"

"Listen to your husband, Mrs. Bartok—"

"For Christ's sake, Scott, tell him!"

"The truth is, Mrs. Bartok, that Victoria Cruz's journalistic hunches, along with whatever your psychic may tell you, just aren't getting us anywhere—"

Susannah ran from Scott past the superintendent at the door and out into the night. The police made no move to stop her.

. . . *179*

28

DECEMBER 23, 8:02 P.M.

At the corner Scott caught up with Susannah, grabbed her shoulders, and spun her around. He slid wet hair back from her eyes. "Baby, be reasonable. What do you want them to do?"

Her breath, white mist, rasped through clenched teeth. Her eyes included him in her accusation.

"Goddammit, Suze. You're not the only one who can feel. He's my son too!"

Her look left him and rose to the dark building. Her voice was bitter as the frosty air. "They only took me in there to shut me up. They didn't believe me."

"I believed you."

She didn't have the energy to challenge his lie. She shook with cold as he nuzzled her face, turning the wool collar of her sheepskin jacket up around her chin. He threaded his arm through hers and was leading her downtown as she twisted back to stare up at the hundreds of dark windows.

"What if Victoria's still in there?"

"The hell with her. My job is to take care of you and find Laddie."

She stopped in the yellow light from a liquor store. A band of black kids fanned out around them, with transistor radios smacking out a fierce, hot beat. The music faded into the roar of traffic.

Again his cold face nuzzled hers. "Come on."

"Where?"

"Trust me. Okay?"

"How about her?"

"I told you."

"She knows—"

"What she knows is how to get headlines. Foy told me all about your dyke friend . . ." He stopped, for he knew he'd said the wrong thing. He dropped his hands from Susannah and plunged them into the pockets of Foy's coat. His hair dripped. He shook as violently as she in this icy rain, his bare feet in sandals, his white Levi's sopping wet. He breathed deeply before he began again. "I'm sorry. Wipe out all I just said, okay? Start over." He reached for her. "Baby, we're both dead on our feet. With all you've been through it's a wonder you can still keep going. You need rest. Me too. I haven't slept since Hawaii . . ." He squeezed a hand over her wet hair. "You should wear a hat."

She shifted her shoulder bag to the side away from Scott.

"You can't keep pushing yourself like this—"

Her face sought his shoulder. "You keep saying I'm going to break . . ."

"I'm here to take care of you, Baby. I love you and I love Laddie. You two are everything in the world to me. I had to learn that the hard way. So please, will you listen? And I'm tired too, so don't, please, twist everything I say. . . . Okay?"

She nodded and allowed him to lead her from the liquor store's yellow light. She slowed. Raising her face, she stared into the lights of 42nd Street. "We shouldn't be walking this way—"

"It's okay."

"No—"

"I got a plan."

She was shaking her head, refusing to move another step. Around them people surged, heads down, huddling against the rain. She turned to walk uptown. A headlight flashed.

"Will you stop for a fucking minute and listen?"

He sprinted ahead to stop her. She turned away but his cold hands turned her face. He kissed her wet brow. In the icy wind his breath came out mist, but his lips were warm, his voice soft. "Don't you even want to hear my plan?"

. . . *181*

"We're wasting time—"

"You don't want to hear what I'm trying to do?"

"Take care of me—"

"Right. What's your plan?"

"To find my son."

"Jesus." He clamped his big, square hands over his face. He fought himself to stay calm. In a quiet voice he began again. "He's our son—yours and mine. And I agree. We have to find him." He moved to keep pace with her. "Nothing in the whole world is more important. But how? Go back in that hotel? Stay out here in this rain till we both come down with pneumonia? Baby, what are you trying to do?"

"Find a telephone."

"And then?"

She shook her head. She didn't want to tell him.

"Haven't I got the right to know?"

"Call Zellner."

"That psychic? Jesus! You don't call that wasting time? That's worse than looking for that damn reporter so she can jerk you around to get more headlines. Baby, face it. These shits have—they've been jerking you around. If they gave a damn you think they'd run out on you like this? Your reporter lady's already written the rest of the story and taken off for Christmas."

Susannah shook her head. Victoria would never do such a thing. Victoria was her friend. . . .

"Baby, answer me this—who cares more about him than you and me? Not her. Not Zellner—"

"The police?" She mocked him, fierce, bitter.

"No. Not as much as you and me. That's why we'll find him." He pressed close and spoke slowly, choosing each word carefully. "Now I want you to listen. Okay? Just listen? Here's the plan. That's the bus terminal right over there across the street. Back at the precinct I had plenty of time to check. There's a bus to your father's—we can be on in twenty minutes. . . . Don't say no. Not yet. Because you're going to stop running long enough to get warm and dry with the only two people in the world who love you. That's right. We're going to your dad's . . ."

He could see the lights of the street shining in her eyes. "You think I'm going to let you turn into one of these wackos, running around in the rain and snow for the rest of your life? How much longer do you think you'd last? Look, you've done everything you can. By now you've got to know in your heart that you can't possibly do anything more. You're dead on your feet and full of pills. Come on. Let me do the worrying for a change. Foy's promised me that if we leave here for a couple of days the police won't let up for a minute. You can call them just as easy from your dad's." He kissed her. "I just came six thousand miles to be with you. God, Baby, I want you back so bad." He was feeling joy, rubbing his hands against the cold. "Your dad's waiting. I called him. At least we'll have Christmas—"

"What kind of Christmas will *he* have?" Laddie again. Always Laddie. Her eyes spilled tears and she sank against his shoulder.

The bus terminal was jammed. People in heavy coats clutching packages pushed and shoved—a world fighting to get home to fires in fireplaces and family dinners and colored lights glowing on trees and Christmas carols. In the long line to buy tickets, Scott never relaxed his tight grip on Susannah's hand. With the tickets, he pulled her close and moved them as one toward a waiting bus.

She slowed.

"For your own good, Suze, face facts. If he'd been killed you'd have to. Life doesn't stop. Those others who pretended to help you? You think they're not going on? At least it's the cops' job to care. They won't stop. We get you some rest and we'll be back. I promise you."

In the line to board the bus Scott tried to force his mouth on hers, hot in the chilly air. She twisted away.

"Baby, I know how you feel—"

"Will you for Christ's sake stop saying that?"

"Okay. Okay, I know. You're his mother. I'm only his father, but by God I can say I love you. I love you and I want you so bad—Baby, I'm here and I don't know what I'd do without you. Look at me. I told you—I'm back for good so I can take care of you for the rest of your life. If the worst happens—and you and I know it won't—there'll be other kids."

She twisted her head so he wouldn't see her agony. They moved up in line.

. . . *183*

"You've made me do all the talking."

"Talk. Everyody talks . . ." Her voice was flat, drained, lifeless.

"Believe me, we're doing all we can. Even if you don't like Foy you got to admit he knows this city a million times better than you and he says you on your own haven't got a prayer . . ."

The line shuffled toward the bus.

"All of us are telling you, you've got to get some rest." He pulled her shoulder to him and they inched next to the steps of the bus behind a woman who heaved herself on board as she balanced two shopping bags and a carton. "You can sleep on the bus," Scott said. "Then let me and your dad take care of you."

"Who's taking care of Laddie?" The question was never asked—not out loud—but hung there in the cold between them. She wrenched from his arms, shoved her way back through the line, and was gone, swallowed up by the crowd.

29

DECEMBER 23, 8:03 P.M.

Ahmed, the guard with the radio, had reported seeing the police and the couple leave the dark hotel. Now he and Candyman waited in an office, watching the doctor push up a white, starched sleeve and move her bare arm under the bright light of a desk lamp. From a physician's steel tray of shining instruments and vials, she worked with precision. She bound her upper arm with a rubber tube. Swabbing the skin with cotton and alcohol, she slid the glinting needle of a hypodermic into the blue-tinged bulge of the vein.

Through the open door to the next room they heard a baby whimper. Another cried. Ahmed's big eyes glittered with fear. Candyman wiped sweat from his face and glanced at an open notebook he held in two shaking hands; a lawyer preparing his case.

"Before you tell me how the police got in here, I want to know about the woman in the basement." The doctor's voice was professional, as uncolored with emotion as the white, starched sleeve or the sterile medical instruments. "What time did she enter this building?"

"Tell her," Candyman said.

"F-five forty-five," Ahmed said.

"How do you know?"

"That is the only time—truly, the only time I went inside the coffee shop—Doctor, I swear!" Ahmed's eyes swam with tears. He stared at the floor and twisted his hands.

"How did she get the key?" The doctor drew out the needle and swabbed the tiny wound.

Ahmed shot a look at Candyman, who said nothing.

"Then we'll have to assume that somehow she found it," said the doctor.

Ahmed bobbed his head. That was it. The woman found the key.

"The only thing we can be sure of is that none of you stopped it from happening. That's unfortunate. If the woman was clever enough to find it, she'd go straight to a hardware store and make a copy."

"I doubt if she had time," Candyman said.

"Change the lock," said the doctor.

"I doubt if we can—"

"Now."

"I mean over the holidays everyone's closed."

"Then get a chain and a padlock. Double the guard." The doctor stopped herself. She had come close to betraying her professional calm. She fixed Ahmed with a hard look. "Do it. Get back down to the street and do it now."

The young man snapped his black, curly head up and down in agreement, only too happy to flee this woman's presence. The doctor kept the tall man standing in front of her desk, waiting in silence until he wiped more sweat. "She got as far as this floor?"

Candyman nodded.

"What time was that?"

He glanced up from his notebook. He spoke with precision, the lawyer he had once been. "She fell at exactly three minutes after six."

"The body is still in the elevator shaft?"

Candyman picked up his scarf and mopped shining sweat from his face and back across dangling strings of hair. "Right."

"I can't hear you."

"Right. She's still there."

"Do you know who she was?"

"A reporter."

"The one who wrote the story in the paper about the boy?"

He nodded.

"You're sure?"

"Here's her wallet." No attorney in a courtroom ever entered evidence before a judge more carefully than Candyman placing his proof on the desk within the circle of light.

The doctor opened the wallet. "Victoria Cruz."

"That first card identifies her. She was with the *Press*."

The doctor flipped through the credit cards and photographs of women. "Apparently she preferred women to men." She slid the wallet across the desk toward the lawyer. "Get rid of it."

"Right away."

"A reporter." The doctor shut her eyes, considering what would bring a reporter here. The man who had been a lawyer wondered if it was a trick of the light that made her face appear softer, more the woman she must have been in the days before she had come to this empty hotel. Candyman, eager to shift the subject, took advantage of that look. "What about the new clients?"

The doctor's face did not change. Was she still thinking about the reporter?

"They have the money."

And still the doctor said nothing.

"We can deliver one of those in there by Christmas."

"That tactic won't work, Candyman. I'm not talking about new clients." Her face hardened. Her eyes were on him, cold and steady, more demanding than before. "I'm talking about security—or the lack of it, that lets her and then the police slip past you and get in here."

"The first time—"

"You're going to tell me why that happened and you're going to tell me exactly how."

Candyman dug a hand into his pocket that bulged with chocolate bars but he drew it out empty.

"I'm waiting."

"We've only got Ahmed and Shelley on guard. You made us get rid of Joanne."

"Don't excuse yourself with numbers. I'm down to one nurse and I'm managing. The fault's your increasing inattention to detail."

"Down there on the street is rougher than hiding out up here—"

"This Victoria Cruz. She's got a Hispanic name."

"So does half of New York."

"The clients who are leaving today and the new ones—they all have Latin names."

"The ones leaving tonight are Brazilians. The new ones didn't say where they're from. I happen to know this Victoria Cruz was Cuban. She was on her own. No connection."

"You can prove there's no connection?"

"The connection hasn't been established." Once again, for a moment, the man sounded like a lawyer, then he faltered. "Believe me, Doctor, there's not any connection."

"The trouble is, I'll never be able to believe you again."

In the next room a baby shrieked and the nurse's footsteps crossed the floor.

"How did the reporter get word to the police and the other woman?"

Candyman stopped a shrug. Instead he straightened his scarves and fought for some shred of dignity. "She must have gotten in touch with them before she came inside."

"She had plenty of time after she saw you to make contact with the couple up at the park—"

"I wasn't followed!"

"Of course you were followed. How else could she connect you with the people from the hotel?"

"If they weren't for real where did they get that money?"

"Not much of a price for the lead she got. And you made it so easy. All three of you—so careless she slipped by all of you and searched till she found that key, had a copy made, and came inside this very building, and got all the way up to this floor—"

"I stopped her!"

"A little over an hour later the police arrived with another woman." The doctor returned the needle to the tray. "Are you going to stand there and tell me she had no connection with the new clients? The police? That other woman?"

188 . . .

"I don't know."

"That's not good enough. I want an answer."

"I don't have one!"

"You better come up with an answer. And I mean fast. Like before you need my professional help." She let the man sweat. "The police and the second woman started their search of this building in the basement?"

"Right." The lawyer's voice was hardly a whisper. He brought his notebook within the circle of light and peered closely. "At approximately a quarter past seven."

"I can't hear you."

"At approximately a quarter past seven."

"Why didn't they see the body?"

"It's in the shaft on top of the elevator. You wouldn't see it unless you were looking for it."

"Where did they go next?"

"Back up to the lobby. The mezzanine. Then floors one, two, three—and finally nine."

"Nine?"

"Nine."

"Why nine?" The doctor had not once raised her voice.

"A spot check. That's only a guess on my part."

"Any pattern to the rooms they opened?"

"Looks like another spot check. I mean they couldn't search them all—"

"What time did they leave this building?"

"Less than twenty minutes ago."

"All three officers? The man and the woman?"

"All of them. They weren't here more than twenty minutes."

"Get rid of the body."

"First thing."

The woman's strong hand, with fingernails trimmed short, arranged the needle, the vial on the metal tray. "You led them here."

Candyman dropped his notebook, then scrabbled it up from the floor. His filthy hands dripped with sweat and he shook violently. The woman's voice never approached losing its calm. "The reporter called the police. They came in here and searched. Now the question is, how long have I got?"

The lawyer struggled to find his voice. "In one way it could be the best thing that ever happened. Look. Say it was just like you say. The reporter tipped off the cops that this big empty hotel isn't empty after all. So the police and the other woman come in. They search. What do they find? Nothing. Absolutely nothing. They don't find a fucking thing. They leave. They're satisfied. They've just proved to themselves this place is empty. Now that they've checked and seen for themselves, it could be years before they bother to look in here again."

"You're saying they won't come back?"

"I'm also saying we redouble security. Doctor, look. Please. I promise you, this won't happen again."

The woman arranged the shiny instruments on the tray. Candyman was desperate. "I've never failed you before."

The hand rolled down the white sleeve that crackled with starch. "Radio the street."

Candyman picked up a radio and drew out its antenna. He snapped on the power. "Ahmed, you there?"

The receiver crackled. "It's Shelley," a voice said. "Ahmed just got down here."

Candyman held the radio. The woman switched off the desk lamp and leaned back in the dark. In the next room a baby complained. Footsteps in that room hurried across the floor.

"He's there." Candyman still held the radio. "They're both back on guard. You want to talk to Shelley?"

"I want you to get out of my sight and do what I told you."

30

DECEMBER 23, 8:17 P.M.

Zellner's black Rolls-Royce glinted in the light from the Broadway theater where crowds surged into a hit musical playing in its third year. A policeman on a horse clop-clopped past.

Inside the car, Kurt splashed alcohol on a towel and handed it over the back seat. Susannah bathed the face and hands of the old man shaking with fever in the black fur rug.

"My God, the way he insisted we race over here!" Kurt wetted and folded another towel. "He shouldn't even be out of bed."

Susannah pushed back the old man's damp hair and bathed his brow. Could the old man understand what she was saying? "The police heard it all on tape, but they still won't believe Victoria's story. I told them about this morning. That we were right here with you on this very street, practically inside the hotel. . . . They don't believe any of us."

"You didn't believe Zellner," Kurt said.

"Not at first."

The old man, glowing with fever, struggled to face the window where he could peer up at the dark hotel.

"You said you saw 'boxes,'" Susannah said. "Could they be, I mean—"

Zellner slumped in defeat. His old eyes blinked. Susannah

bathed his hands. She waited before she returned to her interrupted question. "Could the boxes you saw be rooms?"

Within the fur, the old man shook his head. Did he mean no?

"Please, try and see him again—" Susannah didn't dare push
any further. Was he feeling his way back to what he had seen?

"Nothing's clear . . ."

The mouth dropped open on a rattling gasp. Eyelids fluttered. Sound tore up from deep within the shuddering man, a cry
holding away some dreadful thing. "No!"

"I'm taking him home. Right now." Kurt shoved the towels
and the bottle of alcohol into a plastic bag.

Susannah bent close to the old man. "Boxes . . . rooms . . ."

His mouth moved, fell slack, began again. "I get the most
. . . the most terrible—"

"Stop! Right now!" Kurt's voice rose to a scream.

"Where is Victoria?" Susannah asked.

Eyes shut out pain. The crimson face, shining wet with fever,
shrunk into the fur.

"Please. Can you see Victoria?"

Tears streamed down the red cheeks. "Terrible . . .
terrible . . ."

"Laddie. Where's Laddie?"

She struggled to pull the red mitten from her coat. "Here.
His red mitten." She dug his hand out of the fur and closed the
trembling fingers around the wool.

"I'm telling you," Kurt hissed, "stop this this very instant!"

"Laddie." She urged the old man.

"I . . . I can't see the boy." He fell back with a gasp. "It's the
woman that is so terrible . . . tearing me apart . . ."

"See what you've done!" Kurt struggled over the back seat to
grasp the old man, who slumped into the corner beyond his reach.
Kurt grabbed the wheel. He started the engine. "When you called
I tried to tell him he was too ill to come out."

The driver's automatic release unlatched Susannah's door.
He was dismissing her, ordering her to leave.

She bent to the man huddled in the fur, begging him to look
out the window—up at the hotel. "Up there. There are more than
seven hundred rooms. If you could only tell me where to start—"

192 . . .

The weak voice, a breathy rattle, sounded miles away. What was he saying? The hand rose and suddenly clawed at hers. "Do not . . . do not go in . . ."

"Laddie's in there!"

He rasped, "She went in . . ."

"If they have her they know we've found out about them. They know we'll be coming. I have to get to them before they leave . . . before they take my son—" Kurt now stood at the open door.

Zellner's voice, faint and even farther away, bent her closer. "The Minotaur."

"What?"

"Will you for God's sake get out!" The wind lifted Kurt's white hair.

"The Minotaur—in the labyrinth. The maze. Seven hundred boxes. Seven hundred rooms . . ."

"Sir, we're going now!" said Kurt.

"Promise me," Zellner gasped. "Do not go in . . ." His voice went so thin that Susannah had to strain to hear, to not lose him entirely.

"Where do I start? Is there anything you can tell me to do?"

"Be . . . be as open as you can. Follow your feelings. Your own feelings. But do not go in alone . . ."

"That's all," Kurt screamed.

She kissed the feverish face and grabbed the red mitten from his hand. Susannah reached the curb. The back door slammed. Then the driver's.

"Thank you," she said as the car's heavy tires hissed through the wet and sped away.

She remembered to step quickly back into the shadows of a doorway. The guard at the corner must not see her. From hiding, she looked up at the hundreds of black windows glinting coldly.

"The Minotaur. The labyrinth. The maze. Seven hundred rooms." She repeated Zellner's words. Had he seen the labyrinth? The creature who lived deep within the dark? If only he had been well enough, she felt certain he would have explained his allusion.

She only vaguely remembered the Greek myth. Each year

some city in ancient Greece had to sacrifice seven of its youths and seven maidens—chosen by lot. A ship with a black sail took them to an island and they were sent into the Minotaur's underground maze to await a dreadful fate. Not one of the sacrifices had ever discovered the way out of the maze before the monster reached him or her. Theseus—yes, she was sure it was Theseus—dared to go into the maze to find and slay the Minotaur with the aid of his secret weapon—a thread he unwound as he moved through the labyrinth's black twistings and turnings.

Was Zellner saying to do the same? Once she entered the hotel, must she leave a line to help her find her way back? Is that what he meant? Or was he saying there already was such a line into the maze. Wait, she cautioned herself. Don't go too fast. Consider. When she stood with Foy at that window looking at the hundreds of dark rooms she was the one who suggested that some rooms deep within the dark might be lit through a cable. An electric cable—a line not to follow out through the labyrinth, but to follow in—could lead through the enormous, empty place to the secret warm heart in the midst of all that darkness.

She stood in the night staring at the tower. Icy wind howled around her; newspapers clattered against the wall. The thought warmed her: An electric cable would have to run from within the hotel to connect with some outside source of power. She could prove that if she found a line leading from the back of the hotel across whatever space separated it from the other buildings on the block.

Before she crossed the street she peered through the rain to the corner. The guard outside the coffee shop was deep in talk with someone. Now was her chance! She dashed to the board fence and followed it to a space between the hotel and a theater. Not as wide as an alley, this narrow strip was wide enough for garbage cans, a place outside the stage door where actors probably stood on warm summer nights to smoke.

Susannah peered up into the rain to squint at the dark bricks of the back of the hotel. Back at the sidewalk, a drunk peered in, then staggered into the passage, banging against the garbage cans. He swore. She stood motionless, silent in the black shadows. She heard the drunk piss, sigh happily, and stumble his way back to the sidewalk.

At last, after walking the passage twice and peering up, Susannah admitted defeat. She had felt certain that a single cable had to drop down from one of those hundreds of windows up there and stretch across to the roof of the theater and its secret tap of energy. The falling rain defeated her; she failed to find that cable. She hugged her arms. Her feet, numb with cold, felt nothing.

Under the Yellow Pages' heading "Guns" were forty-eight listings.

A row of shotgun barrels glinted behind the glass and crisscrossed steel of a security curtain. Susannah pushed close. Under a string of Christmas tinsel she saw guns. Revolvers. Pistols. Automatics. Whatever they called them. Guns. Guns and boxes of ammunition. She moved to the door and its sign: CLOSED.

Pressing against the icy steel lattice, she peered inside at a light in the back of the shop. Was this a light left on to fool burglars? Was someone still there? A man moved across the light. With no way to bang on the door behind the lattice, she rattled the steel screen.

The man left the light and moved halfway through the store waving his hands, signaling the place was closed.

She banged the steel.

The man pointed at the sign, but Susannah's commotion made it clear she would not go away. He came close to the glass, a young round face peering out, showing a frown. "Closed!" he shouted. Susannah rattled the lattice until it clanged.

The man within raised and dropped his shoulders in defeat. Bolts moved. Keys unlocked the door, but the crisscrossed steel separated the two.

"Closed." The frown belonged to a young man with a smooth, round face and a close haircut. His hand hovered at his side the way gunfighters in Western movies show their readiness to reach for a weapon.

"Please."

The young man's frown relaxed into an open, almost expressionless face. Was she crazy? Drunk? Why this desperation to come into his shop? He unlatched the steel and rattled up the lattice. Susannah pushed in, and he closed the door and locked it. His hand still hovered above his belt.

"What's the big problem? Last-minute Christmas shopping?"

Susannah had already turned to a glass counter containing shelves of hand guns. Her eyes ran down the line and she pointed to a revolver.

"Thirty-eight, four-inch-barrel Smith and Wesson," he said, but he made no move to unlock the case and draw out the weapon. He waited. His hands gripped the counter. His eyes met the woman's.

She nodded. That was the weapon she wanted. "How much?"

"Got your purchase permit?"

"Right here," she said.

Her hand pulled out of her coat clutching the hundred-dollar bills.

He placed his hands on the counter and shook his head.

"Please."

"Need a permit."

"I need it now—"

The man moved from behind the counter toward the front door. He waited for her, his hand on the lock. He was showing her out of his shop.

"I've got to—" Her hand held out the bills.

"No way," he said. "Not here."

She jerked her head at the lights outside in the street, shadows moving past the latticed windows. "Don't tell me all the people out there who carry guns have permits."

"I wouldn't know."

"Criminals. People with police records. Where do they get guns?"

"No idea." He rattled his keys. He wanted her to leave.

"Please."

"I'm already late," he said.

She resisted moving toward the door. "If you won't sell me one, tell me, where do I go?"

"Take my advice. Don't. With a gun you have to know what you're doing."

"I haven't any choice."

"You'd be asking for more trouble than you can handle."

Susannah found herself on the street, hundred-dollar bills in her pocket, the steel curtain rattling down behind her, but with no weapon.

How could she get a gun? Her mind raced.

She dashed across Eighth Avenue to a porno theatre where she asked the woman in the box office to see the manager. She had reasoned that to protect his box office, the manager had to keep a gun. She asked him where she could buy one. Did this man who looked like a librarian with heavy glasses and a shiny business suit understand her question? He didn't answer. He went back into his office and slammed the door. The middle-aged woman, eating a hot dog with sauerkraut behind the glass window of the box office, told her that if she did not move along she would call a cop. In a liquor store she bought a canned daiquiri as an excuse to wait until the man at the counter, a black man with a thin, long face, was alone. Over a display of peanuts, corn, and potato chips she asked him where she could buy a gun. He shook his head. She showed him her California driver's license to prove she was no policewoman. She pleaded. Did he feel her desperation? He picked up a telephone and murmured something she could not hear.

Less than ten minutes later a young man who looked like a western mountaineer, a backpacker with a yellow beard and hair under a green hooded parka, stood in the shadows of a parking lot, where he filled a .357 magnum revolver with six bullets and showed her how to snap on the release and the safety. She gave him two of the hundred-dollar bills and clutched the cold steel. He even said, "Merry Christmas!"

She gripped the revolver with six bullets in the chambers, the safety catch on, in her hand within her coat pocket as she hurried through the winter's cold throng of Christmas shoppers.

She bought a flashlight and telephoned the operator at the Plaza and left instructions. If she did not call back by midnight, they were to notify the police, Scott, and her father.

She hurried toward the dark hotel.

Peering through the growling traffic, Susannah wondered where the guard at the coffee shop was. He had been there before.

She pretended to hurry toward the bright lights of the theaters and only when she was halfway up the block did she slow enough to turn and look back. Still no guard at the corner.

Across the street, the dark hotel filled the sky. She raised her eyes and her heart sank. God, all those staring, glinting black windows looked so vast, so empty. The police had always believed it was empty. It was only at her insistence that they had made their search. They had satisfied themselves quickly that those seven hundred and twenty-three rooms were empty, dark, and cold. The officers had hurried back to their warm car and gone back to the precinct. Foy had gone home to his family. On Christmas morning his little boy would unwrap an electric train and Foy would take a stack of Polaroids. Now Susannah had come back to stand alone in the freezing rain that mixed with her hot tears. Were the police right? It suddenly seemed all but impossible that the people who had stolen Laddie hid themselves somewhere within all that dark.

But if Laddie was not in there, where was he? She would not allow herself to consider that. She believed with all her heart that he was in there. If she was the only one to believe that, very well then, she was the only one. She alone was left to go in there and find him. She was risking everything. He had to be there.

And those people who hid deep within the vast hotel? She asked herself what they were doing at this very moment. Seeing no guard at the corner worried her. Increasingly, she had come to believe that they had intercepted Victoria. They held her. With the noise and the cigarette smoke from the police, how could they fail to know others had come in and shined their flashlights into the black?

Susannah had a gun. She had a key. If she was ever going to hold Laddie in her arms she could wait no longer to do what she had to do. She must dare to push open that glass door and go back into that dark hotel.

31

DECEMBER 23, 8:48 P.M.

Susannah slipped through the panel and closed it behind her.
The thought that there had been no guard at the corner nagged
her and slowed her steps as she reached the glass door. Perhaps,
because they knew the hotel had been invaded twice, the guard
had moved inside the lobby. Was he waiting in there now? In the
dark? Beyond the door?

She peered through the glass but saw nothing.

She felt the key in her hand. Had they already changed the
lock? Would this key still work? It slid into the lock and turned
perfectly. She eased open the door. Cautiously, she stepped
inside. The door closed; the lock clicked.

At the sound she winced.

She waited. Did anyone else hear the click? Alone in the
dark, she felt very small. Was the lobby even more vast, emptier
now that she stood here alone? The chandelier overhead tinkled
and swayed. On the windows on the Eighth Avenue side, lights
flashed. Drifting newspapers crackled.

Her plan was simple. On every floor she would check each
threshold for a chink of light. In case the light was blacked out,
she would search for a line into the maze, the cable that supplied
that light. She would stand at each door, alert to the faintest,
telltale sound. Each door. Was it possible to check all the rooms

on all thirty-one floors? As Foy had said, a search like this would take until New Year's. Naturally, the detective, reluctant to search, had overstated the time needed, but she had to admit the search could take many, many hours.

Where should she start? Without an elevator, the climb to the thirty-first floor made her quail. She considered. If it loomed as a formidable climb for her, wouldn't that climb prove even more discouraging for the members of the gang, who had to make their way up and down these stairs several times a day? She decided, for no very good reason, that they would go no farther than the fifteenth floor. Very well, they were in one of the more than three hundred rooms somewhere between the mezzanine and the fifteenth floor. Where to begin? Should she start on the fifteenth floor and work her way down, floor by floor? Or would it make more sense to start here on the ground floor and work her way up? She decided to work her way up. Why assume that kidnappers liked to climb stairs any more than she?

She hurried across the lobby's marble floor, toward the stairs.

A faint noise slowed her steps. She peered up at the chandelier tinkling in the draft. No, what she heard was not glass. This was a sharp, animal sound. More like shrill little shrieks. Without turning on her flashlight she peered at the floor. Did shadows move? Did shadows slither across the floor? She held her breath and stumbled back. Around her the shrill shrieks screeched everywhere. Rats leaped and scurried over her shoes. She gasped and clamped her hand over her mouth, blocking a scream.

Behind the door of the stairwell, Susannah reviewed her plan. The police had moved through the lobby, the mezzanine, and floors one, two, and three. At her insistence—and in spite of skipping the other floors—they climbed up to nine. Those had been spot checks and, she decided, proved nothing. This time she vowed to be thorough, even if it meant she would have to check every single door on every single floor.

One glance showed her that the open mezzanine, lit from a wall of glass on Eighth Avenue, stood empty.

On the first floor she pushed the stairwell door open slowly and stepped out onto the carpeting. A window at the end of the corridor showed gray moving with reflected light, framed by the hall's pitch black. Careful to make no sound, she hurried down the hall and grasped the first door handle. Locked. She knelt and felt under the door and found a space, ample space over the threshold that if a light burned within the room it would show its glow. She pressed to the door and listened.

The twenty-five doors on the first floor seemed an endless process. She held her flashlight under her coat to light the dial of her watch. She was astonished at her misjudgment. The first floor had taken only eleven minutes. She would have guessed she'd been searching for more than an hour.

She returned to the stairwell, but the thought of no guard at the corner or the street still haunted her, and stopped her from opening the door to the stairwell. Where was that guard? What if he was coming up these stairs now? The worst thing that could happen would be to run into him, or one of the others, on the stairs. She would be hidden in the dark, but they would have no reason not to use light. Once they saw her, where could she hide? No, they must not come upon her by surprise. She opened the stairwell door without a sound. She listened. No footfalls rang out on the metal steps; she felt their ice-cold steel through her thin, wet California shoes.

She searched the second and third floor.

On the fourth floor she waited long enough to catch her breath before she tiptoed down the hall. There was the window on the street, casting its pale light. Down at the other end of the corridor, before the turn of a corner, icy blasts of air sprayed needles of rain. A window yawned open. Out in the night, city lights sparkled in the wet. Shredded curtains flailed in the black. She stepped around a puddle of water on the carpet.

She found an open door on the court side and stepped into the room. She raised the window. The hall door blew shut with a terrible clang that echoed and paralyzed her with fear. She waited in hiding, but the sudden bang brought no one. When she dared peer out into the court on the inside of the building, she saw no more lights than the police had seen from Eighth Avenue. Only black windows rose more than twenty-five floors in the court, hundreds of coldly glinting windows.

On her way back to the stairwell she found a door ajar and

opened it on a bitterly cold room where a gale from the broken window rattled strips of torn wallpaper. Something in the corner moved. She froze. She forced herself to stand in the dark, perfectly still. A flock of pigeons whirred into her face and battered wildly, fluttering against her. She must not scream. She shrieked inside, throttling panic, but she did not scream. She stumbled out the door, which she closed as quietly as possible against fluttering, banging wings.

She slumped down on the cold steel stairs. Shaking with terror, her legs wobbled, too weak to carry her to the next floor. She was freezing cold, wet, and scared, and the feeling overwhelmed her that Victoria had been on these same stairs and pushed through these same doors and stepped down the same halls. Even stronger was the undeniable sense that Victoria had disappeared forever into one of these rooms within this dark labyrinth, that Victoria was dead. Susannah crumpled against the wall. For a full minute she fought rising and stumbling down the stairs and out the street door to race through the rain to a first-class hotel, where she could lock herself away from everything, crawl into a soft bed, pull the covers over her head, and hide—safe and warm in her own secret place.

But who would look for Laddie?

She forced herself to her feet and began to climb to the fifth floor.

She peered into the dark corridor. Where was the window that should have been a rectangle of gray in the dark? Nothing showed gray, nothing reflected the lights from the street below. The window here on the fifth floor had been blacked out.

"Black!" Susannah's mind raced. "For only one reason! To keep light from showing. They're here! Here on the fifth floor!" Moving in total dark toward the first door, she shrank from daring to shine her flashlight. She stumbled. Her feet scraped along a length of rope. She knelt and, careful to keep the glow of the flashlight hidden under her coat, looked at the carpet. No. It was not rope. It was electrical cable.

The cable ran from an outside room on the Broadway side. All the pieces of the jigsaw puzzle were fitting together. This had to be the cable that tapped the electrical source from the theater across the passage. This was what she had searched for down in the passage and had failed to see in the black rain. She snapped off her flashlight, rose, and, touching the line with her foot, followed it down the corridor.

As she passed doors she listened. Out in the rain a horn honked. Within the hotel she heard no sound. The electrical cable turned a corner. Then she heard it. A baby cried. Unmistakable. A cry any mother would hear rooms away. This was within a few feet. She thrust herself against the wall. She listened. There it was again, the long, sputtering cries of a baby. She edged along the hall. Without warning, blazing light slashed the dark as a door opened around the next corner. A wail rose not more than two or three doors down. She pressed herself back into the shadows, away from the blaze.

32

DECEMBER 23, 9:31 P.M.

A radio switched on and crackled static. "Candyman?" a woman's voice down the hall demanded sharply. "Candyman?"

A radio voice answered through the crackle. "Ahmed and I are on our way up right now—"

"Hurry!" The radio static cut to silence.

Susannah smelled cigarette smoke. She heard footsteps quickly pacing the carpet. Around the corner, only steps away, the woman with the radio was waiting impatiently for whichever one was Candyman. And Ahmed. Her pacing crossed the glare, casting wild shadows on the walls. "On our way right now," the man had said. Susannah realized this meant the stairwell door would open. Candyman and Ahmed would come down this hall in the same direction she had come. If she stayed here against the wall, the two would be bound to see her.

The baby shrieked. Another whimpered. The stairwell door banged open. "Fucking stairs!"

"Candyman?"

A nurse in white with dark goggles raced around the corner, almost brushing Susannah in her dash down the hall to the men.

Susannah made her move. She pressed along the same wall to fit into a door frame's shadow she prayed would be deep enough to hide from the three.

"The Bitch is ready to kill you guys. She's been on the radio for half an hour. There's no one on guard!"

"She wanted that thing in the elevator shaft out of the way, didn't she?"

"That takes all three of you?"

"Shit, man. We can't be everywhere at once," the last voice, a man's, said with a strong accent.

Susannah wondered: Was this the one they called Ahmed? She held her breath. They were coming toward her. A lantern's swinging beam lit their way. The beam flashed closer and closer.

"Shelley's down there now?"

"I told him to call her and tell her we're covered."

"The Bitch is crazier than ever. I'll handle her."

The light and the three strode past Susannah and turned the corner. "Wait. Don't go in yet." It was the nurse whispering. "Not till you calm down—"

"You'd think she'd be grateful," Candyman said. "This afternoon I closed a hundred-thousand-dollar deal and set up another—"

"That's your job. You're the lawyer."

"What you mean is, I deliver and she's ready to cut my fucking heart out."

"Wait right here," the nurse said. "As soon as I radio and make sure Shelley's down there, I'll call you."

A baby whimpered. The door shut, cutting the blazing light. The men's footfalls paced in the dark. Susannah struggled to keep her breathing shallow enough to make no sound.

"Got a cigarette?" asked the voice with the strong accent.

"Better than that if I can figure out how to open this fancy case."

"You think the Bitch is gonna let you stay on?"

"You don't quit her."

"I mean—"

"Don't worry. The Bitch needs me. Like two hundred thousand dollars this afternoon. She didn't need Joanne. Joanne freaked. She tried to quit. You know what Joanne got."

"Are you saying the Bitch did that to Joanne?" Ahmed was hushed, reverent with fear.

Susannah heard the two men down the hall continue to pace.

. . . 205

"Like about Joanne. How do you know, man? I mean for sure?"

The steps approached the corner. Susannah prayed they would turn back. And if they did not turn? Should she run? No? To make the slightest move, the slightest sound, would give her away.

"Jesus." It was Ahmed who spoke, more hushed than before. "You were the one who wasted Joanne?"

Footsteps—three yards away—stopped. Neither man moved.

"I didn't know, man."

"Now you know."

"Really. I didn't know. Wow."

"Here. Try one of these."

"What?"

"Like I said. Something better than your Winstons."

Footsteps turned and came so close to Susannah that her heart beat like a drum thudding through the hall. They stood only a few feet away, around the corner. Did they hear her heart pounding? Her breathing? Did they sense something? In the shadows she made herself as small as she could.

A match flared. An orange flame danced in the dark. Susannah could see the tall man. He didn't look much like a lawyer, but again Victoria had guessed correctly. From the first she had said an operation like this needed an attorney. He held the flame to his partner's cigarette and then his own. The two drew the smoke deeply.

The shorter man spoke in that squeezed voice grass smokers rasp when they hold down smoke. "Good shit."

"The best."

"Hawaiian?"

"Colombian."

"Lucky for you, you found it."

Something metal clicked.

"Nice case. Let's see."

Susannah saw Ahmed pull out a flashlight and shine it on the black enamel and shiny metal of a cigarette case.

"Beautiful."

The two moved from the corner. Acrid smoke reached Susannah.

The door opened. The dazzle, brighter than any ordinary light, blazed in the hall. A woman glaring white in a nurse's uniform and wearing black goggles stood in the door.

"You've got her so edgy I have to go downtown and get the alternate place ready in case we have to run." She stripped off the goggles. "Ahmed, you're coming with me."

"Shit! I just climbed all the way up here—"

"Give me the radio," said Candyman, who carefully snuffed the glow from his toke against the wall and pocketed the roach. Susannah held her breath and shrank into the dark as the nurse, pulling on a coat, and Ahmed hurried past. She heard the fire door open and footfalls ring on the iron stairs. The door slammed.

A baby giggled.

Susannah raced to Candyman, who stiffened in the glare. He felt the muzzle of a gun jammed into his back. "Keep going," Susannah whispered.

A baby shrilled happily.

"Do exactly what I tell you!"

33

DECEMBER 23, 9:35 P.M.

Inside the door a blaze as bright as summer sun burned her eyes. She squinted through tears. What could make this room warmer and brighter than an August day?

Sunlamps? Everything shimmered in sunlight. She could hear the contented gurgles of babies she could not see. One sputtered and cried. Another whimpered.

The lawyer turned. Susannah signaled him to put the radio on a cabinet, and when he banged into a cart stacked with diapers and baby oil it clattered.

A baby shrieked.

For a long moment in this brilliant light she held the man motionless while she strained her seered eyes to make out the sight of cribs in the sitting room of a hotel suite.

Was Laddie here?

A voice, calm but edged with authority, came from the next room. "Candyman?"

The tall man, who never took his eyes from the woman's pistol, made no answer. Susannah thrust its steel against the man. "Answer her."

"Yes, Doctor?"

"You and Ahmed get rid of the body?"

"Yes, Doctor."

"No possibility they can trace it back here?"

"None."

"You're absolutely sure you took care of everything?"

"Yes, Doctor."

"Everything?"

"Everything."

A baby's cries quivered into a demanding wail. The lawyer looked to Susannah, who stole an instant glance over the cribs. She blinked in the burning light. Was Laddie here?

The calm voice called from the office. "Another slip-up and we'll have to get out of here. Right now we're down to you and Shelley."

Susannah signed the man to answer.

"Right."

"Why are we shouting from room to room?" The two heard a chair scrape. "What's going on out there?"

"Stay there, Doctor. I'm coming in—"

Candyman had failed to warn the woman, and now she stood squarely in the middle of the doorway, a doctor in white, a calm, strong woman with long, iron-gray hair. Her black goggles stared beyond the lawyer at the young woman with the gun. Susannah prayed her hand did not shake so much that it betrayed her.

No one spoke.

The baby shrieked horribly. Another crib picked up the screaming. Susannah held the gun she so desperately hoped would not waver on the woman.

"Where's my son?"

The doctor, who betrayed no fear, spoke even more calmly than before she faced the weapon. "You don't know the first thing about guns. You're shaking. Put that thing down before someone gets hurt."

"I want my son. Laddie. Two years old. Blond hair. Blue eyes."

"Candyman," the doctor said quietly. "Tell her."

"Nobody like that here."

The gun wavered, moving between the two, choosing which to make a target—the woman in white or the tall man.

"No two-year-old boy. See for yourself," the doctor said. "If you're not going to wear glasses you'd better turn off the sunlamps."

"You do it."

Lights snapped off, fading the room from midday blaze into sunset warmth. The doctor stood over the shrieking baby. "Do I have your permission to see to the child?"

"No fast moves." Susannah turned to the lawyer. "You get over there with her."

"As you can see," the doctor said, "they receive the very best of care."

The doctor cradled the screaming infant in her arms. Was this love she was showing the child? Susannah's glance slid to include all five cribs. Next to the screaming baby, another cried. A third, oblivious, slept peacefully. Five cribs. Two empty. Three rosy infants, blind as moles with their black plastic goggles tied to their large baby heads.

"You see?" the lawyer said. "Nobody here two years old."

"If you can't buy them from some poor lost girl, you take orders anyway. What do you do? Stay on the lookout till you find exactly the child your customers want?"

"We call them clients," the lawyer said. "It's just us. We don't use tip-offs from outside the group. Too dangerous. Sometimes we look for days. That night with you we got lucky. We needed a blond, blue-eyed boy around two. I take credit for that one. I was the one who thought of going to visit Santa. I figured that's where the kids would be."

Susannah peered at the door to the office. "He's in that room!"

"See for yourself." With amazing gentleness the doctor eased the cooing baby back in the crib.

Susannah feared that in crossing to the office door she could not hold the gun on the two. She stepped back. "Both of you. Ahead of me. In there. Now!"

The doctor's black goggles faced the gun in the woman's trembling hand. As the babies whined fitfully the three entered the office, which had been the bedroom of the suite. A glass cabinet glinted, full of vials, bottles, and silver instruments. Another door stood open on a dark room. Susannah prodded her hostages into the second room and her heart sank. Except for a bed and a hospital chest of drawers, the room was empty. She ordered the doctor to open a closet, which was bare. The three returned to the office and its desk, where a stainless steel tray held a hypodermic needle, a rubber hose, and several vials. Here was the answer—what held this band together. This doctor was an addict. So were those guarding the building down on the street and how many others, Susannah could not guess. All addicts. "Some doctor," she said. "You keep them supplied with dope and they keep you supplied with kids."

"She underestimates you, Doctor," the lawyer said.

From a file folder lying open in front of a digital clock, Susannah found a list of telephone numbers but no names. She spread out a stack of receipts from pharmacies. She found no case histories, no Polaroids of babies or children. She hurled the papers from the desk, banged open a drawer and dumped its contents on the floor. "Where are the files?"

"No files," the doctor said. "No records."

"You lie."

The doctor still wore dark goggles. Her calm made it clear she planned to outwait the nervous young mother. The invader would make her slip-up, the two would make their move. That was their plan. But by God, Susannah told herself, she had her plan too. "You," she snapped at the lawyer, "face the wall!" The man turned. Now only the doctor and her glinting goggles faced her. "Take off the glasses."

The eyes, a surprisingly bright blue in the tanned face, showed nothing, no reaction, certainly no fear, only the simple, steady composure politicians' wives show on television.

"I know he's here. That reporter you just killed saw one of your people wearing his red wool cap."

"There was no reporter here," the doctor said in a voice that was seldom challenged.

"And no police either," Susannah lashed back.

"Look around. See for yourself. No children get better care—"

"And to hell with their mothers?"

The doctor stayed calm, content to wait. There were two of

them against this one woman, whose hand wavered as she held the gun. The doctor was making her point: She had time.

"I know what you're doing. I know how it works. So do the police!"

"Then why didn't you bring them along?"

"Goddamn you, give me my son!"

The pistol aimed at the breast pocket of the physician's white coat. "I swear to God I'll kill you first, then him, then each one of you—one by one—till somebody tells me where he is!"

Susannah reached out, grabbed the doctor's shoulder, and thrust her forward. She pressed the pistol to the gray hair. Her mind flashed on that news photo from the Vietnamese war, the colonel blowing off the bound prisoner's head. Could she do that?

"Where is he?"

The muzzle of the gun at her skull forced no change in the woman. Susannah studied her face. No shiny sweat, no darting eyes. Her hands? Strong, tanned hands hanging at her sides without trembling showed her calm. The doctor spoke without emphasis, but with a finality that said the woman with the gun could never hope to do what she threatened. "Even if you killed me and managed to kill him, the others will never let you out of here."

"Where is my son?"

"Go ahead," the doctor told the lawyer. "Tell the young woman. Tell her the truth."

"He's on his way overseas." The man's face turned.

"Face the goddamn wall!" Susannah shoved the steel muzzle until she felt the woman's skull under the mass of gray hair. "Tell that son-of-a-bitch lawyer not to look at you!"

"We can assume he heard you." If the doctor showed any emotion, it was annoyance.

Susannah shook so violently she took another grip with both hands on the gun. "What does that mean—'overseas'?"

"They're South Americans," the lawyer said to the wall.

"Stop them!"

"Too late."

"You're lying! You're all lying!" Susannah would not, could not believe the man. Zellner had been wrong about seeing Laddie dead. Victoria had been wrong about the morgue. The police believed this hotel was empty. No. She would not, she could not believe any of them, including this lawyer. She could believe only her own feelings.

"I delivered him today," the lawyer said. "What time is it now?"

"After nine-thirty," the doctor said.

"He's in a limousine on his way to JFK—"

"Call the airport . . . the police!"

"No telephone."

"You've got a radio!" Susannah said.

"Not on their band."

The lawyer had answers for everything. Did the doctor allow herself a slight smile? "We can't very well have them monitoring our calls."

"Their names!"

"The doctor just told you. No files. No records."

"The money—was it a check?"

"Cash. Can't be traced."

"They had to have names to stay at the hotel."

"They stayed with friends—"

"More lies! You had to telephone them."

"I remember now. Wiedemeyer. An assumed name. They're Brazilian but originally German or Austrian. Not Latin. They're gone. They took your boy. It's all over, lady."

"Goddamn you, no more lies!"

The pistol roared. There was a puff of dust, and plaster from the wall fell close to the lawyer. "You want me to prove I can come closer?"

A baby shrieked. The doctor's blue eyes never flickered, but the lawyer's hands shook so violently that he clasped them together behind his back.

"You stop those people now and you get my son back or I swear to God none of you leaves this place alive!"

"Doctor—" The lawyer's voice was a croak of fear.

"Do what she wants," the doctor said. "She can't stop them now."

"Yeah, they had to have the kid early today, to buy things and get on this evening's flight.

"What flight?"

"Pan American. To São Paulo."

"Prove it."

"How?"

"I don't care how. Prove to me there is such a flight!"

"Shit. I'm telling you the truth—"

"There's a radio in the next room. Call one of your people to go to a phone and reach Pan American for the flight number and take-off time to São Paulo!"

Susannah's gun forced the two into the nursery where one baby shrieked and another snuffled cries. It took precious minutes to radio the street and send Ahmed to the telephone. They were back in the office when a crackle and a metallic voice from the corner announced that Pan Am's Flight Two-Eleven was scheduled to leave JFK for São Paulo at ten forty-five.

Susannah grabbed the radio from the man and hurled it with a crash through the blacked-out glass. Nothing she had done filled the lawyer with greater dismay than shattering the glass, showing the world where the night insects hid here in the dark, their nest exposed. Even the doctor narrowed her eyes. For the first time her frown asked what this frantic woman would do next. Would she scream from this window? Scream out into the dark? Into the city? Bring the police? No. There was no time to call for help.

"Ten forty-five." The lawyer nodded. "I remember now. They said that flight would get them home by Christmas Eve."

The digits in the desk clock flipped over: 9:48 P.M. Susannah fought despair. The plane would leave JFK in less than one hour.

"Fifty-eight minutes. Too late," said the tall man. "No way you'll ever make it now."

Susannah slammed the gun against the woman. "You're coming with me!"

"Take the lawyer," the doctor said coldly. "He's the one who got a look at them when he took the money. He can take you straight to them—"

"Bitch! Goddamn bitch!" The lawyer's hate for this woman who held his life at the end of a needle spit out in wild rage.

"Take him out of here," the doctor said to Susannah. "He'll get you out the front door."

The man leaped at Susannah and the gun. She fired.

Candyman looked stunned, his mouth fell open, long narrow hands grasped at the red hole in his chest, and he fell. The two in the office standing over the dead man heard the babies in the next room cry.

"Let's go!" Susannah grabbed the other radio and waved her gun.

"What about them?" The doctor's glance went to the nursery.

"When the guard radios and gets no answer, he'll be up here."

The doctor swept the needle and several vials she scrabbled together into a black leather briefcase.

"Move!" shouted Susannah.

With the gun in one hand, Susannah shoved the doctor out the office door and across the room where the babies whimpered.

34

DECEMBER 23, 9:58 P.M.

"It's all right, Shelley," the doctor said in her calm voice that echoed in the black lobby. "This young lady's with me. You can let us through."

The confused guard stood in the dark, his flashlight beam playing its ghostly white on the two women who walked swiftly across the marble toward the glass door. "Doctor, you sure?"

"Open the door for us."

"You want me to radio upstairs?"

"Yes, you do that, Shelley." The doctor had reached the door. "Tell Candyman I've reached the street."

Susannah prodded the doctor through the wooden panel, onto the sidewalk where rain beat down in sheets. The two moved as one to the corner of Eighth Avenue where Susannah, peering into the traffic for a taxi, collided with a woman swathed in wet blankets. From a swirl of wet wool, red eyes glittered. Foul breath spat curses. The bag lady clutched up her monstrous, greasy burdens to drag past the two.

As startled as Susannah had been by running into the old woman, never for an instant did she move from the doctor's side. Her gun, hidden under her sheepskin coat, jabbed into her hostage. Other dark shapes, huddled and bent against the icy rain, dashed past.

Susannah prayed for a taxi with a glowing For Hire light among the moving cars. Headlights bore down on them, silvering the rain into splinters of light.

Wind and rain lashed the doctor's hair. Without a coat, she clutched her black briefcase to her breast and hunched the shoulders of her white uniform. She glanced at her wristwatch. "You've now got exactly forty-seven minutes."

Susannah waved frantically at a free cab hurtling up the middle lane. It shot past.

"Exactly forty-six minutes."

A cab with its For Hire light shining out like the hope of the world, approached the corner. Yes! It was coming toward them! A man with an umbrella leaped out of nowhere to claim the cab. Susannah blocked him, moving herself and the doctor into the street.

"Get in that cab," the doctor warned, "and you won't be able to telephone. Not the police . . . or the airport—"

The cab veered hissing tires to the curb to miss the two. Susannah slammed the woman toward the open door. "One false word to the driver and I blow your goddamn head off."

At gunpoint the doctor bent and crawled into the back seat. The weapon never left the white coat. Susannah ducked in and drew the door shut. The doctor shook rain from her hair and clutched the briefcase. The gun's steel muzzle jabbed her even farther back into the corner.

A black driver with a gold cross dangling from his ear waited, listening with a far-off look to music they could not hear behind the thick plastic and steel mesh that separated him from his passengers. Slits of eyes watched them in his rear-view mirror. A prominent black-and-yellow sign slapped across this plastic wall forbade smoking. NO SMOKING. NO FUMAR. The driver, his eyes still on the two, reached for a Zippo on the dashboard, snapped out flame, and lit a cigarette. Through the cigarette smoke he watched, waiting for one of these two women to speak. Only then would he lean his ear with its glittering cross to the steel mesh.

"Kennedy Airport."

"You gotta be crazy, lady."

. . . 217

Rain thudded the roof, drowning out voices, questions and answers, through the thick plastic partition.

Susannah held the doctor at gunpoint and leaned toward the mesh. "Kennedy Airport!" She was shouting now. "As fast as you can!"

"Kennedy?"

"Hurry!"

"Kennedy?" he groaned. "In all this rain and traffic?"

"Now—dammit!"

He craned his neck to peer up at the rain through the wipers slapping his windshield. "Jesus!"

"Hurry."

"What time's your plane?" His words came from far away, through the mesh of steel and plastic. This wall separating people seemed to sum up all the distrust and fear and violence in the city.

"Ten forty-five."

The driver leaned his head back against the panel, inhaled slowly, and snapped his Zippo. "No way." He shook his head. The cross swung. "No way. The expressway's solid with folks going home from shopping. Very bad."

"It's a matter of life and death."

"Yeah. It always is."

Susannah banged on the plastic. "Look!"

"Can't make it."

"Look!"

The bored driver glanced in his mirror, through cigarette smoke, then twisted around to look at this woman flattening a bill against the plastic. A hundred-dollar bill.

He stubbed out his cigarette and shook off his boredom. "All depends. Like if we can get through the tunnel. Maybe. After that I know another way. You want me to try?"

"I want you to get me there before that plane takes off."

"Hundred dollars?" After the driver made one glance back at the two women and got a nod from the one in the sheepskin coat, the taxi dug out, throwing a sheet of water.

Susannah braced herself against the cab's forward thrust to talk at the mesh.

"You got a radio in this cab?"

"Right there."

"Can you reach the police?"

"What?"

"Can you radio the police?"

The driver slowed. "If you want the police, get out."

"Don't stop! I'm only asking if you can reach the police."

Eyes in the rear-view mirror again narrowed to slits. "Like what do you want the police for? Something wrong?"

"Can you reach them? Yes or no?"

He drove on, windshield wipers slapping. Susannah wondered if he was ever going to answer. "Through dispatch. I can try. Not easy. Not when they is busy like tonight. Hell, if you wanted to call the police you should have called them from a phone."

"No time. It's more important that I get to that plane. Keep going, but call them. Midtown South Precinct. Detective Lieutenant Foy."

The driver turned. In his profile Susannah could see furrows of a worried look. What did he have in his cab? Were these two crazy women? When you drove, you got people like this. "I asked you," he said. "Something wrong?"

"Please. Just get the police. Midtown South. Lieutenant Foy."

Susannah saw the man's long black hand take his microphone from a hook and speak, but the plastic wall and the driving rain blotted out hearing what he said.

Susannah glanced at her prisoner. In the corner of the back seat the doctor's eyes were shut, her strong hands resting on the black briefcase she held on her white coat. The Bitch; that's what the men in the hall had called her. Goddamn her, sitting there pretending to look so perfectly relaxed. Would she look so smug if someone tore that briefcase, with its needles and drugs, from her hands? Susannah ached to bare her nails and claw that masklike face down to the truth. This cool act didn't fool her.

Oh, God it was all real, not a dream. Susannah slid a hand over the torn seat cover of the broken upholstery. This slam-banging cab was rocking through the driving rain of the dark streets. This gun she gripped in her sweating hand, this woman with her tangle of iron-gray hair and her eyes shut, sitting next to her, faintly smiling—all this was happening.

It was happening, and everything that mattered, the only thing that meant a damn in the whole, entire world, depended on this black man she had never set eyes on until five minutes ago and his taxi getting her through the wet night to the airport and her son before he was gone forever.

She tried to ease her fearful, leaping panic by telling herself that at least she had a cab, at least they were moving. The doctor had lied to frighten her, by saying she was passing up her last chance of reaching the police by getting into this cab. That, of course, had been a trick, an attempt to slow her down. She had been right to get in the cab. She peered forward. With any luck they could radio. The driver was working with the microphone right now.

She scrubbed a clear patch in the window's mist.

Outside in the street, in the rain, lights wavered and flashed. Horns honked. She pressed her hot face against the cold glass. They were turning east, jolting through a dark cross-town street that looked like it didn't have a soul on it. At Fifth Avenue they slowed, they stopped, they waited for the red light to change.

Were they going to wait forever?

As they came down Second Avenue and neared 36th Street and the Midtown Tunnel she saw the river of red bumper lights. Was the traffic ahead as bad as it looked? The driver shook his head, his way of saying he did not like the looks of all those red lights.

"Oh, God," she muttered. "What do we do now?"

"Bad," the driver said. "Very bad."

Susannah slid her eyes toward her prisoner. Was the goddamn doctor smiling?

They had one moment before all the other cars trapped them into line.

"What do you want me to do?" the driver asked.

"Can you turn back?"

"Not back. I can either go straight down Second or go into the tunnel and try to wait it out."

"The only way?"

"Only way."

The red lights swarmed around them. "Do it!" she said suddenly. "The tunnel. And keep trying the radio!"

Their move closed them into a solid stream of cars eddying around them. Susannah drew herself away from the back seat so the cold sweat trickling down her bck would not stick. She shifted enough to pull the red mitten from her coat to dry her wet hand that had become slippery and chilled numb holding the gun. Did the doctor see that once she had almost dropped that gun, she shook so much?

Tires hissed down an incline. The rain stopped drumming on the roof. They were in the tunnel, where white tile flared white light. Susannah strained to see ahead through the windshield. Red bumper lights crawled. Were they actually moving? Or, up ahead, had they stopped? With one arm she scraped back her sleeve to bare her watch. 10:07 P.M.

The woman held at gunpoint clamped her eyes shut, but raked both hands through her mass of wet gray hair and settled them in her lap. "Good," she said out loud but pretending to talk to herself. "Trapped under the river. All that black water flowing above us, full of chunks of ice . . ."

Susannah leaned forward. The driver drummed his long fingers on the steering wheel. His lighter blazed. He lit another cigarette. Susannah strained to see ahead. Were those red lights through the windshield ahead moving?

She rapped on the plastic. "The radio?"

The driver pointed up. He was saying that here under the river his radio would not send or receive.

35

DECEMBER 23, 10:18 P.M.

None of the red lights in the tunnel moved and because
Susannah could do nothing, this was the worst time of all. Every
second tore at her as in a fever dream, in one of those mad
struggles, fighting with every ounce of one's life's blood, getting
nowhere. She was trapped, sitting under a black river full of ice,
waiting while seconds ticked into minutes. Above them in the
rainy night, people in other taxis and buses and cars were part of
the holiday rush streaming into the airport and checking in
luggage and moving out to boarding areas and waiting in lines and
climbing onto planes. While she was sitting, waiting, trapped
under a river, were two strangers leading away her little blond
boy?

No. She must not think of Laddie getting on that plane.

And if that plane roared off into the sky—?

Again, she told herself not to think about missing the plane.
That thought, that terrible, chilling thought made her shake. She
wasn't Zellner, but she could see herself in the empty boarding
area standing on carpet, still jabbing this gun at the calm doctor.
They'd be alone. Airline people would come with guards. The
police would come. The doctor would lie. She would calmly tell
them that Susannah Bartok was her patient, one of New York's
crazies. Perhaps, months later, with Victoria's evidence and

222 . . .

Lieutenant Foy backing up her story, she might go free for killing the lawyer; she might even see the doctor, and any of her people who had not long scattered go to jail. Maybe.

None of that mattered. Not if Laddie had left on that plane. Not if Laddie was gone.

Then what could she do? She would eventually prove her son had been kidnapped and taken to another country. Would the FBI or the police help get him back? They might try. The police had tried in New York, where they worked within their own laws. What good did that do? She would hear them tell her about jurisdiction and extradition and red tape and more failure. All this, of course, would be covered with sad little smiles of sympathy. He wasn't their little boy.

Of course, on her own she would spend every minute of every night and day tracing him, following him wherever he was. She would move heaven and earth to find the real names of the man and woman who flew him away. She'd go to their country, but there she'd be alone. They would be rich and powerful, with lawyers who would know how to use their own laws to defeat her. She'd be in their own country. She would never stop fighting, but what chance would she have? They had Laddie. She had her tears and her pleas. She could plead, she could beg, she could cry her eyes out. Would they listen? Would they ever even agree to see her? Why? Would they open the tall iron gates of some estate or some security entrance of a marble town house to her? Would these rich and powerful people with their lawyers and their guards and their police listen to her or allow themselves to see her face to face? She would be asking them to admit they had come to New York, broken the law, paid a fortune for a stolen boy. They wanted the boy didn't they? They had the boy. Give him back? Lose that money? Admit their crime? Never. No. They would never see her. She would whine and beg, become a crazed woman, broken and shuffling throughout hot streets of some strange city, clutching at every passerby, begging strangers to listen to her pitiable story.

Susannah knew that anything she had thought of, this doctor sitting beside her, through her many dealings, had thought of as well. The doctor had thought of far, far more.

"Ten twenty-two," the doctor said.

No. She must not think of Laddie at the airport. Think of him and she would go crazy. She would force herself to think of something else . . . anything else . . .

Think about killing a man. Yes. Think of that. Less than half an hour ago she had fired a gun. She, Susannah Bartok, had actually killed a man. She shook her head at it, for the thought meant nothing. The deed moved her less than watching that moment in *Gone With the Wind* when Scarlett blew the face off the Yankee deserter coming at her up the stairs. In real life, the gun had kicked in her hand. The thin lawyer had clutched himself and fallen . . .

Was Laddie waiting at the boarding gate? Don't let him play with anything sharp. . . so many of the toys they sell at airports have sharp edges . . . don't let him have any of those sugary drinks like Coke or Seven Up. He always spits them up. Sometimes they had little cans of apple juice. Apple juice was all right . . . he liked apple juice . . .

No. Don't think about Laddie. Think about anything else. Think about this doctor sitting next to her with her eyes closed and her strong hands resting so peacefully on that black briefcase. Look at her. Think about her. Susannah had just killed a man. She could kill this doctor if she had to. She would do that. She would do anything . . . give up her own life. . . . Nothing else in the whole, wet, dark, ice-cold night mattered but Laddie, getting to Laddie before that plane left. Get him. Even if something happened to her, if she died to get back that boy, at least he would go back to Scott and live in the sunshine . . .

Why didn't this goddamn traffic move?

She would get out of this cab. She would open this door now and crawl over the cars to that little walkway with a fence up there on the wall. She would run now.

No, of course she would not run.

She must not discourage herself by looking ahead, past the driver who smoked cigarettes in defeat at the sight of that stream of red lights. None of those red lights moved . . .

Looking at those lights was an agony almost as great as thinking of Laddie.

224 . . .

If—by some miracle—those lights did move and they got to the airport, what would be the first thing she would do? Race madly into the check-in area? No. By now Laddie wouldn't be there. He would be in the boarding area with a man and a woman. Those strangers. That's where she would see Laddie—no. First he would see her. He would cry out—tear himself from these strangers and run—and he could run so fast—run into her arms. She would hold him and tell him everything was all right and cover him with kisses. What could these strangers do then? What could they tell the airline people, the security people, the police? Anyone could see that a mother weeping with joy held her own precious son who belonged only to her.

She looked at her watch, and she sensed the woman next to her, even with her eyes closed, knew she was looking at it. 10:21. Twenty-four minutes left. Did that still leave her even an outside chance?

And if the plane roared off into the sky—?

Don't think about that. Think of anything else.

Susannah pushed forward across the torn cover of the broken seat to rap on the plastic. She pounded. The driver finally answered, not by turning and looking at her, but with a shrug ahead at the line of red lights.

Susannah squeezed her eyes shut.

"You didn't call the airport," the doctor said. "You didn't tell them to hold the plane."

Back to the hotel on the windy, rainy corner, Susannah knew very well that such a telephone call was the surest way of all to lose time. Call the airline during the holidays and find herself put on hold to wait while some insane recorded music jangled. Wait. And wait. Before flying to New York she had called the airline nine times before she had gotten an answer.

"You could have told them there's a bomb on board. That would have stopped them."

Get through to the airline and threaten them with a bomb, and they would keep you talking so they could trace the call. That was no guarantee they'd hold the plane. None of that mattered now. As the doctor said, it was too late for that.

The doctor was looking at the white tile in the tunnel. "Are you sitting here now expecting an officer to come along that walkway over there?"

Even if an officer did appear, Susannah expected no help. How long would it take her to tell him her story? Could she convince him? Would he believe her enough to do anything? And if he did want to help, what could he do? Could he magically lift this taxi out of this tunnel's long line of unmoving red lights, into the rain? The most he could do would be to call ahead and have a police escort rush them the rest of the way. He could do that, if he believed her, if they ever got out of this tunnel.

But no cop would come along the walkway. She knew that.

She forced herself back on the seat, switched the gun to her other hand, thrust the weapon into the woman, and wiped sweat on the sheepskin.

God, how many minutes since they had moved so much as an inch?

The doctor pretended to think out loud: "If I told this driver I was a physician in my white coat and you were my patient—a very dangerous patient—who held a gun on me, what could that patient do?"

"Shoot your head off."

"Then? What would the driver do with a dead body on the back seat?"

"Then I hold the gun to his head all the way to the airport."

"He's got that plastic wall to protect him."

"At this close range? Want to bet?"

Apparently the doctor did not want to bet—not with her life. She said nothing to the driver.

In that instant the car moved. Yes. They were actually easing forward. Up ahead red lights crawled. Susannah dared breathe easier. "God, if we can only keep moving . . ."

Suddenly she found herself talking. Maybe if she didn't agonize over the red lights, if she didn't think about them, they'd keep moving. Almost calmly, more like the doctor than the agonized woman fighting hysteria every second, she tapped the woman's black briefcase. "Is it true that more doctors become addicts than anybody else?"

"More suicides, too. My father was a physician." She went

silent. Was she thinking of another life in another city? "He was a suicide."

"An addict?"

"A drunk."

"Being a doctor means you can get enough dope for you and the people who work for you?"

"For that much I can't write prescriptions. It started out that way. Now it takes money. A lot of money."

"So you sell babies."

"We perform a service."

"Kidnapping."

"We take only children mothers give us freely."

Susannah fought anger, raw and red, a hate strong enough that she felt herself capable, hell, eager to kill. "If there's a God in heaven I hope and pray he makes you suffer."

The taxi stopped. Susannah banged on the steel mesh. The driver shrugged.

"You did me a favor, actually," the doctor said, "getting rid of the lawyer. He had to go. And it's not as if another attorney will be hard to find. Certainly easier than moving from the hotel."

The car inched forward. The driver's lighter snapped out flame. He blew smoke.

"Would you ask the driver to give me a cigarette?"

"Sign says 'no smoking.'"

Susannah peered through the plastic and through the windshield. The red lights crept steadily. By an act of sheer will she resisted looking at her watch. The car picked up speed. The doctor spoke:

"The hotel's still the perfect place. I'll stay there."

Victoria was dead. The police had searched and failed. They would not be back. Scott had probably already left town. That left only Susannah who knew about the hotel.

"Perfect," the doctor said.

"With your money you could be anywhere."

"A nice, little clinic I share with other physicians?"

"On your own."

"In a clinic in some respectable building where Hadassah ladies collect for the UJA and little Girl Scouts sell cookies? Or out of the city among green lawns, where everyone knows what's going on? Hardly. No. In the heart of the city everyone moves around us. Nobody cares. That bag lady we ran into when we left the hotel? You know what that bag lady has in her bag? Are you going to ask her, 'Bag lady, what do you have in your bag?' I rather doubt it. In the city you don't want to know. Out in the suburbs you ask. Out there the bag lady wouldn't last an hour."

Susannah thought of Victoria's hat-box man. Now she herself was one of the people on the street. She, Susannah Bartok; two days in New York from California, and she carried a switchblade, a gun. What did other people carry? If the hat-box man did lug a human head around the city in that box, who would bother to stop him? Who wanted, for Christ's sake, to look into that box?

She shuddered. Those thousands, millions of people on the street—all those eyes scrupulously avoiding making contact. Not wanting to know. The heart of the city . . .

The taxi slowed. Susannah twisted in agony. "God, don't let him stop again."

The windshield wipers slapped. Rain drummed on the roof. The taxi had emerged from the tunnel and was creeping through the toll gate. Ahead, the expressway slowed; another river of red lights, bumper to bumper, as agonizing as the crawl under the river.

"Short cut's coming up," the driver slid open the plastic divider and shouted. "You wanna turn off and take a chance?"

"Go!"

The car left the red lights and spiraled onto an off-ramp, down to an empty street. Here no red gleamed; only white street lamps shone in the rain, marking the road through the dark.

The taxi opened up. They jolted and bounced in spine-crunching leaps over the potholes. Susannah shouted for joy. The driver glanced back and grinned. The cross in his ear swung. He nodded happily. At this rate they would reach the airport in only a few minutes. Susannah shoved back into the seat and wiped the beaded window, but all she could make out were dark factories and warehouses sliding by.

"Beautiful," she sighed.

She shot a look of triumph at the doctor, but her hostage had shut off Susannah's victory by feigning sleep. She saw, however, the doctor did not sleep. Her fingers dug nervously at the clasp of her black leather briefcase.

The driver's earring glistened. He pushed back his head. "Can't raise anybody on the radio."

Susannah had all but abandoned hope that the radio would get through. The driver explained that the dispatcher was swamped with calls. "Keep trying!" Susannah was covering every angle, but the radio was no longer her only hope. Soon they would reach the airport.

She loved slam-banging, lurching through the wet night. Every second of the wild ride was making up for time lost in the tunnel.

She stifled a gasp. Did she feel the car grinding down? Were they slowing? Without leaning forward she yelled, "What's wrong?"

The driver jerked his head forward at the splotched windshield, and through the slapping wipers Susannah saw what he saw: more red lights. Another kind of red light, blinking and flaring and sputtering in pink smoke on the wet road.

"Accident."

She bent double in one long groan, then leaned forward. "Can we get around it?"

The driver already had his face out in the rain. He pulled back, shaking his head. "Doesn't look good."

Susannah saw that the blinking red lights were ambulances and police cars, and the pink smoke billowed from flares blocking the road ahead.

The doctor smiled, her hands motionless on the black leather.

The taxi stopped.

Susannah fought the window and found she could not lower it. She rubbed away the mist. Drunken voices sang and shouted the slurred words of "White Christmas." Groups of people with drinks in their hands wandered from the garish, colored light of a tavern that thumped Bing Crosby on the juke box. They strolled happily, singing and shouting the song toward the pink light of the flares, the blinking ambulances and police cars.

"I'll check up ahead." The driver bounded out of the car.

Was the doctor at her side humming the Christmas song? Where the hell was the driver going? Susannah scrubbed the glass and peered into the rain. People wandered past, banging their greetings on the car; people laughing and talking, drinking and singing, waving drinks and shouting, people with all the time in the world . . .

The driver jumped in and mopped the rain from his black face.

At last Susannah worked up her courage: "Bad?"

"Worse than the tunnel. Only way ahead is the ramp and it's blocked by the accident. Even if we go around and get to the expressway it's no better. Solid red lights all the way. Very bad."

"How far's the airport?"

"Fifteen minutes." He wiped his neck. "Shit. And we was so close to making it."

"Can we walk?"

"No way."

"What if I can get up the ramp, get another car—"

"Solid traffic up there."

"No!" Susannah found herself screaming. She jammed the doctor into motion with the weapon, signaling they were leaving the car. The doctor moved into the rain clutching her black briefcase. Susannah opened the driver's door.

The black man shook his head. "Sorry."

Susannah thrust the hundred-dollar bill. He shook his head again. "You keep it. We didn't make it. You want me to try to get the police on my radio?"

"I've got a better idea. I need your help. Come on!"

Two black orderlies and a young intern with a brown beard dripping rainwater worked in shining plastic raincoats to slide a stretcher in the back of the ambulance and close the door.

Drunken carolers surged and police officers waved them back. Bullhorns spat orders. A tall young officer with rain-spattered glasses blocked the taxi driver, the woman in white, and the woman in the skeepskin coat. The driver pushed his face close to the officer. He shouted, "They're both doctors. Can they help?"

The officer pulled off his bleared glasses, saw the white coat, and motioned the three to the ambulance.

The taxi driver took the black ambulance man aside. They spoke, and turned to the young intern with the beard full of rain. He listened, looked first to the woman in white and then the woman in the sheepskin coat. The taxi driver pushed close. "You got to help them, man. I picked them up. An emergency. They've got to get this special medication to a patient at the airport." He pointed at the black briefcase. "You can see I can't make it. Blocked. And it's worse up ahead. But you can get through, and since you're going by the airport, well, like I say, maybe—"

"Sorry." The intern was shaking his head no.

"It really is life and death," said Susannah. She explained her coat. "I was off duty. This is Dr. Dillon. The patient is waiting. The patient would be willing to make a sizable contribution to your hospital—" She held out three hundred-dollar bills.

"Against regulations." The intern moved to the door. "Sorry."

"Please."

Suddenly Susannah felt someone shoving her. "Keep your money." The intern urged the two women into the ambulance around a man on a stretcher. The door slammed. Susannah had no time to thank their black driver, for by this time, under the yelping siren and the blinking light, they were screeching off and bolting into the night. Inside the roaring, shrieking ambulance, Susannah could only hang on, avoid the stretcher, guard her hostage without showing the gun, and hope to hell the driver knew what he was doing. At times they slid through mud nearly out of control, racing along the earthen shoulder of the road. They swerved crazily, edged aside traffic. At times this screaming ambulance seemed to leave the road altogether and fly.

"Doctors, get ready," the intern yelled. "We can't take you all the way into the terminal. If we drop you off up ahead it's not far to walk."

Susannah shoved the doctor out into the rain, and stiff-armed her through the stalled lanes of cars where horns complained in a jam outside the terminal.

36

DECEMBER 23, 10:42 P.M.

The two women burst through automatic doors that snapped open. Susannah missed her footing once but kept the gun in the doctor's back as they struggled on, close together, down a long hall of shining brown tile and glass. At the crowded check-in counters Susannah pushed through long lines of passengers laden with Christmas packages and hand luggage. Gasping, she fought her way to a slender blond woman writing on a ticket with a felt pen.

"Please! Flight Two-Eleven to São Paulo—" She fought for breath.

"Get the hell in line!" a man behind her exploded, so enraged at being shoved out of the way that his face throbbed maroon. Down the line, others picked up his rage.

The cool blond woman continued writing.

"São Paulo!" Susannah fought to make the woman understand.

The clerk made a point of ignoring her. Without glancing up from her work, she spoke crisply. "If you'll take your turn in line—"

"You have to stop that flight!"

The clerk, smiling too sweetly, shut out Susannah by concentrating too closely on a black-haired woman in a fur coat to whom she was explaining boarding-gate procedure in Portuguese.

"Don't let that flight go—please! If you can't stop it—" Frantic now, she was shouting. "Who do I see to stop that plane?"

Though the gun held the doctor, Susannah sensed the woman saw her chance to signal the others. At the same time the line of check-in passengers backed away from the two, police and security guards came on the run and Susannah saw them fanning out, surrounding her at the counter. The doctor wrenched in an effort to twist away, but Susannah held her close. Passengers with packages, the guards, and airline people hurrying in saw that this woman was desperate now that she no longer hid the gun or the fact this woman in white was her hostage. She shoved the gun against the doctor's wet, gray hair. Passengers gasped. A woman screamed and dropped her Christmas gifts. Her three little girls in identical blue coats whimpered.

Security guards and police froze and looked to a senior airline pilot in a blue uniform with four stripes on his sleeve. This tall man with a ruddy face and silver hair parted the crowd. Apparently on a flight himself, he carried a valise, which he handed to a young clerk. More airline people appeared. Everyone waited for the pilot, ruddy and tan and silver, to make the next move. Boldly he took another step toward the woman with the gun.

"Please," she stammered. "You have to stop the flight to São Paulo!"

"I'm a doctor." The woman in white at Susannah's side was speaking with great authority. Every eye was on this motionless woman whose calm matched the pilot's and emphasized Susannah's desperation. "This woman is my patient. As you can see, I'll need your help getting her back to the hospital. I must also warn all of you to be extremely careful—"

"Don't listen to her!" Susannah tried not to scream but her voice broke like a frightened girl's. "She's one of them! I swear to God she's one of them! Call the police in Manhattan—Detective Lieutenant Foy—he'll tell you who I am!"

The passengers, the airport security guards, the police looked to the pilot. No one moved. Those who surrounded the woman at the counter waited for the pilot to speak.

The little girls sobbed.

"Stop the São Paulo flight!" Susannah was begging the pilot and the crowd. "They've got my son!" The raw fear in her voice and a sudden jerk of her shaking hand that held the gun brought a gasp of terror. Was this blond woman in the sheepskin coat, clawing at her wet hair with one hand, holding a gun in the other, crazy enough to shoot?

"Everyone, stand back." The doctor with the unfailingly calm voice, professional, infinitely worthy of trust, willing to be martyred, impressed the crowd. "She's already killed one man."

"She stole my son!" Susannah screamed. "Lieutenant Foy knows all about it, but right now the people who have him are getting on that flight and we have to stop them!"

The silver-haired pilot, this friendly-looking older man who shared the doctor's professional calm, exchanged a glance with Susannah's hostage, a glance to inspire confidence. He was telling her she was magnificent. If she would continue to stay cool he would handle this. He looked straight at the doctor's patient.

"What's her name, Doctor?"

"Bartok. Susannah Bartok."

"Susannah," the pilot said as he became every kind father in the world talking to every child, "give me the gun."

"Stop the plane!"

A police captain jogged into the area fighting for breath. His big, florid face showed ten thousand nights of too many whiskies, but he could still run. He sensed the danger and slowed. He watched the pilot talking to the woman and signaled his men to make no move.

"Give me the gun, Susannah." The pilot's voice was strong, not without warmth, absolutely to be trusted.

"Stop the plane!"

"It won't leave, Susannah."

The woman raked back wet hair and peered with glittering eyes at those who surrounded her. Which one of them had the authority to stop that plane? The silver-haired pilot? The airport security people? The police? The young airline women and men in their uniforms at the counter? Two older men, executives she guessed, hurried in, but, as the police captain had slowed, they joined those who stared at the woman with the gun.

234 . . .

"Who gives the order to stop that flight?"

"This is our Mr. Emerson," the silver-haired pilot said of a softly handsome man in tortoise-shell glasses who squared his shoulders in a dark blue suit. The two men exchanged a few whispered words. The executive nodded. The pilot said, "Our Mr. Emerson's in charge here. He'll tell you himself, Susannah. Listen to him."

"I've stopped the plane, Susannah." The voice was bland as a television announcer's. He took a handkerchief from his breast pocket and wiped his shining brow.

Susannah peered at the executive, then the pilot, and finally the woman at the counter. "She wouldn't stop it. How do I know you have?"

The pilot raised a large red hand and with a minimal gesture cautioned the others to stay in back of him. He glanced at Emerson, who nodded. The pilot spoke: "It hasn't left, Susannah. Believe us. Everything is going to be all right. We're here to help you." He moved his hand slowly toward her. "Now give me the gun."

The doctor waited.

The pilot took one step.

"Don't move!"

"Careful," the doctor warned in her damnably calm voice. "You have to remember that everything Susannah tells you she believes to be absolutely true—"

"She lies! She's the one who stole him! She's the one they call the Bitch—the head of the whole thing!" Susannah heard herself shouting. She saw all of them staring, not believing her. Did *any* of the circle of guards, police, airline people, executives, passengers, crying children believe her?

37

DECEMBER 23, 10:45 P.M.

"Please." Susannah forced herself to speak slowly in an effort to prove she could explain herself with the same calm as these others. She must appear as reasonable as the doctor and those she faced. To show panic would only prove to them the doctor was right. Her eyes pleaded, begging them to believe her.

"Please. A man and woman from South America have got my son and they're taking him on Flight Two-Eleven." Suddenly she heard herself screaming, choking with panic, "Drop that gun!"

The police captain with the big, florid face had raised a pistol.

"Drop it!" Susannah's voice stopped the old man. "Drop it!"

The officer carefully laid the gun on the carpeted floor. He straightened up, fighting for some shred of dignity. He glanced around. He was saying that he had tried, dammit. Was all this talk the pilot and the doctor were doing getting them anywhere?

"Get the passenger list," Susannah said, gulping down panic. "Don't bother to look for the name—they used a fake. Find a couple with a two-year-old boy."

The slender blond woman at the counter picked up a sheaf of papers to make a show of reading them.

"São Paulo. Flight Two-Eleven." Susannah begged desperately. "Please. Please, believe me!"

236 . . .

The doctor spoke: "You see?" She sounded more calm than ever, so calm she might have been in a clinic talking with other doctors. "To her it's all completely real." The doctor was kind, soothing, thinking only of her patient. "Can't you see, Susannah? These people only want to help you—"

"The list!" Susannah hated herself for screaming and she throttled her cry down to a rasp. "He has to be on that list. Not his name. Just a little boy. Two years old. Don't let them take him on board!"

"We're going to do exactly what you say." The pilot, as calm as the doctor, signaled the hostage to prepare herself; he was about to make a move. Holding Susannah with his most sincere look, he moved.

Susannah jammed the gun into the doctor's hair. "One more step and she's dead."

The crowd gasped. Susannah's look held the pilot. He froze.

Her voice fought to sound reasonable, begging all of them to see this from her point of view. "Please. My name is Susannah Bartok. I'm from Laguna, California. Here. My ID." She pulled her wallet from her coat and tossed it on the carpet at the pilot's feet. A young clerk snatched it up, handed it to the older man. The police captain and the executive, who had found no way to speak, moved close to examine a driver's license.

"That's my picture," she said. "Credit cards. A library card."

The police captain apparently felt he had allowed these others to speak for too long, and was ready to show he, too, could be persuasive. "Let me assure you, Mrs. Bartok. Nobody's going anywhere."

"Put down the gun, Susannah," said the pilot. "We've stopped the plane."

"Prove it!"

Mr. Emerson spoke to a younger version of himself, a clone, complete to the tortoise-shell glasses and trimly cut hair. "This young man has radioed the boarding gate."

"Where's his radio?"

"You have my promise," the pilot said.

Susannah searched the men's faces. Could she believe what

she wanted to believe more than anything in the world? Would they, would this ruddy, strong-chinned, silver-haired pilot lie?

"The boarding gate." She jerked her head down the corridor. "This way?"

Several men and women nodded.

Together she and the doctor took one step. They would go to the boarding gate now. Why didn't the others get out of her way?

"First," the pilot said, "give me the gun."

This man with his kind, strong face, who had brought millions of passengers in great silver jets across oceans and through storms, sounded so reasonable; how could anyone not trust him? He waited. The hushed crowd fully expected the woman to do as he commanded.

Susannah spoke only to the pilot: "You'll take me straight to my son?"

"Straight to him."

"In the boarding area?"

"As soon as you give me the gun."

Silence. In other parts of the terminal speakers blared, carols played, people shouted good-byes, but here where everyone waited for Susannah Bartok's next move the crowd held its breath.

The police captain, a man almost as old as the pilot, but with the politician's glibness that eroded any real earnestness, turned on the charm. "Mrs. Bartok. I'm afraid we can't let you through security with the weapon."

"Give me the gun and we take you to your boy," said the pilot.

He said "your boy." That meant he believed her. Susannah felt hot tears spill from her eyes. She nodded. He said he would take her to Laddie. This was the moment she had waited, prayed for.

The metallic voice of a speaker blared, "All passengers for Pan American Flight Two-Eleven to São Paulo should now be prepared to board."

With an animal cry of rage Susannah slammed the gun into the doctor, shoving her into the crowd that gasped and fell back.

"You lied! You said you held the boarding!" she screamed at the pilot.

"Damn!" The captain of police turned to the airline people with his big red face wobbling with fury. "Tell them to shut that thing off!"

Susannah kicked aside a bag of spilled Christmas presents, roughly thrusting the doctor forward. They lockstepped in the direction of the boarding gate. Passengers and airline people, security and police opened their path. Now as the two women moved toward the security check, Susannah forced the doctor into a run. Guards and airline people followed. Security and police officers spoke into portable radios.

Susannah's hostage ran clutching her briefcase, half-stumbling toward the X-ray scanner and magnetometer of the security gate. The airline staff and guards waited for her. A young guard with the build of an athlete touched his moustache as he stepped forward to stop the woman before she reached the others. He was actually smiling. "If you don't want to hurt anybody, Ma'am, give me the gun."

"Has the plane left? São Paulo?"

"The gun, Ma'am."

Half a dozen airline and security people quickly grouped together to block her at the security check. She craned to see beyond them a hundred yards into a boarding area, where close to three hundred passengers stood in a line that wound through the lounge.

Were they Flight Two-Eleven?

"São Paulo?" She shouted at the young guard. He no longer smiled. No one answered. The doctor turned. Behind them in the hall of shining glass the others from the check-in area followed. The doctor allowed herself the luxury of a deep breath.

"Blocked," she said flatly.

The senior pilot, police officers, and the red-faced police captain, security and airline people along with passengers slowed. The captain took command. He had the woman and her hostage trapped between this crowd and the security gate. This time the pilot said nothing to Susannah. His sweeping glance around them was saying it was all over. He reached out. He waited for the gun.

Susannah made no move. The others, feeling it was only a matter of time, waited for that instant when the captain would take the gun, the signal it had ended, that they could take away this desperate, crazy woman and life could return to normal. To their surprise it was Susannah who moved. Her hand shook but she still held the weapon, and dragged the doctor with the other hand as she pushed toward those who blocked her. One by one she peered at them. What was she looking for? A middle-aged man holding his boarding card on top of a stack of magazines and newspapers fell back in shock when she snatched his papers, found one, held it so the passenger faced the front page with its enormous picture of a little white-haired boy. "My son! Read his name!"

The man shook terribly, incapable of uttering a sound.

"Read it!"

"Laddie Bartok," the voice quavered.

Susannah snatched back the paper, thrust up the picture, and turned it for the senior pilot to see. "Two years old. Blue eyes. If you want more proof, look! This picture. You see? It's me!" She jabbed the paper with its photo at the men.

The doctor, forcing calm, spoke to the police captain. "Happens all the time, doesn't it? Whenever there's a story like this you get hundreds of poor souls, psychopaths who come forward—"

Susannah screamed, "Don't listen to her!" She was begging the pilot and the captain of police. "She stole him and sold him for one hundred thousand dollars to those people who are on that plane and I have to stop them—"

"You see the extent of the delusion?" The doctor shook her head, showing admirable compassion.

The airline executive with the tortoise-shell glasses reached the group. The pilot moved to his side, showed him the newspaper. The man nodded. He turned to the airline staff. "Have the Two-Eleven passengers boarded?"

"First class is going on now," a young man in uniform said.

"Hold them."

The young man nodded, turned, and raced through the

240 . . .

security gate into the lounge. The pilot reached out for the third time. "The gun, Mrs. Bartok."

She looked at the pilot, the others.

"You can't very well go through security with a gun," the pilot said.

"You believe me?"

"I believe you."

Susannah carefully placed the gun in the man's hand. In the same instant the police grabbed her; an officer held the doctor.

"Take her through," the pilot said.

The police looked to the captain, who nodded. Two officers led Susannah to the door-frame magnetometer where she squared her shoulders and marched forward. A bell shrilled. She stepped back, pulled a switchblade and a key from her coat, and tossed them on a table. She strode through in silence.

Police flanked Susannah and moved with airline people toward the boarding lounge. Others followed with the doctor. A black guard, a woman with glinting harlequin glasses, reached out for the doctor's briefcase. "This will have to go through X-ray, Doctor. Just a formality."

The doctor shook her head. Fiercely she grasped the case. The guard's eyes met a police officer's. They both saw that her face gleamed with sweat. Until now the doctor had been so calm. What was suddenly wrong?

Between the officers, Susannah raced into the carpeted lounge. Passengers in a long line, holding their boarding cards, approached the door to the jetway. They turned puzzled looks. What brought this woman and a pilot, executives and police racing past them, the woman peering so desperately among them. Near the front of the line Susannah slowed, betraying confusion. She looked back. The pilot and the others saw from her stricken look that her frantic search had failed.

Beyond the first-class door a little boy had disappeared into the loading bridge behind a tall man with gray hair who wore a carefully tailored black overcoat. A woman in her thirties, her brassy hair stiff with hair spray, turned one look back over the shoulder of her leopard coat into the lounge.

A stewardess stopped the couple, who stiffened with annoyance as she led them back to the door. The sleepy little boy, hanging by both hands between the man and the woman, stared blankly back into the lounge and the hundreds of people who waited behind them; the guards, the woman in a sheepskin coat— a coat he had never seen. He suddenly jerked his hands from the man and woman. His fists scrubbed his eyes that grew wide.

All eyes were on the boy and for an instant no one else moved. He raced from the couple who snatched out to stop him. He dashed free. He ran wildly, crying out until he threw himself into the outstretched arms of the kneeling woman.

38

DECEMBER 23, 11:17 P.M.

Laddie giggled into the telephone.

"Hey, Laddie Boy, how you doing?"

At his father's voice, Laddie giggled again and reached for his mother. Susannah took the phone.

"He's really there?"

"Yes."

"He sounds all right."

Susannah nodded. "He's here. That's what matters."

"How are you doing? You all right?"

"I will be once I get some sleep."

"The police can take it from here."

"They've just left. This is the first chance we've had to be alone. I called you as soon as I could. The airline's put us in their VIP waiting room . . ."

"What's he doing now?"

"He's asleep—all wrapped up in a blue blanket."

She had called Foy's office, and, as she'd expected, Scott had raced back there through the rain from the bus station. She closed her tired eyes, which felt rubbed with sand, and saw him standing by the lieutenant's desk with its empty coffee cups and Christmas poinsettia, tall and tan in his tropical shirt and white pants and sandals, running a big hand through his bronze curls.

"Thank God, uh?" he sighed.

"Yes."

"Okay. Here's what we do." His voice was up; he could have been planning a weekend at the beach. "You stay there and I'll be right out. We're getting on the first flight back to California. Foy says it's okay—"

"Scott—"

"Don't worry. I know they're booked solid for the holidays but you can always get a flight if you stand next to the check-in counter—"

"Listen for a minute?"

"No time, Baby. We're going to have Christmas at home!"

"No."

"I'll be right out. Don't move—"

"I'm not going back."

"Suze, Baby, you just said yourself, you're dead on your feet. My God, after all you've been through. . . . Look, you rest up till I get out there. I'm taking you home—"

"Please, will you just listen?"

"Baby, I know how you feel—" He stopped himself abruptly. "Damn! I'm sorry. You told me never to say that and I agree— but I got a right to tell you how I feel, and I gotta tell you I love you and that boy more than anything in the world and I want you both back."

Even the way he breathed told her he didn't dare say more. She knew everything about this huge man; she knew how much courage it took for him to beg. "Suze, I love you."

She held her breath and swore to God she wouldn't cry.

"Suze?"

Her voice dropped to a whisper, although she was alone in the room with the sleeping boy. "In a lot of ways I'll always love you . . ."

Her answer brought more silence. She shut her eyes and felt his pain, which might, at this moment, be even greater than her own. She could see him standing there with that helpless look she had seen only three or four times in their marriage—like the time his father died. She could see the day in the blazing sun he held a sixpack of beer, looking around the beach at Haleiwa where some guy had ripped off his surfboard. He'd had that look a few hours ago in the rain on Eighth Avenue. Was he crying?

"At least let me see him?"

"Okay, but I mean that's all. Really, I mean it. I'm not going back."

In the airline's deeply upholstered and dimly lit VIP lounge, raindrops gleamed as they slid down the windows where lights flashed out in the wet night. Huge, silver jets moved past the glass. Engines roared in the black. Scott entered without a sound and found mother and son wound in blue blankets. He brushed Susannah's face with a kiss and lifted Laddie to his unshaven cheek. The boy stirred, woke up long enough to run his arms around his father's neck and kiss him.

Sleet sparkled in the beam of automobile headlights as Scott watched Susannah, shivering in the wind, telling the cab driver to take her and her son to the police precinct. With one hand he held his canvas bag until he found himself holding Susannah's hand with the other. Shaking hands. He knelt at the car door, and kissed his sleeping son. "See you."

39

DECEMBER 24, 7:23 A.M.

In the bus terminal Susannah and Laddie, in their thin California clothes, sipped hot chocolate. Over his cup the little boy's eyes followed his mother's every move. Very carefully he returned the cup to the saucer. She wiped a drip of chocolate from his chin. "We're going to be home by Christmas."

The boy very carefully raised his cup with two hands and sipped more hot chocolate. For the first time his mother took her eyes from him as she unfolded a newspaper in such a way that he would not see his picture on the front page. Another reporter had finished Victoria's work. Today's big, black headlines. Today's story. Today's pictures. A few days from now the world would forget the story of the little boy in Times Square at Christmastime and the empty hotel. Susannah told herself that with luck her son might also forget these three days. On the second page Susannah found Victoria looking out solemnly from a photograph which, with a different hair style, did not much resemble her friend. The caption told of her death.

Victoria.

The boy carefully put down his hot chocolate and tugged his mother's sleeve. "Why are you crying, Mama? I'm here."